CW00705081

MURDER AT
WHITECHAPEL ROAD STATION

MURDER AT
WHITECHAPEL ROAD
STATION

JIM ELDRIDGE

Allison & Busby Limited
11 Wardour Mews
London W1F 8AN
allisonandbusby.com

First published in Great Britain by Allison & Busby in 2024.

First Edition

ISBN 978-0-7490-3146-6

Typeset in 11.5/16.5 pt Adobe Garamond Pro by
Allison & Busby Ltd.

By choosing this product, you help take care of the world's forests.
Learn more: www.fsc.org.

Printed and bound by
CPI Group (UK) Ltd, Croydon, CR0 4YY

For Lynne, who lights up my life

CHAPTER ONE

Monday 31st March 1941

The phone in DCI Saxe-Coburg's office rang and was picked up by Coburg's detective sergeant, Ted Lampson.

'DCI Coburg's office,' said Lampson.

'Is that you, Ted?' asked a male voice. 'It's Joe Harker at Whitechapel.'

'Joe,' said Lampson cheerfully. 'Long time no speak. How are you? If you're after my guv'nor, he's in with the superintendent at the moment.'

'Actually, it's you I was after,' said Harker. 'We've got a murder here at Whitechapel and there's a couple of strange things about it. Really strange. And knowing that Scotland Yard will be getting involved, I wanted to make sure we had the best people. That's why I'm calling.'

'Flatterer.' Lampson chuckled. 'Who is it? Who's been murdered?'

'It's a woman. By all accounts she was a prostitute.'

'And what's so strange about it?'

'I'd like it if you could come and see for yourself. You and your guv'nor, that is.'

'Sounds mysterious,' said Lampson.

'Mysterious is the right word for this one,' said Harker.

'We've left everything in place at the scene so you can see it just as it was found.'

'And where is the scene?'

'The old Whitechapel Road Tube station. Also known as St Mary's.'

When Coburg returned, Lampson told him about the phone call.

'He didn't say what was particularly mysterious about the situation?' asked Coburg.

'No, he said it was best if we saw for ourselves.'

Lampson was elected to drive as he knew the way around Whitechapel better than Coburg.

'How reliable is Sergeant Harker?' asked Coburg as they made their way east from Central London.

'Very,' said Lampson. 'If he says there's something strange, there is.'

'He didn't give you any idea as to what it was?'

'No. All he said was they've left everything as they found it for us to look at, before they have the body taken away.'

'A murdered prostitute,' said Coburg thoughtfully. 'In Whitechapel.'

Lampson chuckled. 'Don't start trying to guess. From the way Joe was talking, it's best if we keep an open mind on what we're about to see. So, no jokes about Jack the Ripper. Prostitutes are getting killed all over the place. Not just in Whitechapel. Maida Vale. Ealing. Hampstead. Soho.'

'Yes, alright,' said Coburg. 'How long have you known Sergeant Harker?'

'Years,' said Lampson. 'We both used to play football for the Whitechapel police squad. We were both defenders; Joe was right back and I was left. That was when we were both constables. In the end I found it a bit much having to travel to Whitechapel all the time, so I had to abandon it. But Joe kept it up. He's a good bloke.'

They pulled up outside the former Whitechapel Road Tube station and saw that part of the front wall was missing. Attempts had been made to fix wooden boards across the gap, but it looked a precarious piece of carpentry.

'It got hit during the early days of the Blitz,' said Lampson. 'Badly damaged. We won't talk about that in front of Joe. His sister, Joan, was killed in the blast.'

Lampson then went on to fill Coburg in on the recent history of the abandoned station.

'The station was closed in 1938. Before then it was always a bit of an oddity. A lot of people used to confuse it with Whitechapel station. When it was opened it was known as St Mary's Whitechapel Road. The thing is the station was very close to Whitechapel and Aldgate East Tube stations. In fact, Aldgate East was only a couple of hundred yards from St Mary's Whitechapel Road, so it was decided to shut Whitechapel Road and let Aldgate East be the main station for the area.

'When the war began, the borough of Stepney leased the abandoned station from London Transport for use as an air raid shelter. Because the railway tracks were still in use, they bricked up the edges of the platforms to make the area safe for people sheltering in it. Joe's sister, Joan, was going in when the front of the old building was hit by a bomb, destroying part of it.'

'Hence the boards that have been put up,' said Coburg.

'No, the boards were put up after it was hit a second time, a couple of months later, wrecking the repair work that had been done the first time. Remember, this area, the whole of the East

End, has suffered more from the bombing than most other areas of London.'

Coburg reached for the handle of the passenger door. 'This is where we get out, I presume?'

Lampson nodded. 'The entrance to the old station is a brown door a bit further on. Joe told me to look out for it. He said he'll be down on one of the former platforms, where the air raid shelter is, waiting for us.'

They got out of the car and locked it. Then Coburg followed Lampson along Whitechapel Road. After a short while they came to a nondescript-looking door sandwiched between two boarded-up shops.

'This is it,' said Lampson.

They walked into what looked to be a rear service entrance to the station. The former ticket office had obviously been destroyed along with the front of the old station during the recent bombing. They walked down a circular staircase, which seemed to go on for ever, before they came to what had once been a station platform. A brick wall had been erected at its edge, and as they arrived a train went past, and they saw the wall shake.

'How safe is that wall?' asked Coburg.

'I'm told it's safe enough,' replied Lampson. 'It may not stop a bomb, but we're deep below ground and the only thing likely to mess it up is if a train hits it, which is unlikely.'

A tall man in the uniform of a police sergeant approached them from along the platform.

'Joe Harker,' Lampson muttered to Coburg, who stepped forward with his hand outstretched. 'Sergeant Joe Harker, I presume.'

'Indeed, sir,' said Harker. 'I'm glad you could come, Chief Inspector.'

'You told Ted it was strange.'

'It is,' said Harker. 'If you'll follow me.'

They walked along the platform, passing a few groups of people, mostly elderly or women with small children, who appeared to have set up camps.

'People who are afraid to go up top,' explained Harker. 'This area's been so badly bombed, and it's not always at night. The Germans come along the Thames Estuary and this area's one of the first built-up places they come to. Also, people want to know they've got a place here when they come down, and they like a spot further away from the edge of the platform.'

They reached a halfway point, where curtaining had been set up. The smell gave away what was behind the curtains.

'Earth buckets,' confirmed Harker. 'They're due to be cleared and changed later.'

He turned a corner and they followed him along a short corridor, which came out on the other platform.

'Eastbound,' explained Harker.

As they walked along this platform they passed more small groups of people who had set up camps, with mattresses and chairs.

At the far end of the platform they came to a hole in the brick wall. Harker produced a torch and switched it on, illuminating the darkness beyond the hole. They walked into what appeared to be an access tunnel.

'There's a warren of these tunnels from here,' Harker told them. 'They're left over from when they were building the station way back.'

They walked along the narrow tunnel and Coburg saw that at various places there were alcoves leading off from the main tunnel, and some of the alcoves had further tunnels leading off into darkness. Coburg caught the smell of stale urine and excrement.

'Toilets,' he remarked.

'Unofficial ones,' said Harker. 'Not everyone has the time to stand and queue by the earth buckets on the westbound platform.'

He stopped by a space where an alcove had widened out into a sizeable aperture and shone his torch into it. A uniformed constable was guarding the area and he saluted as the visitors arrived. He had set up an oil lamp to illuminate the large alcove, enabling Harker to switch his torch off.

'PC Dixon,' Harker introduced the constable.

Coburg and Lampson nodded to the constable, then turned their attention to the body of a woman, lying on her back on the floor at one side of the space. She was obviously dead.

'Stabbed in the heart,' said Harker. He reached down to take hold of the bottom of her long flowing skirt.

'This is the first thing,' he said.

He lifted the skirt and pulled it up to her shoulders, revealing the horror it had been hiding.

'She's been eviscerated,' Harker said. 'Her womb, her bladder, her intestines, everything down there cut out.'

'Not left here?' asked Coburg.

'No. He must have taken them away with him.'

'Who found her?'

'A woman who came in to use it as a toilet in the early hours of the morning.'

'Where is she? Can we talk to her?'

'She went home as soon as the all-clear sounded. She was all for leaving after she'd found it, but there was a serious air raid on and her husband told her she'd have to wait. I've got her address. She reported it to one of the officials from the council who was down here, and he reported it to the local police as soon as the all-clear had gone.' He looked at Coburg. 'Seen enough?'

'For the moment,' said Coburg. 'I assume the medics have been contacted.'

'They have,' said Harker. 'Hopefully the doctor's on his way. But the body isn't the strangest thing.'

He led them to a side wall where they saw what appeared to be a large leather case on the ground.

'There,' said Harker.

'It looks like an old-fashioned surgeon's case,' said Coburg.

'That's exactly what it is,' said Harker. 'It's full of surgeon's tools. I've seen one just like it in a local museum. They reckon it's from Victorian times.'

Coburg and Lampson exchanged looks. Harker gave a weary sigh. 'Someone's sending us a message about You-Know-Who.'

'Perhaps, when the doctor arrives, he might be able to throw some light on the old case,' suggested Coburg.

'He might,' said Harker.

Coburg caught the note of doubt in the sergeant's voice and looked at him inquisitively.

'There are two doctors on call for this area from the London Hospital,' explained Harker. 'If it's Dr Webb, we've always found him helpful. Dr McKay, on the other hand, can be rather . . . dour.'

'Not helpful?' asked Coburg.

'He's a man of strong opinions who doesn't suffer fools gladly. And he seems to view most people as fools. Or, at least, people who take up his time unnecessarily when he's got more important things to do.'

'Such as?'

'I get the impression he'd prefer to be treating sick people than looking at corpses.' He sighed. 'But then, he doesn't seem fond of sick people either. The fact that the doctor hasn't arrived yet suggests to me that today's on-call doctor is Dr McKay.'

The sound of footsteps approaching made them turn towards the entrance. A constable, carrying a torch, entered, accompanied by a short, thin, bearded man in his late fifties.

'Dr McKay's here, sir,' announced the constable.

'What have we got?' demanded McKay gruffly.

'A dead woman who's suffered extreme injuries,' said Harker.

McKay approached the dead woman, then carefully lifted the bottom of her skirt and raised it.

'My God!' he said. 'These aren't just extreme injuries. She's been eviscerated.'

'Yes,' said Harker. He gestured towards Coburg and Lampson. 'These gentlemen are from Scotland Yard. DCI Coburg and DS Lampson.'

'Why have you called them in?' demanded McKay disapprovingly.

'Because of something we found at the crime scene,' said Harker. He pointed at the ancient doctor's case.

McKay walked to it.

'Be careful about touching it,' cautioned Coburg. 'We'll need to check it for fingerprints.'

McKay looked at Harker. 'Has it been opened already?' he asked.

'Yes,' said Harker. 'I opened it.'

'So there'll already be fingerprints on it.' McKay took out a handkerchief, with which he covered his hand and flicked the lock. The case fell open, revealing a set of old-fashioned surgical instruments.

'Victorian,' announced McKay.

'You're sure?' asked Coburg.

'Absolutely,' said McKay curtly. 'My grandfather had one identical to this.'

'Where did he practise?' asked Coburg.

'Why?' asked McKay.

'I wondered if it was a design made to a particular area.'

'No,' said McKay. 'But, for the record, my grandfather practised in Edinburgh.' He turned to Harker. 'I brought an ambulance with me to take the body. I told them to wait outside until I gave them instructions.' He turned to the constable. 'You may instruct them to come down and collect the body.'

The constable departed, and McKay stood looking thoughtfully down at the body. 'Do we know who she is?'

'Not yet,' said Harker. 'There's been no purse or any sort of identification found here. We'll start asking questions locally once she's been taken away.'

'I suggest a police photographer takes a picture of her, which we can show around,' said Coburg. 'With your permission, of course, Doctor.'

McKay nodded in agreement.

'I'll send a photographer to the London,' said Harker.

McKay turned to Coburg. 'What's your opinion of the surgeon's case being left so obviously, Chief Inspector?'

'We'll be looking into that,' replied Coburg guardedly.

The doctor gave a sniff to show he wasn't impressed by this answer.

There were footsteps outside, then the constable returned, accompanied by three ambulance men carrying a stretcher. McKay watched as they loaded the dead woman's body onto the stretcher, then he followed them out after saying, 'I'll give you my report, Sergeant, after I've examined her.'

Coburg waited until he was sure the doctor was well out of earshot before he commented, 'Not exactly a ray of sunshine, is he.'

'He is what he is,' said Harker resignedly. He pointed at the surgeon's case. 'What do you want to do about this?'

'We'll take it with us for a proper examination. If you need it, it'll be at Scotland Yard. Can you get your men to do a detailed inspection of the station, checking in case there's anything that looks suspicious. After all, you know this place better than we do, so if there's anything that looks odd – like the surgeon's case – your people are more likely to spot it. I hope you didn't mind my suggesting that your people arrange the taking of the photograph. My thinking is that your men know the people of this area and will know best how to use the photograph of the dead woman, who to specifically show it to and talk to, for example.'

'That makes sense,' said Harker. 'We'll start with the people who were in the air raid shelter last night, see if anyone knows who she is. And if anybody saw her going off with any men.'

'Excellent,' said Coburg. 'Thank you, Sergeant.'

As Coburg and Lampson left the station and walked to their car, carrying the case, they were watched by a shadowy figure on the other side of the road.

So, they've taken the first two bites of the bait. The Watcher smiled. *The body and the case. Good. It's begun.*

CHAPTER TWO

Rosa walked with John Fawcett, her producer, into the small theatre deep below ground at the BBC Maida Vale studios.

'You've been here before, I believe,' said Fawcett.

'Yes. Before the war,' said Rosa. 'It was a programme of piano jazz, and I was lucky enough to be one of the artistes featured.' She looked around at the rows of plush red seats. 'I love this theatre. Three hundred seats means it has an intimacy you rarely get in the larger concert halls.'

'Which is why I thought it would be perfect for *Rosa Weeks Presents*,' said Fawcett.

He strolled down the aisle to the slightly raised stage where two chairs had been placed by the grand piano. 'We'll be broadcasting the first show next Tuesday evening. I thought we could chat through the programme and presentation, see what we'll need. Did I tell you your guests for the first show?'

'Yes. Flanagan and Allen, and Vera Lynn. That's wonderful. You were lucky to get them; they're so busy.'

'I've known them for some time, worked with them before on different shows, which helped. I also think they were quite intrigued by the idea of doing a show with just a small trio instead of the usual big band. Do you have anyone in mind for your drummer and bass player, or do you want me to find your sidemen?'

'I was going to ask if you'd agree to Wally Dawes and Eric Pickup. Wally is a drummer I've worked with before at different venues, and Eric I've worked with on recordings.'

Fawcett looked thoughtful, then said, 'Yes, I've worked with Eric, he'll be superb. But are you sure about Wally?'

'Why?' asked Rosa.

'Well, I haven't worked with him for a while, and he was always good, but lately I've heard he's got a bit of a drink problem.'

'A drink problem?' said Rosa, surprised. 'I hadn't heard that. But then, I haven't seen him for a while either. The war has interrupted a lot of sessions. But if you'd prefer another drummer?'

'No, no,' said Fawcett. 'If he's your choice, I'm happy to try him out. I do remember him before the war. Always excellent, especially on the backbeat. However, I believe he was caught in a raid that brought down part of the building he was in, and he's had some difficulty recovering. Shall we try a session with you, Wally and Eric and see how it works out? If he's alright, I'm happy to go ahead. When are you free? I know you're driving the ambulance . . .'

'For this, my boss, Mr Warren, has said he will give me whatever time off I need.'

'In that case, how about the day after tomorrow? Wednesday. I suggest early afternoon.'

Rosa smiled. 'Seeing how Wally is after lunchtime?'

'Just a cautionary measure,' said Fawcett. 'I'll make the arrangements with their agents. Will half past two suit you?'

'Half past two will be perfect.'

'We won't have Flanagan and Allen or Vera for the run-through, but I'll be happy for you to take the vocals. After all, I just want to see how the trio fits together. Bud and Chesney will be doing

"Underneath the Arches" and "Shine On, Harvest Moon"; and Vera will be singing "We'll Meet Again" and "Red Sails in the Sunset".'

'Excellent,' said Rosa. 'I've got the music at home so I'll practise those.'

'I was thinking for your opening song to be "Up A Lazy River", if that's alright with you. I know you admire Hoagy Carmichael. I feel "Lazy River" has a gentle quality about it that will be perfect for bringing the audience listening at home in. My thought is to begin with the opening verse and chorus, then you say: "Good evening, listeners. I'm Rosa Weeks and this is *Rosa Weeks Presents*. In tonight's show you'll be hearing from my special guests, Flanagan and Allen and Vera Lynn, and I'll be putting in a few songs of my own. I hope you enjoy the show." Then you return to the song. We'll have applause from the audience, which someone will signal, and then you do your second number, after which we'll have Bud and Chesney. Then Vera comes in to do a number; then you do one. Then Vera does her second, followed by you, then Bud and Chesney. And finally, you again to round off the show. Then, while you and the trio play out with a musical version of "Lazy River", an announcer comes on and gives the closing credits, and we end with more applause from the audience. How does that sound?'

'It sounds very well worked out,' said Rosa. 'Very impressive. I hope the boys and I can do you justice.'

'I'm confident you and Eric will,' said Fawcett. 'However, I reserve judgement on Wally until the day after tomorrow.'

As Coburg and Lampson entered the large reception area at Scotland Yard, Coburg noticed the duty sergeant at the desk, Sergeant Crawford, hailing him and walked over.

'Yes, Dan?' asked Coburg.

'Superintendent Allison is looking for you,' said Crawford. 'He seemed quite agitated about something.'

'Did he say what it was about?'

'No, just asked where you were. In fact he's phoned down twice since to see if you'd come in, so I get the impression that whatever it is, it's urgent.'

'Thanks, Dan. I'll go and see him straight away.'

Coburg and Lampson made their way up the wide marble staircase to the first floor and Coburg headed for the superintendent's office, while Lampson made for theirs. Coburg knocked at the superintendent's door, and at the command 'Enter' walked in.

'Ah, there you are at last, Coburg,' said Allison impatiently. 'Where have you been?'

'Out on a case, sir.'

Instead of asking for details of the case, the superintendent said brusquely, 'Forget that. You're to go to the palace at once.'

Coburg looked at the superintendent and asked, puzzled, 'Which palace, sir?'

There were so many palaces in London: Lambeth Palace, Alexandra Palace, Crystal Palace, not to mention the royal palaces. Allison looked at him in disapproval, as if his chief inspector was being deliberately obtuse. 'Buckingham Palace,' he said. 'The King wishes to talk to you.'

Coburg was on the point of asking, *King George VI?*, just to make sure he'd heard right, but a look at the expression of annoyed impatience on Allison's face made him instead ask, 'For what purpose, sir?'

'You'll be told that when you meet him. I told the palace

you'd be there as soon as you returned. Unfortunately, I had no way of knowing where you and Sergeant Lampson had disappeared to. You left no message of your whereabouts.'

'No, sir, for which I apologise. We'd had a call about a dead body in Whitechapel.'

'Whitechapel? Couldn't the local force handle that?'

'It was the local Whitechapel force who contacted us because of some strange circumstances in the case.'

The superintendent chose not to ask further questions about Whitechapel; it obviously held little interest for him. Certainly not the same interest as a request from the King of England.

'Very well, but I urge you to get to the palace.'

'Yes, sir. I'll just inform Sergeant Lampson.'

Allison shook his head. 'Just your presence is requested.' He looked at his watch. 'I suggest you leave now. We don't want His Majesty to feel he has been kept waiting.'

'Yes, sir.'

Allison stopped Coburg as he was about to leave. 'One thing, Chief Inspector. I have to make a telephone call to alert the palace that you are on your way, and another to a third party. I understand that there may well be someone else in attendance when you meet the King.'

'Yes, sir. May I ask who?'

'As that depends on whether this person is available, I'm afraid you will have to wait and see who awaits you.'

All very mysterious, thought Coburg as he walked towards his office. Despite the superintendent urging speed, he couldn't just leave without letting Lampson know he was going out. He opened the door of his office and looked in. Lampson looked enquiringly at him.

'Everything alright?'

'Hopefully I'll tell you when I come back,' said Coburg. 'I've got to go out.'

With that, he pulled the door shut and made his way downstairs and out to his car.

On his arrival at the gates of Buckingham Palace he was stopped by two uniformed policemen. He showed them his warrant card and told them, 'I have an appointment with His Majesty.'

They had obviously been briefed to expect him, because he was waved through, after being directed to drive through the arch to the rear of the palace.

No sooner had he parked than a man in a footman's uniform appeared and asked, 'DCI Saxe-Coburg?'

'Yes,' said Coburg.

'If you'll follow me,' said the footman. 'His Majesty is in his study. He's expecting you.'

Coburg followed the footman into the palace, then up some stairs and along a series of corridors, until they arrived at a large oak door. The footman knocked at the door, then opened it and announced: 'Detective Chief Inspector Saxe-Coburg, Your Majesty.'

The footman opened the door wider and Coburg entered.

The King had been seated in an uncomfortable-looking wooden armchair and he rose to his feet as Coburg entered.

What do I do? wondered Coburg. *Do I bow? Offer to shake hands?*

His dilemma was resolved when the King held out his hand towards Coburg and they shook hands.

'Thank you for coming, Chief Inspector.'

'I'm flattered to be asked, Your Majesty,' said Coburg. 'I am at your complete service.'

The King gestured for Coburg to sit, then seated himself.

Although Coburg had seen the King in newsreels, it was the first time he'd seen him face to face. A slender man in his mid-forties of medium height, there were still traces of the stammer that had plagued him in his young life, but he'd obviously learnt to control it, taking short breaks between sentences. Coburg recalled being told that an Australian speech therapist called Lionel Logue had been the one who worked with him to help him overcome his stammer, and that the King – although at the time of this therapy he'd still been Prince Albert, only becoming King after the abdication of his elder brother, formerly King Edward VIII and now the Duke of Windsor, who abandoned the throne in order to marry the divorced Mrs Wallis Simpson – had worked on his vocal and breathing exercises with his wife, Elizabeth Bowes-Lyon, now Queen Elizabeth.

'Saxe-Coburg,' said the King thoughtfully. 'I assume we must be related to some degree.'

'It's possible, sir. Although I've never really explored my family history.'

'Your father was the Earl of Dawlish, a title now held by your elder brother, Magnus.'

'That's correct, sir.'

'The House of Saxe-Coburg and Gotha was founded in 1826, by Ernest Anton, the sixth duke of Saxe-Coburg-Saalfield. It was a cadet branch of the Saxon house of Wettin. Various branches of the family were extant throughout Europe in the last century. Ernest Anton's younger brother, Leopold, became King of Belgium in 1831, and his descendants continue to rule. It was Ernest's second son, Prince Albert, who married my great-grandmother, Queen Victoria. Victoria was herself a niece of Ernest and thus a first cousin of Prince Albert. There are other branches of the family in Portugal, Austria, Bulgaria and even Brazil. So it is quite feasible that somewhere along the line, some of our mutual ancestors intermingled.'

'Yes, sir.'

The King smiled. 'When I was growing up, part of my education consisted of my family history. It has stuck with me rather than my deliberately seeking it out to study. Of course, the family interest in the Saxe-Coburg-Gothas rather waned after my father changed the family name to Windsor in 1917, but I've always been interested in where we came from. It might be of interest to ask your brother about your family's particular roots to see where we intersect.'

'I will, sir. Thank you.'

'However, that is by the by. The reason I have asked you here is because one of my valets has disappeared.'

'Disappeared?'

'Yes. Bernard Bothwell. Three days ago he did not report for work. A messenger was despatched to his residence to see if he was indisposed, but his family reported that he seemed to have vanished. He left for work as usual, but never returned home. They reported his disappearance to the local police, who checked the hospitals and other places where he might have gone, but there has been no trace of him.'

'So the local police are aware of his disappearance?'

'Yes. But that is all they know.' He paused, then said, 'Unfortunately, coinciding with his disappearance, a personal item of mine has also gone missing.'

Before he could continue, they were interrupted by the door opening and the bulky figure of a large man hurried in.

'My apologies, Your Majesty,' boomed the new arrival in fruity rich tones that Coburg immediately recognised as belonging to the Prime Minister, Winston Churchill.

Immediately, Coburg rose to his feet.

'Detective Chief Inspector Saxe-Coburg,' said Churchill, and walked towards Coburg, his hand outstretched. Coburg shook it. 'I know your brother Magnus well. We were comrades in arms during the First War.'

'Yes, sir,' said Coburg. 'He often talks of you.'

'Well, I hope?' asked Churchill.

'He always sings your praises, Prime Minister.'

Churchill smiled. 'A good man. A very good man. It was he who suggested we contact you about this appalling situation.' He gestured at the chair behind Coburg. 'Sit, man. Sit.' He turned to the King and said, 'Again, my apologies, Your Majesty. My lateness is due to reports of enemy action that came in this morning, which I needed to deal with. North Africa. Have you filled the chief inspector in on what has occurred?'

'Only the disappearance of Bernard Bothwell. I was just about to inform him of my personal loss when you arrived.'

'A watch,' said Churchill. 'And not just any watch. It was a gift to His Majesty from his late father, King George V, and therefore particularly precious. There is no doubt in my mind that this villain Bothwell has taken it.'

'We cannot be certain of that, Winston,' cautioned the King.

'The disappearance of Bothwell and the disappearance of the watch at the same time shows the two are connected. Find

Bothwell and we find the watch. Or, at least, what he did with it. I'm sure you agree, Chief Inspector?'

'With respect, Prime Minister, I agree with His Majesty. There may be another explanation. My experience as a police detective has taught me it is best to keep an open mind on any investigation.'

'Hmph,' grunted Churchill, obviously not pleased with Coburg's reaction. 'Very well. But it is important that this timepiece is recovered. And without publicity. We cannot let news of this theft, if that is what it is, and the strange disappearance of the King's valet become public knowledge. It could lead to a loss of morale in the security surrounding the royal family, and that is the last thing we can afford to happen. So, you can use every instrument at your disposal, but the item that is sought – this precious watch – is not to be mentioned outside this room. Concentrate on the valet. His disappearance is already known to the local police, so we can contain any harm the story might do as a personal tragedy.'

'You said that my brother, Magnus, recommended me to you,' said Coburg. 'Do I understand from that, that he knows about the situation?'

Churchill hesitated momentarily, before saying, 'He knows about the disappearance of the valet, and the fact that something precious to His Majesty is also missing. The people who know about the watch are limited to those of us in this room: His Majesty, me, and you. And we'd like to keep it that way.'

'I understand that,' said Coburg. Hesitantly, he asked, 'There is one exception I would be grateful if you would consider. My detective sergeant, Sergeant Lampson, has shown himself to be brave, patriotic and the ultimate in discretion. With your agreement, I would like to share that information with him. He is highly intelligent and has the best nose of any police officer in sniffing out the truth. I can assure you he would not pass on the information about the watch, but if he knew what we were looking for, I believe it would mean we would have a greater chance of recovering it.'

The Prime Minister looked enquiringly at the King. 'What do you, say, sir?'

The King looked at the two men thoughtfully, then said, 'I believe we should accept the advice from the chief inspector.' He looked at Coburg. 'If you can assure us this will not lead to the story of the watch getting out.'

'I can assure you of that, sir. Sergeant Lampson would give his life rather than disclose that information.'

'Very well,' said Churchill. 'You may tell this Sergeant Lampson. But no one else.'

'And who should I report to?' asked Coburg.

'To me,' said Churchill. He looked at the King. 'Will that be alright, Your Majesty? We both know that you are often out and about on affairs of state, whereas I am usually contactable.'

The King nodded. 'Yes, that is acceptable.'

'One last question,' said Coburg. 'You told me, sir, that the disappearance of your valet had been reported to the local police. Could you let me have details of the local station it was reported to, and the senior officer who was tasked with looking into it?'

Again, the King nodded. 'Certainly. I'll get my secretary to find those details and contacts and messenger them to you at Scotland Yard.'

CHAPTER THREE

On his return to Scotland Yard, Coburg sought out his sergeant in their office, and gestured for him to follow him. Curious, Lampson followed the chief inspector downstairs and then outside into the street.

'I've got something to tell you that's very private, so we need to be somewhere we can't be overheard,' said Coburg. 'There's a small public gardens just along the road; we'll find ourselves a bench there.'

When they got to the small ornamental garden area, Coburg and Lampson found a bench and settled themselves down.

'I've just come from Buckingham Palace,' Coburg told his sergeant. 'I was summoned there to meet the King and the Prime Minister.'

'Blimey,' said Lampson, impressed. 'What is it? Are you up for a knighthood or something?'

'Nothing like that. It seems the King's valet, a man called Bernard Bothwell, has vanished and they want us to find him.'

'Why us?'

'Because of what they say he's taken, and absolutely no one else is to know about this. At first they didn't even want me to tell you; it was just supposed to be between me, the King, and Churchill. Luckily, I was able to persuade them that you wouldn't tell anyone.'

'Does that include Eve?'

Eve was Lampson's wife, who he'd married just a few weeks before.

'I'm afraid so.'

'Okay,' said Lampson. 'What did this bloke take?'

'According to them, he took a watch that was given to the King by his father, which makes it special.'

'A watch?' said Lampson in disbelief.

'I don't believe it either,' agreed Coburg. 'I'm sure there's something else going on that they don't want mentioned. But we have to go through the paces, looking for this Bernard Bothwell and this mysterious watch. Churchill said "Find the man and you find the watch." My belief is that it's the man they want, but they don't want anyone knowing about it if we find him, and they certainly don't want anyone knowing what he took from the King, if he took anything.'

Lampson looked concerned. 'It sounds like we're getting into murky waters. Are Special Branch involved? Or the intelligence services?'

'Not according to Churchill, which makes the whole thing even murkier.'

'So how do we go about it?'

'The King said he'll send me the details of Bothwell, and also of the local police station which his wife reported his disappearance to.'

'So the local police are involved?'

'But only in the fact the valet's disappeared, not about this alleged watch. Until those details arrive there's not a lot we can do, so I suggest we return to the office and see what else we've got on our plates.'

'There's the Whitechapel murder. And that series of jewel robberies.'

'Yes. We might have to offload the jewel robberies. I've got a feeling this search for the valet is going to be very time-consuming, and as it's for the King and Churchill, they'll expect a quick result.'

As Coburg walked into their flat in Piccadilly, Rosa was sitting at the piano playing.

'That's nice,' he said. '"Up a Lazy River". Hoagy Carmichael.'

'My BBC producer wants that to be the theme song for my *Rosa Weeks Presents*,' she told him. 'If we get a series, that is. This is just a pilot show, as they call it. So I'm making sure I can play it fluently.'

'Oh yes, you were seeing your producer today. How did it go?'

'Very good. I'll tell you all about it later, but first, Magnus phoned for you.'

'What did he want?'

'He wants your advice about the East End.'

'Did he say why?'

'Something to do with Churchill. He said he'd tell you himself later.'

'I'd better speak to him and see what's going on.'

Coburg picked up the receiver and asked the operator to connect him to Magnus's number. It was Magnus's old friend and general factotum, Malcolm, who answered.

'Malcolm, it's Edgar. Is Magnus there?'

'Yes he is, Master Edgar.'

A few second later, Magnus was on the phone.

'Rosa tells me you want my advice about the East End,' said Coburg. 'Something to do with Churchill.'

'Yes. Churchill got in touch with me because he's very concerned about the amount of damage the Luftwaffe is doing to the East End. Apparently the Home Secretary passed him a petition signed by the people of the Stepney area protesting about the lack of proper air raid facilities. By all accounts Whitechapel is one of the worst affected. They seem to be bearing the brunt of the Nazi bombing.'

'They are,' agreed Coburg. 'I was in Whitechapel today and saw the effects for myself.'

'Churchill is concerned about morale being low there.'

'It is. The death rate there is worse than almost anywhere else in London.'

'The thing he's asked me to do is go to the area and look around, for places that can be quickly converted into air raid facilities. I must admit it's not an area I know well, so I was hoping you might be able to give me some guidance. I intend to visit the area with Malcolm, but it would help us enormously if you could make suggestions about where we should look.'

'My advice is to have a word with Sergeant Harker at Whitechapel police station. Joe Harker, that is. He's a really good man with a comprehensive knowledge of the Whitechapel area. I'd be happy to phone him and tell him you'll be calling on him.'

'Would you? That would be enormously helpful, Edgar.'

'My thought is he'll also know who it's best for you to get in touch with about the rest of the area. Stepney, Poplar, Canning Town. And the south side of the river: Bermondsey, Wapping, the Isle of Dogs.'

'Thank you. That would be excellent. Sergeant Joe Harker at Whitechapel police station, you said.'

'That's right. I'll see if I can get hold of him now. If he's not at the station, I'll call him first thing tomorrow morning.'

'Thank you.'

'There's another thing I wanted to talk to you about. I had a meeting today at the palace.'

'Ah,' said Magnus, a tone of caution and warning in his voice. 'I don't think this is something we should talk about over the telephone.'

'I agree,' said Coburg. 'I was going to ask if I could call on you.'

'Certainly,' said Magnus. 'When?'

'As you're in, would it be alright if I came over now?'

'Could you make it an hour?' asked Magnus. 'Malcolm has prepared our evening meal, which is hot, and he's just putting it on the table.'

'An hour will be fine,' said Coburg.

He hung up and Rosa asked, 'A meeting at the palace?'

'Yes,' said Coburg. 'With no less a person than the King himself.'

'A gathering of policemen?' asked Rosa.

'No, just myself, the King, and Churchill.'

'My God!' said Rosa, impressed. 'You do move in exalted company. What was it about?'

'Officially I'm not allowed to tell you,' said Coburg. 'But because I know my life would be unbearable if I didn't, I'll tell you as much as I can, but you are sworn to secrecy. If it gets out that I've told you anything, my career will be over and I'll possibly end up in jail.'

'I promise,' said Rosa. 'No one will hear it from me.'

Coburg told her about his meeting with the King because one of his valets had gone missing, along with a personal item of the King's that had gone missing at the same time.

'What sort of personal item?' asked Rosa.

'Well, that's the thing I'm not allowed to tell anyone,' said Coburg. 'To be honest, it's all very strange and I'm not sure if I'm being told the whole truth. In fact, I wouldn't be surprised to find it's all a red herring. As it is I'm not supposed to even tell you about the valet going missing. If it got out that I'd told you I could well be tried for treason or something.'

'I promise, not a word about it will cross my lips.' She thought it over, then asked, 'If you think there's something else going on, do you think Magnus might know what it is? He's close to Churchill.'

'I don't know. It seems it was Magnus who recommended to Churchill that I look into what's happened, but I'm not sure how much he's been told. As he and Churchill are old comrades, it's possible Churchill may have told him. But, even if he did, knowing Magnus, his first loyalty is to Churchill and the King.'

'So this could be a pointless visit.'

'It could be,' admitted Coburg. 'But I like to know what I'm getting myself into. Anyway, that's my day. You said you'd tell me about your meeting at the BBC. When does your pilot show go out?'

'Next Tuesday evening. We're broadcasting from the theatre at the Maida Vale studios.'

'Can you arrange a seat for me?'

'I'll ask Mr Fawcett. He seems very amiable, so I'm sure it'll be okay.'

'There's something else, isn't there?' said Coburg. 'Something that's bothering you.'

'That's the problem with being married to a detective.' Rosa laughed. 'I can't hide things. Yes, it's the drummer. The music is to be by a trio, me on piano and two old chums of mine, Wally Dawes on drums and Eric Pickup on bass. What with one thing and another, mainly the war, I haven't seen either of them for a few months. But John Fawcett told me that a while ago Wally was involved in a bombing raid that rattled him.'

'So, he's unsteady?'

'I'm not sure if "unsteady" is the right word. According to Mr Fawcett, Wally drinks. Heavily.'

'And he wants him replaced?'

'He does, but he's agreed to give him a chance. The day after tomorrow we're going to have a session to go through the music for the show, the three of us with Mr Fawcett, but mainly I think it's to see how Wally is. How he handles himself.' She sighed. 'I hope it goes okay. Wally's a really nice guy; I've always got on well with him and worked well with him.'

'I suppose you'll just have to wait and see the day after tomorrow. If he turns out to be falling short, at least you'll have time to get another drummer.'

'Yes, but that's not the point. It's how it will affect Wally if he gets dropped. It would finish him off.' She looked at the clock. 'Anyway, that's for another day. You'd better get off. Magnus will be waiting.'

'I will,' said Coburg. 'But first I'll see if Sergeant Joe Harker is still at work.'

Coburg was told that Sergeant Harker had left Whitechapel police station, so he left a message that he'd get in touch with him in the morning. He then drove to Magnus's flat.

Magnus was indeed waiting. For once, he was on his own.

'As we're going to be talking about your discussion with the King, Malcolm has tactfully taken himself off for an hour.'

'We met at the palace,' said Coburg.

Magnus said nothing, waiting for Coburg to continue.

'The Prime Minister was there as well.'

'I imagined he would be.'

'What's really going on, Magnus?'

'What do you mean? I assume they told you His Majesty's valet has disappeared, and by all accounts he's taken an item precious to the King, and they'd like you to look into it, with the greatest discretion and without telling anyone else.'

'Have you been informed of what that item is?'

'No. Churchill didn't tell me and I didn't ask.'

'And you recommended me to find the valet and the item.'

'Possibly,' said Magus guardedly.

'What do you mean, "possibly"?'

'Churchill asked me who was the best detective at Scotland Yard, and I told him in my opinion you were. But I got the impression he'd already reached that conclusion. You really do have a good reputation amongst the chattering classes, Edgar. All those cases you've solved involving foreign royalty, top diplomats. Even Charles de Gaulle, I'm told. And he's not the sort to praise anyone English easily. All I will say is to wish you well and hope you can sort this out. The King is a really good man.'

CHAPTER FOUR

Tuesday 1st April

When Coburg and Lampson arrived at their office the next morning, they found a uniformed constable standing outside the door.

'Apologies for disturbing you, sir,' said the constable. 'But Superintendent Allison has asked that Chief Inspector Coburg see him as soon as you arrive.'

'Thank you, Constable,' said Coburg, and set off for the superintendent's office, leaving Lampson to go into their office.

The superintendent was sitting at his desk when Coburg entered his office.

'You wanted to see me, sir?'

'Yes.' Allison reached inside one of the drawers of his desk and took out an envelope, which he handed to Coburg. 'This came by messenger for you this morning.'

The envelope bore the crest of Buckingham Palace, and was stamped *Private and Confidential*.

'Thank you, sir,' said Coburg.

'I assume this is a result of your meeting with the King yesterday,' said Allison.

'I assume so, sir.'

'Did the meeting go well?'

'It seemed to, sir. The Prime Minister was also present.'

'Just the three of you?'

'Yes, sir.'

'Are you able to tell me what happened at that meeting?'

'Yes, sir. One of His Majesty's valets has disappeared. The valet's family reported his disappearance to their local police station, but without success, so His Majesty has asked me to investigate and locate the valet.'

Allison thought this over, then asked, 'Did he say why he wanted this valet found?'

'No, sir. Just that he wanted him found. His Majesty and the Prime Minister have given me permission to enrol Sergeant Lampson to help me with the investigation.'

'Just the two of you?'

'Yes, sir. With the assistance of the local police as they've already been notified of the man's disappearance.'

'And which local station is that?'

'They did not advise me of that yesterday. His Majesty informed me he would be sending me details.' He held up the envelope. 'I imagine that's what this envelope contains.'

'In that case you'd better open it,' said Allison.

'I will, sir. Thank you, sir.'

As Coburg headed for the door, Allison added, 'And if you need any assistance, don't hesitate to contact me. As the King and the Prime Minister have requested you for this, this must be considered top priority.'

'Thank you, sir. I will make sure it is.'

Coburg returned to the office, where Lampson was keen to know what the superintendent had wanted. Coburg showed him the envelope. 'I think he was hoping I'd open this there and then. He wanted to know how I got on at the palace yesterday.'

'What did you tell him?'

'About the valet going missing.'

'Nothing else?'

'No.' Coburg smiled. 'I don't know anything else.'

He opened the envelope and took out a sheet of paper with lines of information. A smaller piece of paper had been attached to it with the handwritten message *As per*, and signed *G.*

'G?' said Lampson, looking over Coburg's shoulder.

'George,' said Coburg. 'As in George VI.'

'Bloody hell!' exclaimed Lampson. 'That'll be worth a bit, that will. Autograph hunters will pay big money for the King's signature.'

'No one's paying any money for this,' said Coburg firmly. 'I shall hang on to it in case it's needed to get people to co-operate, but after that I'm burning it.' He read the details on the sheet of paper. 'It's all here. Bernard Bothwell's address in Wilton Road, Pimlico. His wife's name, Jean Bothwell. They have two children, a son aged fifteen and a daughter aged twelve. Their telephone number is also here. As is the telephone number of the police station at Pimlico, along with the name of Sergeant Walter Radford, the officer they reported Bothwell's disappearance to.' He looked at the list of contacts. 'We'll start with Sergeant Radford at Pimlico, then we'll make contact with Mrs Bothwell and arrange to call on her,' he told Lampson. 'I get the idea we're in for a busy day.' He looked at the telephone on his desk and said guiltily, 'I said I'd call

Sergeant Harker this morning, but with the superintendent on my back about this business with the King, I'd better do that a bit later.'

Coburg's and Lampson's first visit was to Pimlico police station, where they found Sergeant Radford on duty.

'DCI Coburg and DS Lampson from Scotland Yard,' said Coburg, introducing themselves. 'We've been tasked by His Majesty King George VI to look into the disappearance of Bernard Bothwell, the King's valet. We understand you're already looking into it.'

'The King!' exclaimed Radford, awed. 'Scotland Yard! This is big, then?'

'We're not sure,' said Coburg. 'If he turns up then it won't be. What have you found so far?'

'Nothing,' admitted Radford unhappily. 'Mrs Bothwell came in and said her husband had gone missing, but we get a lot of that, husbands going missing for a day or two. Usually they turn up.'

'Did she mention that her husband worked for the King as his valet at Buckingham Palace?'

Radford looked very uncomfortable. 'She may have done,' he said awkwardly. 'I'll have a look at the notes we made when she came in.'

'Did you talk to her yourself?' asked Coburg.

'I did, at first,' said Radford. 'But when I realised there hadn't been a crime, as such, I passed her over to one of the constables to take details. We were really busy on that day. There'd been a robbery at a jeweller's, someone had been stabbed. There was a lot going on.'

'I'll need a full report of what action you and your men took, and the continuation of your investigations,' Coburg told the sergeant sternly. 'The King and the Prime Minister have asked me to make a full report on how this was handled. They will be looking into your actions personally.'

'I think you put the fear of God into him, guv.' Lampson grinned as they left the police station.

'Good,' said Coburg, annoyed. 'I can't stand laxness and inefficiency in anything, and even more so in a police investigation. I'm hoping the fear of what might happen to him might make him pull his finger out.'

They reached the car. 'Where to next, guv?' asked Lampson, sliding into the driving seat.

'Wilton Road, to talk to Bernard's missus.'

Jean Bothwell was obviously relieved when Coburg and Lampson introduced themselves and the reason for their visit.

'Scotland Yard?' she said, surprised.

'At the personal request of His Majesty, King George VI,' said Coburg. 'He's very worried about Bernard's disappearance and has asked us to look into it.'

'Do come in,' she said, and took them through to the living room. 'I hope you do a better job than that sergeant at Pimlico station,' she said, obviously aggrieved. 'He wasn't interested. He pretended he was, but I could see he just thought I was some silly woman.'

'Rest assured, Mrs Bothwell, we are taking this very seriously. When did you last see your husband?'

'Friday morning. Six o'clock. He left to go to work. He goes in at that time because the King likes to sort his wardrobe out for the day. Bernard's one of two valets, so there's always one of them to look after the King. They do shifts. Bernard does the day shift from seven o'clock until four. The other valet does from four in the afternoon until seven in the morning.'

'What's the other valet's name?'

'Hector McBride. He's Scottish.'

'How do he and Bernard get on?'

'Very well. At least, I've never heard Bernard complain about him. Mr McBride usually stays overnight at the palace, unless the King and Queen have gone to Windsor. In which case, Mr McBride goes with them, because the King depends on his valets. The two princesses are at Windsor, you see, for safety because of the air raids, but the King and Queen like to spend time with them as often as they can.'

'How does Bernard travel to work?'

'He gets the bus that goes up Belgrave Road. It drops him close to the Palace.'

'And he finishes work at four in the afternoon. What time does he get home?'

'Depending on how the buses are running, he's usually home at five.'

'But on Friday he never came back?'

'No. I did wonder if he'd gone to see his sister, Ethel. He'd had a letter from her saying she was worried about her daughter, Sarah, and he thought he ought to go and see if there was anything he could do to help. But when Bernard still hadn't arrived by eight o'clock I went to see Ethel and she said she hadn't seen him.'

'You didn't telephone her?'

'Ethel's not on the phone.'

'Where does Ethel live?'

'Whitechapel Road in Whitechapel. Her name's Ethel Mars.'

'Do you have her address?'

Mrs Bothwell wrote the address down on a piece of paper and handed it to Coburg.

'Can you think of any reason why your husband would vanish like this?' asked Coburg. 'Was he happy at work? Had he had any rows with anyone recently?'

'No,' said Mrs Bothwell. 'And he was very happy at work. He loved working for the King. It made him very proud.'

'Did he have any money worries?'

'No. We've been lucky that way. Bernard's always worked in good jobs.'

'Is there anyone he might have gone to stay with? A friend for some reason?'

'He doesn't really have many friends, as such. He's pally with George Moore next door and occasionally they go to the pub together. But only now and then. He prefers to be at home. And, if he had been going anywhere, he'd have let me know. He's good that way.'

'Do you have a photograph of your husband I could borrow?' asked Coburg. 'I'd like to distribute it to the other local police forces, see if there's been any sighting of him. I promise I'll return it.'

'Of course,' said Mrs Bothwell. 'And thank you for this, Chief Inspector. It's so unlike Bernard.'

As Coburg and Lampson left the house and made for their car, Lampson asked, 'D'you think she was telling the truth?'

'I do,' said Coburg. 'The question is was her husband telling her the truth?'

'Where to now?' asked Lampson. 'His sister in Whitechapel?'

Coburg nodded. 'While we're there, I'll be able to call in and talk to Sergeant Harker face to face about Magnus, which is always better.' Then he added thoughtfully, 'I wonder if this business with the valet is connected?'

'With the murder over there?'

'Just a thought.'

'I don't see how, guv.'

'Nor do I at the moment. But we've got this mystery of the missing valet, as well as a murder, and both look as if they might involve Whitechapel. I don't like coincidences.'

CHAPTER FIVE

Ethel Mars lived in a terraced house in Whitechapel Road, not very far from the former Tube station, now an air raid shelter. She was intrigued when they showed her their warrant cards and introduced themselves, and she invited them in.

'Is this about Bernard?' she asked. 'Jean was very worried when she called, said him not coming home wasn't like him at all.'

'And would you agree with that?'

'Oh, certainly. Bernard's always been a very responsible person. He's a couple of years older than me, so he was the man about the house after our dad died.'

'What happened to your father?'

'Pneumonia. Twenty-four years ago, it was. Is it true that Bernard's gone missing?'

'That's how it appears. You haven't heard from him?'

She shook her head. 'No. I'll tell you the same I told Jean. I haven't seen him or heard a word from him.'

'I ask because Jean told me you'd got in touch with your brother because you were worried about your daughter, Sarah.'

Ethel Mars was silent at this, unable to look Coburg in the eye.

'What's the problem with Sarah, Mrs Mars, and why did

you think your brother might be able to help?'

'It's the lack of a man about the house,' she finally said reluctantly. 'Her dad was taken prisoner at Dunkirk. Sarah was always a bit wild, but since her dad's not been here, she's got worse.'

'In what way?'

'The worst way,' said Mrs Mars. 'I think she's been getting money off men.'

'Prostitution?' asked Coburg.

For a moment she didn't say anything, kept her head down; then she nodded. 'She goes out and comes back with money.'

'Where does she go?'

'Pubs mostly. She won't listen to me. I thought if Bernard had a word with her he might be able to straighten her out. What she's doing is not just wrong, it's dangerous.'

'I know,' said Coburg. 'I was here yesterday at the air raid shelter.'

Mrs Mars shuddered. 'The woman who got killed. Carved up, they said. Is that right?'

'I'm afraid it is.'

'I told Sarah about it this morning. Warned her. She just laughed. Told me it wouldn't happen to her, she was careful. Maybe if you had a word with her?' she asked hopefully.

'I'll certainly try,' said Coburg. 'Where's Sarah now?'

'She's out. She's always out.'

'Where does she go?'

'Pubs. The shops. Now she's got money she buys herself things. Rubbish trinkets mostly. Before she had the money, she used to shoplift.'

Coburg nodded, then asked, 'Do you know Sergeant

Harker at Whitechapel police station?'

She gave an unhappy sigh. 'Yes. He's a good bloke. She got picked up a few times, drunk and disorderly, and soliciting. He tried to talk to her, but she just abused him.'

'How old is she?'

'Twenty-one. Too old to be put in juvenile protection.'

'I'll have a word with Sergeant Harker and ask him to get his men to pick her up and put her in custody, then phone me at Scotland Yard. I'll come down and talk to her.'

'She may not listen to you.'

'She may not. But, in the absence of your brother Bernard, I guess I'm all there is. I'll do my best, Mrs Mars.'

'Thank you.'

'Have you always lived here? In Whitechapel?'

'Yes. Me and Bernard grew up here. He and Jean lived here, just a few streets away, until he got the job at Buckingham Palace. He decided to move to be nearer to it. That's how he and Jean ended up in Pimlico. He's certainly gone up in the world.'

'Well, there's definitely a link there,' said Coburg as they left the house. 'The niece is obviously working as a prostitute here in Whitechapel. And we've got a dead prostitute here.'

'It doesn't mean the two cases are connected, guv,' cautioned Lampson again.

'True,' said Coburg. 'But as we're in Whitechapel I suggest we call on Sergeant Harker and see if there's any news. Even if there isn't, I can fill him in on Sarah Mars, and also tell him about Magnus.'

As it turned out, there was news.

'Good day, Chief Inspector,' Harker greeted them. 'I'm glad

you've called in. I was just about to phone you.'

'Oh?'

'We've got an identification for the dead woman at Whitechapel Road. She was Georgia Brand, a known prostitute. She was identified from the photo by a friend of hers, a Jess Windward, who's another one with a record for prostitution. We've talked to Windward but I wondered whether you'd like to have a word with her yourself.'

'Yes, I would. Thank you.'

'There's another thing. Someone else saw a man going off with her. His name's Brendan Riley, a local man. We pulled him in. At first he denied going off with her, but then he admitted he had. We took him into the tunnels and asked him which one he and Georgia Brand went to. It turned out to be the one where her body was found.'

'Strong evidence,' said Coburg.

'However, Riley insists she was alive when he left her. We've still got him here. We're holding him until we can confirm the victim was still alive when he left her. Would you like to talk to him?'

'I would indeed.'

'There's an interesting thing about Riley. Before the war he used to do walking tours of the Ripper murders, the sites where the women were killed, and he had all the details. Who was killed where, what was done to them. I thought it was a horrible thing for anyone to do, but people used to turn up. I cautioned Riley, told him I didn't like what he was doing. But, legally, there was nothing I could do about it.'

'But he stopped, anyway.'

'Yes, the bombing in this area put a stop to his activities.

People don't want to go for a night-time walk when bombs are falling. While you're talking to Riley I'll get one of my men to bring Windward in.'

'Thank you,' said Coburg. 'The reason we called in is because I believe you know Sarah Mars.'

Harker groaned. 'We do. What's she done now?'

'Just the usual, according to her mother, Ethel. I had occasion to call on Mrs Mars in respect of another investigation we're conducting.'

'In Whitechapel?'

'No, but some information we received led us to talk to Mrs Mars. She's worried about her daughter.'

'I'm not surprised. She's out of control. I told her myself when we had her in here, she'd come to a bad end if she didn't change her ways. But all she did was laugh at me.'

'Well, I've promised to have a word with Sarah. Personally, I doubt if it will do much, but Mrs Mars is at her wits' end.'

'It might have more impact than just me, a local sergeant, you being a chief inspector from Scotland Yard.'

'We'll see. All I can do is try. But I need to get hold of her, and she seems to be pretty elusive. So, can you ask your people if they see her to bring her in and hold her in custody, then I'll come over to talk to her.'

'What charge?'

'Whatever you think will hold her for a bit. Living on immoral earnings, drunk and disorderly, whatever fits.'

'No problem.' He produced a couple of sheets of typed-up paper and passed them to Coburg. 'This came from Dr McKay. It's his report on the woman who was found at Whitechapel station.'

Coburg read through McKay's report, then read it again, absorbing the information it contained.

'Two knives?' he said.

'That's Dr McKay's opinion,' said Harker. 'A broad blade with a sharp point dealt the initial killer blow, thrust into her upper body and penetrating the heart, then a narrower and very sharp knife was used to carry out the removal of the organs.'

'So it wasn't a spur-of-the-moment thing,' commented Coburg. 'Whoever did it went well prepared. Did Dr McKay have any thoughts on what sort of weapon this broad-bladed one was? He says that it was sharp on both edges.'

Harker picked up a small piece of paper. 'He attached this with it. He says he didn't want to put it in his report in case it sent us off on the wrong track but he believes it could have been a short sword.'

'A sword?' queried Coburg.

'Yes. You'd have thought that something like that would have been noticed.'

'Indeed,' said Coburg. He handed the report back to Harker. 'I'll leave this with you for the moment. If you can get hold of a copy, I'll put it in the file at Scotland Yard.'

Harker nodded. 'I'll ask at the hospital, see if they've got a copy for you. Do you want to see Riley now?'

'Yes,' said Coburg. 'Before we do, there's another thing I wanted to see you about. It concerns my brother, Magnus, the Earl of Dawlish.'

'An earl?'

'I'm afraid so.'

'Is he in trouble?'

'Fortunately not. It seems he's been tasked by the government with finding suitable places for more air raid shelters in the East End.'

'About time!' said Harker.

'I agree. The problem is, he's not familiar with the East End.'

Harker chuckled. 'Him being an earl, I'm not surprised.'

'The thing is he's taking this very seriously. He really wants to do a proper job. So I wondered if it would be alright if he came to see you to ask your advice on where might be the best places for him to look.'

'I only really know where the best places would be here in Whitechapel. I can't speak for places like Canning Town and the Isle of Dogs.'

'My hope would be that after he's looked Whitechapel over, you might be able to pass him on to your counterparts in the other areas around you. If you wouldn't mind, that is.'

'Not at all. Anything that saves lives over this way you can count me in to help. He's a genuine good bloke then, this brother of yours?'

'He is, and he has the ear of the Prime Minister, so you can be sure anything he comes up with will be put in action.'

'Excellent. Tell him to get in touch with me, he'll be very welcome.'

'He'll undoubtedly be accompanied by a chap called Malcolm Grant. They're old pals; they were in the trenches together during the First War. They still work together. Both good chaps.'

'Right. Tell him I'd be delighted to help. In the meantime, if you both go to the interview room, I'll bring Riley in.' He was about to leave, when he stopped. 'I thought it might be interesting for you to talk to Riley without me there. I've already quizzed him at length, so I thought we could swap our impressions of him afterwards, if that's okay.'

'Fine by me,' said Coburg.

Brendan Riley presented a sorry sight when he was led into the interview room. He was unshaven and he stank - a mixture of an unwashed body and unidentified odours emanating from his stained clothing. He was in his mid-fifties, with long hair curling over the velvet collar of his jacket, reminding Coburg of some of the pretentious actors he'd known, especially those of the Shakespearean school. As it turned out, Coburg wasn't far wrong, because Riley's opening words to them were: 'I used to be an actor, you know. Perhaps you remember me? I gave a memorable Hamlet at the Lyceum.'

'I'm afraid not,' said Coburg.

Riley sighed. 'Ah, such are the vagaries of a life on the stage. One moment lauded, the next treated with derision. And now fallen this low. Why am I being held here?'

'You were seen with a woman called Georgia Brand, a prostitute, at Whitechapel Road, the former Tube station.'

'I didn't ask her name,' said Riley dismissively. 'It was a commercial meeting, mine for relief, hers for cash.'

'She was murdered that same night. By all accounts, you were the last person she met with.'

'Obviously not,' said Riley pompously. 'That would be the person who killed her.'

'Which could be you,' said Coburg. 'What time did you meet her?'

'Alas, I no longer have a watch. It is currently residing in a pawn shop.'

'We have a witness who says she saw you with Georgia

Brand shortly before two o'clock in the morning.'

'This person was not asleep at that time? How strange.'

'Where did you go with her to have sex?'

'Into one of the tunnels. She had a torch. Sergeant Harker has already asked me this. In fact, he took me to the old station and asked me to show him where our *amour* took place. I'm surprised he hasn't told you all this already.'

'He has, and the tunnel you showed him to was the very one where her body was discovered.'

'I assume that's where she took all her clients.'

'Possibly, but until we've got some proof that she was alive when you left her, you're going to have to remain in custody.'

Riley shrugged. 'It's as comfortable as any other place. I suppose there's no chance of any liquid refreshment?'

'Water and tea.'

Riley gave a wry smile. 'A sense of humour, I see, Chief Inspector.'

'Sergeant Harker informs us that you used to do walking tours of Whitechapel.'

'In the steps of the Ripper!' declaimed Riley proudly. 'And very popular they were, before the war put a stop to them.'

'You know a great deal about the activities of Jack the Ripper?'

'I do indeed. When it became obvious to me that I was becoming *persona non grata* in the thespian world, I realised I needed a new string to my bow. There had always been a huge interest in the Ripper and his activities so I decided to bring him to life.'

'You played the part of the Ripper?'

'Great heavens, no! I was the storyteller, in the storyteller tradition as laid down by the Greek dramatists. Aeschylus and the like.'

'Where did you get your information from about the murders?'

'The public library. Books and also old copies of the local newspaper. Mary Ann Nichols, the first victim, killed and butchered on 31st August 1888. Then, 8th September, Annie Chapman's mutilated body is discovered.' He stopped and asked, almost challengingly, 'Do you want me to go on?'

'If you would,' said Coburg calmly.

'Testing my knowledge?' asked Riley.

'If you can't remember them . . .' said Coburg calmly.

'Of course I can remember them!' burst out Riley angrily. 'Catherine Eddowes, 30th September. Elizabeth Stride, the same date, 30th September. Mary Jane Kelly, 9th November. And then there are the others, unproven as victims of the Ripper, but to my mind there is no doubt they were also victims of the same murderer: Annie Millwood. Emma Elizabeth Smith. Martha Tabram. Do you want the dates?'

Coburg shook his head. 'No thank you, you've proved you have the knowledge. But how about the identity of Jack?'

Riley gave a smug smile. 'Now that information would be worth a fortune, and *if* I knew it, I would hardly share it with you.'

CHAPTER SIX

Jess Windward was in her forties, tall and thin with her face heavily made up, the excessive rouge and thick eyeliner emphasised by her dark hair being pulled back into a bun.

'You and Georgia were friends?' asked Coburg.

'We looked out for one another,' said Windward. 'This can be a dangerous game to be in.'

'So why do you do it?'

'Money. What d'you think? A girl's got to earn a living.'

'There's always factory work,' said Coburg. 'Especially with a war on. Lots of opportunities.'

'Have you ever worked in a factory?' demanded Windward.

'No,' admitted Coburg.

'I thought not,' said Windward scornfully. 'Not with that posh accent. And, even if you had, you'd have been a manager or something.'

'Did you see Georgia the night she was killed?'

'At the start. But then she got a punter, so I went off to look for one of my own.'

'Did you find one?'

'Yes.'

'What was his name?'

'I've no idea. I don't ask to see an ID card, just the money.'

'Did you see Georgia later during the night?'

Windward shook her head. 'No. But then, I didn't go looking for her. The last thing a girl wants is to be interrupted when she's working.'

'Did you have many clients that night?'

'No. And the ones I did have, we did it up against a wall.'

'So you didn't go into the tunnels like Georgia.'

'With that stink of shit? No. I've got some professional standards. Lie down there and you don't know what you're lying on.'

'So you didn't see Georgia again?'

'No. I found somewhere to sleep, and when the all-clear sounded I went home. It was the next morning when I went out to a café for a cup of tea I heard that a woman had been killed at the old Tube station. Then, later in the day, a copper came round knocking on doors with a photograph of Georgia. I knew at once from the photo she was dead; the dead have that look about them, no matter how hard funeral directors work to make them look alive. I told the copper I knew her, and he took me to the station to see Sergeant Harker.'

'You already knew Sergeant Harker?'

She nodded. 'Yes. He's a decent bloke, not like some of them. He's picked me up but let me off with a warning. He wanted to know if I had some bloke minding me.'

'A pimp?'

'That's right. I told him no. I know what them blokes can be like. They take your money and treat you bad. If I was stupid enough to do that I might as well be married to some bloke.'

'What about Georgia? Did she have a minder?'

'No. That's what brought us together. We were both

independents. We both had the same attitude: what I earn is mine. Neither of us had any intention of giving a cut of it to some bloke.'

'Did she ever mention a man called Brendan Riley?'

Windward smiled. 'Old Stinky, she called him. He was almost a regular. When things were hard she could usually count on him for a ten-bob shuffle.'

'You didn't see him on the night she was killed?'

'No.' She sighed. 'Poor cow. Who'd want to do a thing like that?'

After Windward had gone, Coburg and Lampson met with Harker in his office.

'What do you think?' the station sergeant asked them.

'I think Jess Windward is a tough and careful woman,' said Coburg. 'I don't think she's got anything to add to what we know. *If* she's telling the truth, that is.'

'I'm sure she is,' said Harker. 'I've picked her up a few times, and I've always found her to be honest, even though what she does is criminal. I've heard that in some countries prostitution is legal. In those countries, someone like Jess would be thought of as a hard and conscientious worker. As it is, she could be in jail.'

'Has she ever been inside?'

'No, but I've warned her it could happen. When I've done that she usually keeps a low profile for a while. She's sensible enough. I suggested to her she should get a proper job.'

'Yes, I did the same,' said Coburg.

'What did she say?'

Coburg gave a wry smile. 'She said she wasn't interested. I get the impression she's careful.'

'The trouble is, can she be completely sure?' asked Harker. 'If this bloke strikes again she could be a victim.' He looked at Coburg. 'What do you want to do about Riley?'

'I'm not sure about him,' said the chief inspector. 'For the moment I'd prefer you to keep him here while we make some enquiries into him. Has he got any history of attacking anyone? Women or men?'

'No. At least, nothing officially.'

'Any record of mental illness? Has he ever been locked up?'

Again, Harker shook his head. 'Nothing. Not in this neck of the woods, anyway.'

'And he comes from this area?'

'Born and bred.'

Coburg and Lampson returned to their car.

'Not much to go on,' commented Lampson as they got in and he turned the engine on.

'I think if we get any joy it'll be through the local coppers picking up rumour and gossip,' said Coburg thoughtfully as they drove off. 'Someone's bound to know something, or at least have suspicions about someone.' He looked at his watch. 'When we get to the Yard, you can get off, Ted. I've got to get this photograph of Bernard Bothwell copied and distributed.'

'Do you want a hand with that?'

'No. I'm sure Eve will be glad to see you home early for once. How's she doing?'

'Recovering bit by bit,' said Lampson. 'The thing is to try and stop her doing too much.'

'Give her our regards and tell her Rosa and I are thinking of her.'

When they got to the Yard, Lampson left to catch his

bus home, while Coburg went into Scotland Yard and made arrangements for the photograph of Bernard Bothwell to be copied, and for the copies to be sent out to every police station in London, with instructions for them to contact DCI Coburg urgently at Scotland Yard if there were any sightings of the man.

A difficult day, he thought, with two very difficult cases to worry about.

CHAPTER SEVEN

Wednesday 2nd April

In the small terraced house in Purchese Street in Somers Town that the newly-wed Mr and Mrs Lampson, and Lampson's son, Terry, called home, Eve put three bowls of porridge on the table, bringing them to the table one at a time with her one good arm. The month before, just before her wedding to Ted Lampson, she'd been the accidental target of a hit-and-run driver and had suffered a broken arm and a fractured skull. She still wore a light protective skull cap of bandage as a precautionary measure, and a flexible splint on her arm to aid its recovery. The hospital had also recommended she use a walking stick when she was out to make sure she didn't overbalance and risk injuring her skull, but so far Eve had resisted this, except when she knew she might be crossing uneven ground, like the local park, if Terry was playing a football game at the weekend. Lampson and Eve had set up a football team for the boys of Somers Town and they played against other local teams from boys' clubs, churches, schools. The next game was the coming Sunday, against a team from Warren Street Boys club.

'You should have let me and Terry do that,' said Lampson as Eve set the last of the three bowls down.

'I need to exercise the arm,' said Eve. She sat down and

picked up her spoon. 'The hospital told me yesterday I should be able to stop using the splint next week. With a bit of luck I should be able to get back to work once the splint's off.' She looked at Terry. 'Back to making sure you behave.'

Eve was a teacher at the local school, on leave while she recovered from her injuries.

'I always behave,' said Terry defensively.

'That's not what I heard,' said Eve. 'I was told this temporary teacher they've got in for your lot while I'm away is thinking of quitting because of the trouble you cause him.'

'It's not our fault,' said Terry. 'He's useless. He can't keep order. He keeps telling us to be kind to one another. What he means is, be kind to him. Every now and then he walks out of the classroom and cries in the corridor.'

'Nonsense!' snorted Eve.

'He does,' insisted Terry. 'Jenny Evans looked through the glass and saw him.'

'In that case, the sooner I come back the better,' said Eve.

Terry spooned the last of his porridge into his mouth, then pushed his bowl away.

'Finished,' he said. 'This is just like Goldilocks. Except we get to eat our porridge.'

There was the sound of a car drawing up in the street outside. Lampson looked through the window and saw the police car park outside.

'Here's the guv'nor,' he said, getting up. 'I'll see you two later. Take care of yourselves.'

As was their regular routine, Coburg switched to the passenger seat and Lampson drove them to Scotland Yard. Lampson loved to drive, but couldn't afford a car of his own. Coburg's much-loved Bentley had been garaged for the duration of the war on the orders of politicians who felt a chief inspector driving such a car belied the austerity measures the country had been instructed to observe.

As the duo walked into the reception area at the Yard, they were hailed by the duty sergeant at reception.

'There was a telephone call for you from Sergeant Harker at Whitechapel station, sir. He asks if you can phone him as soon as you get in.'

Coburg and Lampson hurried up the stairs to their office.

'I wonder what's happened?' asked Lampson. 'Think Riley may have topped himself?'

'Unlikely, in my opinion,' said Coburg. 'He might threaten it, but Riley's too vain and self-absorbed to do anything like that.'

A few moments later he was talking to Sergeant Harker.

'Sarah Mars has turned up.'

'Good. '

'Not so good, I'm afraid. She was found at Whitechapel Road Tube station in the tunnels, in the same condition as the last one: ripped to bits. All her internal organs cut out.'

'Damn!' cursed Coburg. 'Sergeant Lampson and I will be right over.'

Coburg and Lampson were taken straight down to the same alcove in the shelter where Georgia Brand's body had been found. Sergeant Harker was there with a different doctor and two ambulance people, one holding a stretcher.

'Dr Webb from the London Hospital,' the doctor introduced

himself, giving them a friendly smile and shaking their hands. 'Second time for you here, I understand. Although last time I believe you met my colleague, Dr McKay.' He gave them an apologetic smile and added, 'I'm afraid he can sometimes appear a bit brusque, but he's an excellent doctor.'

'I'm sure he is,' said Coburg. He pointed at the body of Sarah Mars, which lay face up on the ground. 'What can you tell me about the deceased?'

'I'm afraid to say her injuries are the same as those of the previous victim,' said Webb. He walked over to Sarah Mars's body and raised her long skirt to show the detectives her wounds. As the doctor had said, they appeared to be identical to the wounds Georgia Brand had suffered: long jagged incisions that laid her abdomen open, revealing that her internal organs had been removed.

'I'll be able to give you a fuller report once I've had a look at her at the London,' said Webb. 'I decided to wait until you'd seen her, and looked at her in situ, as it were, before I had her taken away.'

'Thank you, Doctor,' said Coburg. He began to move in a circle around Sarah Mars's body, gradually widening his circle as he examined the ground, which was splattered with dried blood. He looked at Sergeant Harker. 'Did the constable who found her notice anything out of the ordinary? Any footprints, for example?'

'No. Although chummy left us a gift, like before.'

He pointed to where a large leather apron had been left lying away from the body, close to the wall.

'It's the sort worn by slaughterers, butchers and shoe menders,' said Harker.

'He's definitely taunting us,' said Coburg. 'One of the

original suspects in 1888 was a man known as Leather Apron.' He looked at Dr Webb and said, 'Thank you for waiting, Doctor. You can take her away now.'

Webb gestured to the two ambulancemen, who lifted the body onto the stretcher and carried it away. Dr Webb followed them.

'I assume Riley's still in custody?' Coburg asked Sergeant Harker.

'He has been all the time.'

'Then we know he didn't do this.'

'Shall I let him go?'

Coburg thought it over. 'I'm still not convinced he isn't involved in some way. He may not be the actual killer, but he's got an obsession with the original killings.'

'Keep him locked up?' asked Harker.

'No, we've got no evidence to hold him. Let him go, but have him watched. If he is involved, he may lead us to whoever's doing it.'

'I've decided to put a small team of constables on duty at the shelter at nights, just in case he tries again. I was also thinking of barring any known prostitutes they see coming in, but then I thought they'd be safer here than outside. In the end I've decided that if my men see any women known to be prostitutes they're to take them into custody overnight. We might end with overcrowded cells, but at least it should put a damper on Jack's activities.'

Once more, Coburg studied the patch of ground where the body had lain, this time bending lower. He spotted something in a puddle of thick blood and took a pair of tweezers and an evidence bag from his pocket. Using the tweezers, he picked up what looked like a pen or a pencil, although it was difficult to see it clearly because of the clots of blood clinging to it. He dropped it into the evidence bag, and put the bag in his pocket.

'It looks like a fountain pen,' he announced. 'Although we'll know more once we hand it to forensics to take a look at. The leather apron was left here deliberately for us to find, but I don't think that was the case with this pen. Hopefully, we'll have something to reveal about the killer.'

Coburg and Lampson returned to the Yard, where they collected the Victorian surgeon's case. Remembering how upset the superintendent had been when he couldn't get hold of the chief inspector to tell him about the palace, Coburg took the precaution of letting the desk sergeant know that he and Lampson would be at Scotland Yard's Curtis Green annexe.

'All these items are from the scene of the murders of two women at a disused Tube station in Whitechapel,' Coburg told the leader of the forensics team at Curtis Green, Arnold Ridley. 'The surgeon's case was found on Monday; the leather apron and fountain pen were found today. I need to know anything you may be able to find about the person who handled them. If possible, where they came from. In short, everything.'

Ridley nodded. 'Looking at these, someone's sending a message from the past,' he said.

'Yes, that's my thought,' said Coburg. 'We need pointers towards who.'

They walked out of the building and stood for a while on the Embankment, looking at the flowing waters of the Thames.

'You've had a thought, guv?' asked Lampson.

'I have. Whoever this killer is, he's taunting us with the surgeon's case and the leather apron. I think the pen was accidental. If he's following the original Ripper, we need to be ready for where he's going to strike next.'

'Whitechapel, like before,' said Lampson.

'But where in Whitechapel? The old Tube station again? Sergeant Harker is going to have a squad of constables patrolling inside, warning off the prostitutes. The chances are that when our killer strikes again it might well be at one of the places the original Ripper struck.'

'You think he's going to strike again? Mightn't he just leave it at these two and sit back smugly watching us blundering around blindly?'

'No, he's playing a game. That's what gives him his pleasure. He'll strike again. What we need to do is go back into the archives.' And he gestured back at the building they'd just left.

'The Black Museum?' asked Lampson.

Coburg nodded. The Black Museum was the general name for the Crime Museum. It had been set up in 1874 in the basement of Scotland Yard as a collection of crime memorabilia, aimed at giving police officers practical items from crimes in order for them to study and assist their detective skills. It included articles of clothing and items belonging to murder victims, burglars' tools, printing plates used for forging bank notes, shotguns disguised as umbrellas, as well as death masks from executed murderers. It also housed much of the information gathered from the time of the original Jack the Ripper enquiries, including letters supposed to have been written by the killer, as well as the notebooks of Frederick Abberline, the detective in charge of the case. A few years before, the collection had been moved to the building at Curtis Green.

'I thought they'd closed the Black Museum, on account of the war,' said Lampson.

'They have,' said Coburg. 'But I know the man in charge,

and I think he owes me a favour.'

'What sort of favour?'

'One it's best not to talk about,' said Coburg.

Coburg walked back into the building, Lampson following, and asked the receptionist to see if Gerald Plomley was available. When he was told that Mr Plomley was, he asked her if she'd call him to the reception area.

Plomley was a man in his forties, very well groomed and expensively dressed.

'Edgar,' he greeted Coburg. 'What can I do for you?'

'I need access to the museum.'

'You know that officially we're closed,' said Plomley.

'I do,' said Coburg. 'But we have someone bumping off prostitutes in Whitechapel copying a series of such killings in Victorian times.'

'Not that old chestnut,' groaned Plomley.

'I'm afraid so, and real people are dying,' said Coburg. 'I promise we won't say who let us in to examine the archives. If asked I'll say I picked the lock.'

'You can't pick locks,' said Plomley.

'No, but my sergeant can,' said Coburg.

Plomley looked suspiciously at Lampson, who gave him a smile and a wink. Then he looked at Coburg with a weary sigh. 'I suppose you're going to mention my father.'

'Why would I do that?' asked Coburg.

'You've done it before when you wanted a favour from me.'

'True,' admitted Coburg. 'But in this instance I'm just appealing to your good nature and you, like me, wanting to see a vicious criminal taken off the streets.'

Plomley sighed. 'Follow me,' he said.

CHAPTER EIGHT

A short time later, Coburg and Lampson were sitting at a table in the Black Museum's reading room. With the museum officially closed for the duration of the war, they were the only ones in it. They had an array of box files with everything the museum had on the original Jack the Ripper cases from Victorian times.

'We're lucky that Inspector Abberline was meticulous, and also worried about things going missing, so he had copies of his notebooks made,' said Coburg. 'It means we can both study them at the same time.'

He slid one of the notebooks across the desk to Lampson. 'Here's yours.'

Coburg and Lampson pored over the Abberline notebooks from the Scotland Yard archives.

'"The first victim, Mary Ann Nichols, née Walker,"' read Coburg, '"was killed on 31st August 1888. She married William Nichols in 1864 and had five children. After William had an affair, the couple separated in 1880. Mary became an alcoholic with a taste for gin. She became a prostitute, living in casual lodging houses. According to her friend Ellen Holland, who Nichols shared a bed with in the lodging house at 18 Thrawl Street, on the evening of 31st August, the deputy at the lodging house turned her out because she did not have the four shillings lodging fee. At 2.30 a.m., Holland saw Nichols at the corner of Brick Lane and Whitechapel High Street. She was drunk and hardly able to stand. At 3.40 a.m. two carmen, Charles Cross and Robert Paul, discovered her body at the entrance to the stable yard in Buck's Row."'

'He's very good on details,' said Lampson.

'That's one of the reasons he was considered the best detective at Scotland Yard,' said Coburg.

Lampson turned to the autopsy reports.

'"Autopsy report on Mary Anne Nichols by Dr Rees Ralph Llewellyn",' he read. '"Five of the teeth were missing and there was slight laceration of the tongue. There was a bruise running along the lower jaw and the right side of the face. This might have been caused by a blow from a fist or pressure from a thumb."' There was a great deal more about bruising and cuts to the face and a description of cuts to her throat and neck, which had 'severed the tissues right down to the vertebrae,' before he came to '"There were no other injuries about the body until just about the lower part of the abdomen. Two or three inches from the left side was a wound running in a jagged manner. The wound was a very deep one and the tissues were cut through. There were several incisions running across the abdomen. There were also three or four similar cuts running downwards on the right side, all of which had been caused by a knife".'

He then turned to the autopsy report by this same Dr Phillips on Elizabeth Stride.

'Elizabeth Stride's body wasn't mutilated like the others',' he pointed out.

'No, but the injuries to her face were the same,' said Coburg. 'The suggestion was that, with all the people around at the time, the killer abandoned the idea of mutilating her, but he was able to carry that out shortly after on the body of Catherine Eddowes.'

Lampson turned to the autopsy report on Catherine Eddowes, and after a few moments said: 'He really was some sort of demented monster. He cut out her vagina and her rectum, along with her intestines.'

'Wait till you get to the autopsy on Mary Jane Kelly. The others were bad, but that was by far the worst. He had more time with Mary Jane than with the others. All the others were killed and eviscerated in the open. Mary Jane was killed in her room. The killer had all the time to do what he wanted.'

Lampson nodded, then read Abberline's notes recording the events leading up to Mary Jane Kelly's death. She was killed on 9th November in her room at 13 Miller's Court.

'Why did he stop the killings?' asked Lampson.

'Some suggested he'd died. Others said he'd fled abroad. Certainly, there were reports of similar murders in America within a year of them ending in England.' He flicked through the notebook. 'Ah, Abberline's list of possible suspects. This will make interesting reading, seeing why he listed some and not others.' He read down the list of names, until he came to: 'Leather Apron. Here we are.'

'Where?' asked Lampson.

Coburg showed him the page, and Lampson turned to it, then read the section.

'He lists a series of possibles, but then dismisses them all,' said Lampson. 'A cobbler or bootmaker? Here's a John Piser.

Also, a Polish Jew called Kosminski. Then Seweryn Kłosowski.'

'Who was later executed under the name of George Chapman for murder,' said Coburg. 'But he was executed in 1903, some years after the Ripper killings. And the murders he committed were by poison.'

'So we can discount him.'

'I don't know. There must have been a reason Abberline included him in his list of suspects.'

Suddenly Lampson stopped flicking through the pages.

'This is interesting,' he said. 'There's one page that has been partly blocked out.'

'Ah, that could well be the royal connection,' said Coburg.

'The royal connection?'

'Surely you know about that. Queen Victoria's personal physician, Sir William Gull, and the Queen's grandson, Prince Albert Victor. That they trawled Whitechapel picking up prostitutes, who Gull killed and dismembered.'

'Yes, but I was told that was all a rumour spread by radicals to undermine the royal family.'

'Well, *I* was told it was quite likely authentic.'

'Who by?'

Coburg smiled. 'Let's just say, someone who might know.'

CHAPTER NINE

In the control booth at the back of the theatre, John Fawcett listened as Rosa on piano and vocals ran through the reprise of 'Up A Lazy River', the play-out for the show. She, with Eric Pickup on bass and Wally Dawes on drums, had run through all the music for the show, from opening with 'Up A Lazy River' as the introductory theme, then Gershwin's 'Summertime', followed by 'Shine On, Harvest Moon', which Flanagan and Allen would be doing, then 'Red Sails in the Sunset' for Vera Lynn, followed by 'We'll Meet Again', then 'Underneath the Arches', and the upbeat 'When the Saints Go Marching In'. Now they were wrapping up the proceedings with a final version of 'Up A Lazy River'. As well as listening to the music, most of John Fawcett's attention was on Wally Dawes, looking for any tell-tale signs of inebriation, any slip-ups in his handling of the stick or brushes, any missed pedals.

He pressed the button on the control desk, which sent his voice out into the small theatre.

'Just checking the disc,' he said.

In reality, it gave him time to assess what he'd heard and seen from Wally Dawes, which had appeared fine.

He got up and walked out of the control booth and down the aisle towards the stage.

'Excellent!' he announced. 'I think we have a hit show on our hands. Well done, you three. You sound as if you've been playing as a unit for a long time.'

'On and off, we have,' said Rosa.

'That's true,' said Eric. He looked at Rosa and Wally. 'A late-night session at the Blue Parrot about ten years ago, as I remember.'

'Was it as long ago as that?' asked Rosa.

'It must be.' Wally grinned. 'I had more hair then.'

'Well, that's enough for today, I think,' said Fawcett. 'I'll see you all here next Tuesday. Rehearsals start at three o'clock. We'll take a break about six, then we start the broadcast live at half seven. See you next week.'

Eric began packing his double bass into its cover, and Wally wandered over to where Rosa at the piano was putting her music away.

'I just wanted to say thanks, Rosa,' he said quietly.

'For what?' asked Rosa.

'You must have heard about the problem? The drink?'

Rosa shrugged. 'I hear lots of things about many people. Not all true.'

'Yes, well, it was true. After the building I was in came down, I was lost. I made a right mess of myself. Missing gigs. And those I did make . . .' He gave a rueful look. 'I messed up. But I've been working hard to get myself straight. I really have.'

'You sounded great today.'

'It felt good. But that's because you're great to work with. You and Eric. I just wanted to say thanks for giving me the chance.'

Rosa went to Wally and took his hand in hers. 'I never had any doubts,' she said.

* * *

72

Coburg and Lampson returned the documents to their box files, then went to the reception desk where they asked if she could let Mr Plomley know they'd finished. 'We've left the box files on the table for him. Please tell him we're very grateful for his assistance.'

As they left the building and made their way back to Scotland Yard, carrying the notes they'd made in a briefcase, they discussed what they'd learnt.

'It looks like he's replicating the original murders. He knows exactly what sort of injuries were carried out. Where'd he get that much detailed information?'

'Same place as us? Abberline's notebooks?'

'Not necessarily. There's been loads written about the original Ripper. What he did to these two women is identical to the injuries the original victims suffered. This is someone who's spent time researching the original murders in great detail.'

'That actor bloke, Brendan Riley. Or it's a copper, someone who knows the details.'

Coburg frowned. 'Maybe, but that's not something I care to think about.'

'You may not like the idea, but it's still a possibility.'

Then a thought struck Coburg. 'There's another thought. Knowing what sort of injuries the women received is not enough – we're looking for someone who knows *how* to commit those sort of injuries. A knowledge of female anatomy. Skill with a surgical knife.'

'A surgeon?' said Lampson.

'Or a pathologist. Someone with medical experience. Maybe a butcher who's used to cutting up animals. After all, a pig and a human are pretty much the same under the skin.'

'Back to Leather Apron,' said Lampson. 'What about a funeral director? They do embalming, so they have to know what to do with the internal organs.'

Coburg groaned. 'Just like Abberline faced in the original investigation: so many possibilities.'

When they got back to the Yard, Coburg handed the briefcase to Lampson.

'You take the notes we've made up to our office,' said Coburg. 'I need to check that the photograph of the missing valet has been distributed to the stations around London.'

Once Coburg had checked that the photograph had indeed been sent out to every station in London, he made for his office, where Lampson told him in ominous tones: 'The superintendent's looking for you.'

'Did he say why?'

'No, but he doesn't look happy.'

Coburg walked along the corridor to the superintendent's office and knocked. At the command 'Enter', he walked in.

'You wanted to see me, sir?'

Allison regarded him with a grim expression of dissatisfaction that did not bode well. 'I came looking for you today, and was advised that you were at Curtis Green.'

'Yes, sir. That is correct.'

'What were you doing there?'

'Sergeant Lampson and I were going through the archives looking for connections to the current Whitechapel murders. There was another this morning.'

'Yes, so I understand. However, Chief Inspector, I instructed you to concentrate your energies on the King's missing valet.'

'Yes, sir. That is part of it.'

Allison looked at Coburg, puzzled. 'What do you mean, part of it?'

'The latest victim turns out to be the niece of the missing valet.'

The superintendent stared at the chief inspector in astonishment. 'Are you suggesting that the King's valet has something to do with these murders in Whitechapel?'

'It's just a line of enquiry we're following up.'

'No, Chief Inspector,' said Allison firmly. 'Your immediate priority is the search for the missing valet. Anything to do with the murders in Whitechapel can be handled by the local police force. If it is felt Scotland Yard need to be involved, *I* will appoint one of our own detective inspectors. I want you to disregard the Whitechapel murders and put all your efforts into the search for the King's missing valet. Is that clear?'

'Perfectly, sir,' said Coburg. 'In fact, yesterday I sent out a photograph of Mr Bothwell to all London police stations. I believe that boots on the ground may be the only answer to finding him.'

'If it doesn't turn up anything very quickly indeed, I want you to instigate some other course of action. Have you talked to the people he worked with?'

'Not yet, sir. That's next on my list.'

'You should have already done it instead of wasting time with these Whitechapel murders. This is the King we are talking about!'

Coburg made his way back to the office. Lampson looked at him sympathetically.

'You look upset, guv,' said Lampson.

'I've just received a dressing-down for looking into the Whitechapel murders. The superintendent has made it very clear to me that I'm to concentrate on one thing only: the King's missing valet. Leave the Whitechapel murders to the local police. If a Scotland Yard detective is needed, he'll choose one. And it won't be me.'

Lampson gestured at the notes they'd made at the Black Museum. 'So, what do we do with these?'

'We hang on to them. If someone else is given the investigation, we pass them on to him, if he wants them. But that will depend on who it is. Some will welcome our notes; some will want to do their own. They won't like the idea that we may share some of the credit.'

'There'll only be credit if the murders are solved and the killer caught,' pointed out Lampson. 'Which didn't happen with the original investigation into the Ripper.'

After work had finished for the day and Lampson had made his way home to Somers Town, Coburg sat in his office pondering that afternoon's confrontation with Superintendent Allison. Yes, the vanished valet was a very real issue, but was it of more importance than the savage murder of two prostitutes in Whitechapel? Obviously, it was to the superintendent. Unless Coburg could get to the bottom of the missing valet, he'd have the full weight of the King and the Prime Minister hanging ominously over him. He needed to do something to allay the situation. *Contact me*, Churchill had said. *Very well*, thought Coburg, that's exactly what he'd do. At least it would be something he could report back to Superintendent Allison.

He left the office and made for this car, then headed to

the former Tube station at Down Street, close to Green Park. The Tube station had closed in 1932, but the outside decor remained in place: the coloured tiles familiar throughout London's underground stations along with a three-arched semi-circular window. A sign by the street door proclaimed it to be the headquarters of the Railway Executive Committee.

It was also the secret headquarters of Winston Churchill's War Cabinet and government, a temporary accommodation while the Cabinet War Office at Horse Guards was being strengthened.

Coburg pressed the intercom beside the door, and, when a voice answered, said, 'Detective Chief Inspector Saxe-Coburg from Scotland Yard to see the Prime Minister.'

There was a moment's pause, then the voice said, 'Someone will be with you shortly.'

Coburg waited. After about five minutes the door was opened by a tall man in a smart dark suit who Coburg guessed to be a civil servant.

'DCI Saxe-Coburg,' he said in formal tones. 'May I see your warrant card?'

Coburg showed it to him.

'Thank you,' said the man. 'If you will follow me. The Prime Minister is in, but tied up at the moment. I'll take you to the waiting area. Have you been here before?'

'Yes, but then it was to see Mr Purslake at the Railway Executive Committee on the lower level.'

The man nodded and led Coburg to a circular staircase that wound down to deep below ground. The staircase continued further down, but the man led Coburg off the staircase and into a corridor. Halfway along the corridor he stopped beside a door. A wooden chair had been placed outside the door.

'Please make yourself comfortable,' said the man. 'The Prime Minister will be with you shortly.'

Coburg sat. The man walked off, going further into the depths of the underground bunker. Coburg sat, checking his watch. He knew the Prime Minister had a lot on his plate and rarely had time to take a break from the demands of his role. He even had a bed in this bunker as often he never made it home. It was forty minutes before the door opened and Churchill himself looked out at Coburg. There was no apology from Churchill for keeping him waiting, which Coburg found understandable. The man looked strained.

Coburg walked into the small office, which contained a desk, three chairs, filing cabinets and a telephone.

'I hope you have news for me, Chief Inspector,' said Churchill, a note of accusation in his voice as he took his seat behind his desk, gesturing for Coburg to take one of the chairs.

'None that's positive, sir,' said Coburg. 'I've issued a photograph of the missing man to every police station in London in the hope that someone might have seen him. There is the possibility that he might be suffering from some kind of amnesia and doesn't know who he is.'

'Unlikely, surely,' grunted Churchill.

'There have been such cases as a result of the bombing,' said Coburg. 'But my main purpose in coming to see you, sir, is to ask if it would be possible for me to interview the King's staff at the palace.'

'To what end?'

'So far we've drawn a blank. My hope is that he might have mentioned something to one of his fellow workers. Even a casual remark in passing that might give us a lead as to what's happened to him, where he's gone. It's been five days now since he vanished.'

Churchill thought it over, then nodded. 'I'll give His Majesty's private secretary, Sir Jasper Connor, a ring, and tell him you'll be calling at the palace. He'll make the arrangements for you to talk to the staff. But there must be no mention of the watch,' he added firmly.

'I understand, sir,' said Coburg. 'Although I shall be listening carefully in case anyone there mentions the watch unprompted.' He hesitated, then said, 'I'd like to take Sergeant Lampson to the palace with me, if I may. It will speed up the interviews if there are two of us are carrying them out.'

'You seem to have a high regard for this sergeant of yours,' grunted Churchill.

'I do, sir.'

Churchill nodded. 'Very well. But he is not to have contact in any way with Their Majesties. Is that clear?'

'Very clear, sir,' said Coburg.

'Is there anything else?'

'No, sir,' said Coburg.

Churchill nodded. 'Report to me if you find anything.'

'Yes, sir,' said Coburg.

And he left.

CHAPTER TEN

Thursday 3rd April

Rosa and her co-crew in the ambulance, Doris Gibbs, were on their way to pick up an elderly patient in Edgware Road and take her to the hospital for a check on her recently amputated leg.

'It makes a change for us not to have to hurtle along with the bell ringing because we've got an emergency, with every second counting,' commented Doris. 'This is nicer.'

'What's the address again?' asked Rosa.

'147. It's just along here on the left. Mrs Pickford. She's got a wheelchair, according to the note, so it's just a case of hauling her and it on board. The sooner we get an ambulance with a tail lift, the better.'

'I asked Mr Warren and he said there was a shortage because all the factories are tied up making weapons. He said we just have to make do with what we've got, for the moment. At least we've got a ramp.'

'We still have to pull the wheelchairs up,' pointed out Doris. 'It's doing my back in. It's not too bad when it's someone thin and frail, but that bloke we had last week was about thirty stone. I was tempted to just tie him behind the ambulance and haul him along behind us in his wheelchair.' Then she changed the topic to Rosa's forthcoming radio broadcast. 'How did rehearsals go yesterday? Were Flanagan and Allen there? And Vera Lynn?'

'No, it was just to run through the music with me and the rhythm section. Bud, Chesney and Vera don't come in till next Tuesday, the day we do the broadcast. The thing is they know the numbers they're doing really well, because they've done them so often.'

'What will they be doing?'

'Bud and Chesney will be doing "Shine On, Harvest Moon" and "Underneath the Arches", and Vera will sing "Red Sails in the Sunset" and "We'll Meet Again".'

Doris chuckled. 'Listen to you. Bud and Chesney and Vera.'

'That's what the producer's told me to call them.'

'So I suppose they'll call you Rosa.'

'If they talk to me at all,' said Rosa. 'I've never met them before, so it's all unknown.'

'You are lucky,' said Doris. 'Mixing with all these famous people. Doesn't it feel strange?'

'Well, yes and no,' said Rosa. 'When I was touring I appeared with some pretty famous people, and found that they're just . . . well, people. Some are nice, some are not so nice. In fact, some of the most famous were among the nicest. It was the ones who weren't famous and were jealous of those who were, who weren't so nice.' Suddenly she slowed the ambulance and pulled in to the kerb, and said in a puzzled voice, 'You did say number 147?'

'Yes,' said Doris, checking the job sheet. Then she looked out at where 147 should have been, and saw that a whole row of houses had been demolished, smoke still rising from the ruins of the collapsed buildings. Two fire engines had been parked just ahead of them, and they could see firemen sorting through the smoking rubble.

'Poor Mrs Pickford,' said Doris. She looked at the working firemen amid the wreckage and opened her door of the cab. 'You wait here. I'll go and have a word and see if there's anyone who needs to be ambulanced anywhere.'

'Good morning, Sergeant Harker!'

Harker looked up from the reception desk and his heart sank as he saw the plump check-suited figure of Charlie Brown, or Cheerful Charlie Brown as he liked to style himself, breeze into Whitechapel police station.

'Good morning, Mr Brown,' said Harker guardedly.

'Charlie, please, Sergeant.' Brown beamed. 'I hear there's been another New Ripper killing at the old Tube station.' He grinned. 'The New Ripper is what we're going to be calling him at the *Chronicle*.'

Brown was a reporter for the *Whitechapel Chronicle* and a constant visitor to the local police stations in his quest for the Big Story that would lead him to the hallowed buildings in Fleet Street where the big circulation dailies like the *Daily Mirror*, *The Sketch*, *The Telegraph* and *The Times* had their offices. For Brown, the New Ripper presented the best opportunity he'd had to make this happen in years.

'A young woman, I hear,' said Brown. 'A prostitute like the previous one?'

'We're still looking into that,' said Harker.

'Oh come on, Sergeant!' Brown appealed. 'This is the biggest story in this area since . . . well, the last time it happened.'

'We don't know if the two murders are connected,' said Harker.

'Oh come on!' said Brown again. 'Two women killed and their bodies ripped to bits, just like in the olden days.' He leant forward confidentially. 'I hear you've arrested Brendan Riley, the bloke who used to do the Ripper walking tours. Is that right?'

'No,' said Harker. 'Mr Riley was discovered the worse for wear, so we took him in for his own safety.'

'So he was here when the last one got done?'

'He was.'

'So he can't have done it.'

'At the moment I have no official statement to make,' said Harker.

'I heard that Scotland Yard attended. Who was it? One of their top bods?'

'I'm not allowed to divulge that sort of information.'

'Not to worry, I'm sure they'll be able to answer that at Scotland Yard. I hear the bodies were taken to the London Hospital.'

'Yes,' said Harker. 'It's the nearest.'

'Who was the attending physician?'

Harker thought this question over as he looked at Charlie Brown, and then gave half a smile as he said, 'It was Dr McKay.'

Brown looked aghast. 'Oh, not that old misery!'

'I'm sure he'd be happy to talk to you,' said Harker.

The disgruntled expression on Brown's face showed that, just like Sergeant Harker, he doubted this very much. He forced a smile and said, 'Thank you, Sergeant. You've been very helpful.'

With that, he left. *Bastards*, he thought. *They're doing everything to stand in my way, stopping me getting the story.* The story that could put him on the map as far as Fleet Street was concerned. Well, they weren't going to do it. After years of poking around in Whitechapel to get his stories, Cheerful Charlie Brown had grown a thick skin. The soul of a poet and the skin of a rhinoceros, that's how he saw himself. If the police weren't talking to him, they wouldn't be talking to the bigger newspapers. Which meant there was an opportunity for him to make this an exclusive. And then the Big Boys would come calling.

Lampson looked ahead in awe as Coburg drove down The Mall towards Buckingham Palace. They had agreed that Coburg should take over the driving for this visit as he'd been to the Palace before and should be recognised by the guards on duty.

'I can't believe it,' said Lampson. 'Me, going to Buckingham Palace. Are you sure it's alright?'

'I asked permission for you to work with me on this case from the King himself, and the Prime Minister, and they agreed.'

'You spoke about me to the King?' said Lampson, stunned.

'No, I did it by mime,' said Coburg sarcastically. 'Of course I told them about you.'

'So they know who I am?'

'I expect they've already forgotten,' said Coburg. 'But they know my sergeant is working with me.'

'I can't get over it,' said Lampson. 'Wait till I tell Eve and Terry I was here.'

'You can tell them, but not what it was about.'

'Looking for a missing valet,' said Lampson. 'I promise I won't say a word about the watch. Or anything else that's gone missing.'

'And I'd advise not saying that it's a missing valet we're looking for. Best to just leave it that we're looking into someone at the palace who needs our help. Terry's bound to say something to his pals and next thing the tale of the King's valet going missing from the palace will be in every household in North London.'

'I'll tell Terry not to say anything.'

'Oh come on!' scoffed Coburg. 'He's twelve years old. Could you have kept that quiet when you were twelve years old?'

'Nothing like that ever happened to me when I was his age,' said Lampson. 'Anyway, I take your point. We've been asked in because one of the staff has some information for us. How about that?'

'That's good,' said Coburg.

An alarming thought struck Lampson. 'What do I do if I meet the King? Or the Queen? You know, walking along a corridor or something?'

'I think it's unlikely, but if you do just stand still and let them pass. If they speak to you, you can respond. But don't speak to them unless they speak to you first.'

'So no "Hello, King mate. How you doing?"'

'Ha ha, very funny,' said Coburg, not amused.

They reached the entrance gates and Coburg showed his warrant card. The police on guard had obviously been apprised of their impending arrival because they were waved through, with the same instruction as previously about driving through the arch to the rear entrance.

Coburg pulled up and a liveried footman opened the car door for them.

'DCI Coburg and DS Lampson from Scotland Yard to see Sir Jasper Connor,' said Coburg.

'Yes, sir,' said the footman. 'Sir Jasper is expecting you. He's in his office. If you'll follow me.'

They followed the footman up a flight of stairs and along a heavily carpeted corridor. As they were approaching a door, it opened and King George VI walked out. He stopped when he saw the two policemen.

'Ah, Chief Inspector Saxe-Coburg,' he said, enunciating his words carefully. 'You have returned.'

'Yes, Your Majesty.'

'Jasper was just telling me you were coming today. Any news about the – er – person?'

'Nothing yet, I'm afraid, sir, but our enquiries are continuing. I've sent his photograph to all the London police stations and we're here today to talk to some of the staff.'

'Very good,' said the King. 'I assume this is your colleague you mentioned?'

'Yes, sir. Detective Sergeant Edward Lampson.'

'Edward,' said the King. 'A good regal name. Welcome to the palace.'

'Thank you, Your Majesty,' said Lampson, and bowed.

'I'll leave you with Jasper,' said the King, and he walked off along the corridor.

Charlie Brown walked into the reception area at the London Hospital and asked if it was possible to see Dr McKay. 'I'm Charles Brown from the *Whitechapel Chronicle*. The local police have told me to see Dr McKay with some important questions I've got.' From his past experiences of meeting Dr McKay, he knew the doctor would not be impressed by Cheerful Charlie.

The receptionist made a phone call, and ten minutes later the grim-faced figure of Dr McKay strode into the area.

'Dr McKay,' said Brown, holding out his hand. 'Charles Brown of the *Whitechapel Chronicle*.'

'I know who you are.' McKay scowled, ignoring the reporter's outstretched hand. 'What do you want?'

'I understand you were the attending physician at the scenes of the recent murders in Whitechapel Road's old station, the air raid shelter. I wondered what you could tell me about the victims.'

'Nothing,' said McKay flatly. 'I do not agree with medical details being used as entertainment.'

'This is hardly entertainment, Doctor,' said Brown. 'This is a story of vital interest to everyone who lives in this area.'

'Then I suggest you direct your questions to the police who are investigating,' said McKay.

'I have done, but the local police directed me to you, or to Scotland Yard.'

'In that case I suggest you contact Scotland Yard.'

'I will, sir,' said Brown gratefully. 'I remember they said the person in charge was Detective Inspector . . .' He paused and looked at McKay inquisitively.

'Detective *Chief* Inspector,' McKay corrected him sternly. 'Saxe-Coburg. Now, I wish you good day.'

With that, McKay turned on his heel and walked off.

Brown grinned to himself. DCI Saxe-Coburg. He

recognised the name from reports in the top-quality newspapers. Married to the jazz singer Rosa Weeks. This case was starting to get even more interesting.

Hector McBride was a dapper young man in his early thirties, dressed immaculately in a perfectly cut suit of an expensive brown material. He had been relaxing in his private room in the palace when he got the message from Sir Jasper Connor that two detectives from Scotland Yard wished to speak to him about Bernard Bothwell.

'Thank you for seeing us, Mr McBride,' said Coburg when he invited them into his room. 'I understand your shift is in the evenings and you're on call during the night, so you must excuse us taking up your time when I assume you should be sleeping.'

'That's perfectly alright, Chief Inspector,' said McBride. 'I sleep very lightly, and His Majesty rarely calls on me during the night. My duties are mainly during the late afternoon and evenings if he has a function to attend, and first thing in the morning if he has an early appointment.'

'And then you hand over to Bernard Bothwell.'

'Yes.'

'Can I ask, what steps have been taken to find a replacement for Mr Bothwell since he vanished?'

'I've arranged for a cousin of mine, Terrence Kilbride, to do the day shift on a temporary basis until Mr Bothwell is found.' He looked with wariness at Coburg and asked, 'Do you think he will be found?'

'We hope so,' said Coburg. 'How well do you know Mr Bothwell?'

'On a social level, not really at all. Our lives are very different. He's married and lives out with his family. I am single and live here at the palace. The only time we meet is when we hand His Majesty over, in the morning and late afternoon.'

'How do you get on with him?'

'Fine. We exchange pleasantries when we meet and pass on anything that's happened during our separate shifts that needs to be taken into consideration. But, honestly, His Majesty is no problem. He is the perfect master. He knows what he wants, and as long as we make sure it's provided, he appears content to let Mr Bothwell and myself get on with it.' He gave a rueful smile. 'Unlike some other people I could mention. Not that I'll name names, because confidentiality is important in any such relationship, but I used to work at some of London's top hotels, and some of the people we had to work for were appalling in their taste and manners.'

'Have you any idea why Mr Bothwell would vanish?'

'None at all. It is completely unlike him. He has always been so reliable. Absolutely dependable. And devoted to His Majesty, as I am.'

'Was he close to anyone here at the palace? Did he have any special confidantes?'

McBride shook his head. 'Not to my knowledge. The thing is, he didn't live in. The staff who live in the palace form friendships, or at least social interactions, having evening meals together, that sort of thing. Bothwell often had his midday meal here, though sometimes he brought a packed lunch from home.' He remained thoughtful for a few moments, then said, 'On reflection, I can't honestly think of anyone he spent any time with, except His Majesty. When he wasn't sorting out

His Majesty's wardrobe and preparing clothes, he would be ironing, or sometimes doing repairs, if they were very minor and didn't necessitate one of the repairers.'

'Do you have many repairers?'

'Lord, we have a whole clutch of them on hand!'

'Well, what did you think of him?' Coburg asked Lampson after they'd left McBride's room.

'Why isn't he in uniform?' asked Lampson.

'The same reason many people aren't,' said Coburg. 'Including you, Ted. Restricted occupation. Being valet to the King of England is not something everyone can do, not successfully, anyway.'

The Watcher frowned thoughtfully as the large Bentley pulled up outside Whitechapel police station. Two well-dressed men got out and walked into the station. Who were they? The Watcher wondered. Sergeant Harker had called in Scotland Yard in the form of DCI Coburg and DS Lampson, but these two didn't look like Scotland Yard detectives. Both men looked to be in their late fifties or early sixties, although the older of the two could well be in his middle sixties. Maybe they were Home Office. Or perhaps Special Branch.

They had to be here about the murders; it was the only reason top people like that would be in Whitechapel. It was time to be careful.

Scare them off. That should be easy; they didn't look like much, physically. Old soldiers from the way they held themselves, yes, but The Watcher guessed that had been a long time ago. Not that The Watcher would do the dirty work on these two; the best thing would be to get some of the local tearaways involved. That would be the trick. Give the two old geezers a going-over; that would get them scurrying back where they belonged. And send a message as to what would happen to anybody else Whitehall might send. Stay out of Whitechapel. But first, The Watcher had to find out for sure why they were here. If they weren't here to look into the murders, then launching an attack on them would only make the situation worse.

Inside the police station, Sergeant Harker had invited Magnus and Malcolm into his office, while a constable took over the reception desk.

'What do I call you?' asked Harker. 'Is it Your Grace? DCI Coburg said you were an earl.'

'Magnus and Malcolm will do fine,' said Magnus. 'We're very grateful for your help in this way.'

'We'll be very grateful if you can get us more air raid shelters,' said Harker. 'Would it be helpful if I arranged for a constable to walk the area with you, pointing out possible locations?'

'It would indeed,' said Magnus. 'However, I must tell you that, although our visit to the East End is not exactly a secret, we have been asked by the Prime Minister not to let it be known why we are here.'

'The Prime Minister?' said Harker, impressed. 'Churchill?'

'Yes,' said Magnus. 'He's the one who's given us this task. He's very much aware of the damage and loss of life there has been to the East End. The problem is that he's concerned about property speculators. There are some owners of buildings that might look to make a large profit if they believe the government is ready to take them off their hands. So we thought we'd concentrate

91

our search on properties owned by the local council, along with buildings that may be temporarily out of use as a result of the bombing. Small factories or large shops, that sort of thing.'

'To that end, I wonder if the sight of a policeman walking around with us might make people suspicious,' put in Malcolm. 'Wonder what we're up to.'

'Yes, that's a good point,' said Harker thoughtfully. Then he brightened up. 'We can say you're from the Home Office come to look into the murders here.'

'Murders?' asked Malcolm.

'Two, so far,' said Harker. 'Tragically, in the style of the original Jack the Ripper.'

'Ah yes, Edgar mentioned one such murder to me.'

'You never told me,' complained Malcolm.

'It wasn't necessary,' countered Magnus. He looked at Harker. 'Two murders, you said?'

'Yes, the most recent body was discovered yesterday morning.'

Magnus nodded. 'That would be a good cover story. Excellent thinking, Sergeant. Can you arrange for a constable to be our escort?'

'No problem,' said Harker. 'If you come back tomorrow, I'll have someone ready for you. I'll select one of the older men. The man I've got in mind will know the area. I'll have to tell him the real reason about why you're walking around, what you're looking for, but this man will keep his mouth shut and won't tell anyone else. If anyone asks, he'll stick to the story about you being from the Home Office about the murders.'

Coburg had chosen McBride's cousin, Terrence Kilbride, as the next person to talk to. Like his cousin, Kilbride had a gentle

Scottish lilt to his voice, Border Scots or Edinburgh, thought Coburg, rather than the broader dialect of the Highlands and Islands or Glasgow. However, Kilbride had even less to offer in the way of information than his cousin. He'd never even met Bothwell, and was only at the palace following a call from his cousin, Hector.

'I'm afraid I know nothing about Mr Bothwell, Chief Inspector,' he said. 'You need someone who worked with him.'

Yes, I do, thought Coburg. *But who did he work with? We're going to need to widen our search.*

When Coburg and Lampson got back to Scotland Yard there was a message for DCI Coburg to call Dr Webb at the London Hospital in Whitechapel.

'Dr Webb,' said Coburg when he got through. 'I got your message.'

'Thank you for calling,' said Webb. 'I wanted to let you know the result of my autopsy on Sarah Mars. It's the same as Dr McKay's on the first victim. The fatal blow was done with a pointed double-edged blade straight into the heart, then a knife was used to cut out the organs.'

'This double-edged blade, Dr McKay mentioned it could have been a sword.'

'Yes, that's possible. But if so, a short sword with a narrow blade, not anything like a broadsword. Dr McKay and I have discussed it and agree both our victims were killed by the same person in an identical manner.'

That evening at home, Lampson sat and read the paper, while Eve did the exercises to strengthen her arm, and Terry read a comic. Then, in deliberately casual tones, Lampson said,

'You'll never guess where I was today.'

'Where?' asked Eve.

'Buckingham Palace.'

Both Eve and Terry stared at him, then Terry said, 'Did you meet the King?'

'I did, actually,' said Lampson.

'Never!' said Terry in disbelief.

'I did,' said his father.

'How?' Eve asked. 'Why were you there?'

'What did he say?' asked Terry.

'He told me that Edward was a regal name.'

'What were you there for?' demanded Eve impatiently.

'I'm not allowed to say,' said Lampson. 'But we were called in because they wanted my guv'nor's advice about something.'

'What?'

'Something to do with one of the staff,' said Lampson. 'But I'm not allowed to say any more.'

'Will you be going back?' asked Eve.

'Possibly,' said Lampson. 'It depends on the guv'nor. Apparently, he's a cousin, or something. Of the King, that is. The royal family's name used to be Saxe-Coburg-Gotha, and he's Saxe-Coburg. Different branches of the same family.'

'So is he royalty?' asked Terry.

'He says he isn't, but his brother's an earl, and the guv'nor's an Honourable, so I reckon it's likely.'

'What's an Honourable?' asked Terry.

'It's what you get called if you're the younger son of an earl. His dad was an earl, and when he died, the guv'nor's elder brother Magnus became the new Earl.'

'And your guv'nor's just a detective, like you?'

'Only he's a chief inspector.'

'Did he say what football team he supported?' asked Terry.

'I don't think the guv'nor supports any football team,' said Lampson.

'No, I meant the King,' said Terry.

'I didn't ask him.'

'I hope it's Spurs,' said Terry.

Lampson looked at the clock and said, 'Bedtime, Terry. You've got school tomorrow.'

'Right,' said Terry. He headed for the door to the stairs, taking his comic with him.

'G'night, Dad. G'night, Eve,' he said.

'Goodnight, Terry,' said Eve. 'Don't read for too long.'

After Terry had gone, Lampson gave a sigh and said quietly, 'I said to him about calling you Mum, now we're married. But I haven't heard him say it.'

'He will, when he's ready,' said Eve. 'It'll take him time to get used to it. He's never known what it's like to have a mother, with his own mother dying when he was just a baby. It's always been just him with you, and his nan and grandad.'

Lampson nodded. 'I know, but I wish he'd get used to the fact that you're his mum now.'

'I'm sure he is,' said Eve. 'It's just he doesn't put it into words yet. But he will, in time.'

In their flat, Coburg and Rosa were also swapping tales of their separate days. Coburg told her about his and Lampson's encounter with the King, and Lampson's reaction, which made her laugh, and then he told her about the second murdered woman at Whitechapel, though without going into gruesome details.

'I expect I'll be bumping into Magnus and Malcolm as this case continues,' he said. 'They're over there sorting out potential sites for air raid shelters.'

'How did they get that job?' asked Rosa.

'I believe Churchill gave it to them. Old comrades, that sort of thing.'

'Talking of dead people, we had an incident today.' And she told him about going to pick up elderly Mrs Pickford, and finding the row of houses had been destroyed during the night. 'The call had been booked a few days before, so as far as we were concerned it was alright. Until we got there. Four houses gone. A neighbour told us Mrs Pickford and her son had decided to stay in the house rather than go to the shelter because she was in a wheelchair after having a leg amputated, and she couldn't get up and down the stairs.' She sighed. 'Poor them.' She looked at her husband. 'Is this going to go on for much longer?'

'I wish I knew,' said Coburg. 'All we can do is get through each day and night as they come and hope.'

Suddenly they heard the familiar sound of the air raid warning wailing through the streets.

'At least we've got a solid shelter in the basement,' said Coburg, getting up and handing Rosa her coat.

CHAPTER ELEVEN

Friday 4th April

As Coburg and Lampson walked towards the main staircase across the reception area of Scotland Yard the following morning, they found a short, tubby, smiling man in a brown checked suit in their way.

'Excuse me,' he said apologetically. 'DCI Saxe-Coburg?'

'Yes,' replied Coburg warily.

'Charlie Brown from the *Whitechapel Chronicle*. Dr McKay at the London Hospital and Sergeant Harker at Whitechapel nick suggested I contact you. It's about the women who were murdered at the old Whitechapel Road Tube station. I'm writing a story about it for the *Chronicle* and I wondered if I could ask you a few questions.'

'I'll leave you to it and see you upstairs, sir,' said Lampson, and departed.

Resignedly, Coburg gestured at a wooden bench at one side of the reception area.

'We'll talk there,' he said.

Brown followed the chief inspector to the bench and sat down next to him, taking a notepad and pencil from his pocket.

'Thank you for seeing me,' he said. 'First, do you know the names of the victims?'

'Yes. We'll be issuing that information to the press shortly.'

'The talk in Whitechapel is that both women sustained dreadful injuries, which were very similar to those sustained by the original victims of Jack the Ripper in the 1880s. Would you agree with that?'

'They were certainly badly mutilated, I'm sad to say.'

'Their reproductive organs were removed, I'm told.'

'Again, details of the injuries they received will be issued to the press shortly, once we've received the full medical reports.'

'We've been told both women were prostitutes. Is that fair to say?'

'Again, that is to be ascertained.'

'As a result of these murders there's a great deal of panic in and around Whitechapel. What steps are being taken to protect the public?'

'You'll need to talk to the local police about that.'

'That would be Sergeant Harker.'

'It would,' confirmed Coburg. 'Though how much he'll be able to tell you, I don't know.'

Suddenly they heard the sound of fast footsteps coming to them from the staircase. They looked up to see Sergeant Lampson hurrying towards them.

'Sorry for interrupting,' apologised Lampson, 'but there's an important telephone call for you, sir. *Very* important.'

'About the Ripper victims?' blurted out Brown.

Coburg got to his feet. 'We'll have to continue this conversation another time,' he said to Brown.

As Coburg and Lampson hurried towards the stairs, Brown called out after them: 'You can always get me at the *Whitechapel Chronicle*!'

'What's the phone call about?' Coburg asked Lampson as they hurried up the stairs. 'Or is it a ruse to get me away from that man?'

'It's real enough,' said Lampson. 'It's Shadwell police station. That photograph you sent round of the missing man. They think they've got him.'

'Excellent!' said Coburg. 'Where is he?'

'At the moment he's on a slab at the London Hospital.'

'He's dead?'

'He is.'

'How did he die?'

'I'll let the station sergeant at Shadwell tell you. He's still on the phone, I hope, unless the operator's cut him off.'

Coburg ran into the office and snatched up the phone.

'DCI Coburg,' he said. 'I'm sorry to have kept you waiting.'

'That's alright, sir. Sergeant Paulson from Shadwell station here.'

'My sergeant tells me you've found the missing man.'

'Yes, sir. His body was pulled out of Shadwell Basin yesterday. He'd been stabbed in the heart. According to the medical people, he'd been in the water since last Friday. From brick dust in his pockets we think his body had been weighed down, but after nearly a week in the water his body bloated and rose to the surface. Unfortunately, he had no wallet on him, no form of identification. It was only when we got your flyer with his picture that we clicked.'

'Who was the attending doctor?'

'A Dr McKay.'

Yes, it would be Mr Misery, thought Coburg, not the genial and more amiable Dr Webb.

'Who found his body?' asked Coburg.

'A bloke who was fishing.'

'In Shadwell Basin?'

'There's carp there, but this bloke never catches anything. I think he just goes there to get away from his family. It's an excuse.'

'Can you arrange for him to come in. And I'll need to talk to everyone else who was involved in recovering the body.'

'Including Dr McKay?'

'Yes.'

'Do you know Dr McKay?'

'I've met him,' said Coburg. 'I'll go on to the London Hospital and see him after I've talked to everyone at the station. Has anyone informed the man's family of his death? We'll need a formal identification.'

'I'm not sure if that's a good idea,' said Paulson. 'The body's in quite a mess, as you can imagine after all that time in the water. Perhaps you can ask Dr McKay if he can make the face look presentable.'

'I can ask him,' said Coburg. 'I'll appeal to his better nature and his sense of humanity.'

Paulson gave a derisory laugh. 'Good luck with that,' he said.

Magnus and Malcolm arrived at Whitechapel station and Sergeant Harker introduced them to Constable Bert Watts, a man in his mid-fifties. His left arm was missing, his sleeve pinned up.

'This is PC Bert Watts,' Harker told them. 'These gentlemen are Magnus Saxe-Coburg and Malcolm Grant.'

'You look like an old soldier, sir,' said Magnus. 'Or am I wrong?'

'No, sir. I served during the First War. The Middle East. Palestine.' He patted his empty sleeve. 'That's where I lost this, sir. Luckily for me, the shortage of men this time has meant I'm able to get back in uniform. Did you serve, sirs?'

'Yes, we were both in the trenches in France,' said Magnus.

'The Somme,' added Malcolm.

'I believe that was a hard time, sir,' said Watts.

'No harder than for anyone else, I suppose,' said Magnus. 'But yes, it was pretty bloody.'

'Especially the first day, July the first,' said Malcolm. 'The worst day in the history of the British army, they said. We took fifty-seven thousand casualties, nineteen thousand killed and thirty-eight thousand wounded.'

'Yes, well, that's all in the past,' said Magnus brusquely. 'It's the present we have to contend with. I assume Sergeant Harker has told you what we're here for?'

'Possible locations for new air raid shelters.'

'And our cover story?'

'Investigating the murders by the New Ripper.'

'The New Ripper?' queried Malcolm.

'That's what the local paper are calling him. Not that I approve, but I suppose it differentiates between him and the original Ripper. I've got a few places lined up that may be of interest. I assume you're looking for something with a big basement so people can shelter? I mention that because some of the early shelters were just brick buildings on flat waste ground, which fell down when a bomb fell on them, or even just dropped nearby.'

'Yes, that was what we were thinking,' said Magnus. 'There's always the possibility that cellars can be excavated, but that takes time to do it properly. Whereas somewhere with cellars would be ready for immediate use.'

'There's a couple of abandoned churches, with crypts,' said Watts.

'That would be good,' said Magnus. 'Are they available?'

'I'm sure you could negotiate with the church authorities,' said Watts. 'Actually, only one of them's an actual former church; the other was a synagogue.'

'As long as it saves lives, I can't see people being bothered what sort of denomination it was,' said Malcolm.

'In that case, I'll show you them,' said Watts. 'Would you prefer to drive, or are you happy walking?'

'Walking,' said Malcolm firmly. 'It's always the best way to get to know an area.'

Coburg and Lampson had arranged to meet Sergeant Paulson and Desmond Downs, the man who'd found the body, at Shadwell Basin. Both men were standing waiting for them by the lock that connected the open area of water to the Thames. Downs was a tall gloomy-looking man. 'Four years I've been coming here and never caught anything, until yesterday,' he groaned.

'I believe your hook became entangled with the corpse,' said Coburg.

Downs nodded. 'Ruined my line. It got tied up with the poor bloke. I had to cut it.' He groaned again. 'They're not cheap.'

'We'll see if we can get you reimbursed,' said Coburg. 'Do you come here often?'

'When I'm not at work.'

'Where do you work?'

'At the power station. Yesterday was my day off so I thought I'd get some fishing in. A fortnight ago, my pal Joe Wrigglesworth caught a really big carp here.'

'Where were you standing when you hooked the dead man?' asked Coburg.

'I've already told Sergeant Paulson,' said Downs.

'I know, but please humour us,' said Coburg. 'We're not that familiar with this place.'

Downs gestured them to follow him. They did, and he

stopped a short distance from the lock gates.

'It was here,' he said. 'I saw something bobbing about near the shore, and as I reeled in my line it came towards me, so I realised my line had got caught up with it. I brought it right into the shore, and saw it was a body.' He shuddered. 'The face was all white and the fish had been biting at it. Horrible it was. Made me sick to my stomach. Well, I wasn't going to pull it out. One look at the state it was in, and the putrid smell, and I thought it was likely to fall to bits. So I tied my line to the lock gates to make sure it didn't float away, and then went to look for the lock keeper. He phoned the police. Sergeant Paulson sent two men.'

Coburg looked at Paulson, who said, 'My men dragged him out and I phoned the London Hospital to get a doctor to come out. When I got here I could tell he'd been in the water for about a week; we get quite a few drownings here. Dr McKay arrived and took him to the London in an ambulance.'

'Have you ever seen him before?' Coburg asked both men.

'No,' said Downs.

'Me, neither,' said Paulson.

'Was anything else found?' asked Coburg. 'A bag, or anything?'

'No,' said Paulson. 'I was planning to get the lake dragged, but I decided to wait until you got here. The basin's quite shallow around the edge, about four feet deep, but then it goes to twenty feet deep in the middle, and there's lots of silt, so it's not easy to drag. There's a local diving club. I could get them to have a go in it, but all the silt makes the water quite dark and thick.'

Coburg looked thoughtful. 'That's a good suggestion, but for the moment I suggest we leave it and see what Dr McKay has to tell us.'

'He'll tell you to go away and not bother him,' sighed Paulson.

'Yes,' agreed Coburg ruefully. 'We've met Dr McKay before.'

CHAPTER TWELVE

Dr McKay was his usual abrasive self when Coburg and Lampson entered the mortuary in the basement of the London Hospital.

'Dr McKay,' said Coburg, forcing a smile of greeting.

'Chief Inspector,' responded the doctor dourly. 'I suppose you've come to look at the body that was fished out of Shadwell Basin?'

'We have,' said Coburg. 'Although after six days in the water I shouldn't imagine there'd be many clues as to what happened to him.'

'He didn't drown, if that's what you're wondering,' said McKay.

'No, I was told he was stabbed.'

'That is correct. Right in the heart with a long-bladed and sharply pointed knife.'

'Similar to the one that killed the women at Whitechapel?' asked Coburg.

'No,' said McKay firmly. 'You've read my report?'

'I have,' said Coburg. 'You suggested that blade at Whitechapel might have been a short sword.'

'Or a similar weapon,' said McKay. 'I've been thinking about it since and it's possible it could have been a bayonet. Both sides of the blade having sharp edges.'

Coburg thought about this, then nodded. 'Yes,' he said.

'I mention this because I was in the last war and saw many

injuries inflicted by bayonets,' said McKay. 'I mentioned this to Dr Webb and he agrees, although he has no experience of bayonets. Too young.'

'Yes,' said Coburg. 'I saw action in the First War, too. And saw many wounds caused by bayonets.'

McKay walked them to a body lying on a table covered with a sheet. 'This wound was altogether different. More like a commercial knife, or a kitchen knife. Sharp point with just one side of the blade sharpened.' He pulled the top half of the sheet down, exposing the dead man's head and chest. The white skin had the usual rubbery look of skin immersed in water for any length of time. It had also been torn by the teeth of fish.

'It looks like the carp have made a meal of him,' observed Coburg.

'And eels,' said McKay. 'I hadn't realised before there must be eels in Shadwell Basin. I expect they came through the lock.'

'Time of death?' asked Coburg.

McKay gave an ironic laugh. 'I assume you mean date of death,' he said.

'Yes,' said Coburg.

'From the state of the body and internal organs I'd say he's been in the water for about a week.'

'He was reported missing a week ago,' said Coburg. 'Last Friday.'

'Then I think we can conclude that he was killed last Friday and his body dumped in Shadwell Basin the same day,' said McKay.

'He was clothed,' said Coburg. 'Are his clothes here?'

'Stored in a box, as is the case with all cadavers who come in to be examined. They were soaking wet, but I decided not to have them dried, because I was fairly sure the police would want to examine them in the condition they were discovered.'

'Indeed we would,' said Coburg. 'I'd like to take them to Scotland Yard for proper examination. They might give us some clues as to who killed him, and why.'

'To be frank, I doubt that,' said McKay. 'His pockets were empty. The local police looked through them searching for a wallet, or anything that would give the man's identity. You're welcome to take them, but I would remind you that the man's relatives will surely want them, possibly for his funeral.'

'Talking of the relatives, we're going to bring in his wife for a formal identification. Just the face, there's no need to subject her to what the fish and eels have done to his torso. Would it be possible to make his face presentable for her, do you think?'

'Of course,' said McKay in a terse tone that showed he was offended at the request. 'I left him in this state for you to see him. I am sensitive to the feelings of the relatives who come here to identify their loved ones.'

'I apologise, Doctor. And thank you for that consideration. Sergeant Lampson and I will be visiting his wife as soon as we return to central London. One last question: have you looked through the clothes yourself?'

The doctor regarded the chief inspector with a look of superiority. 'My responsibility is the dead body, not his accoutrements,' he said curtly.

'Thank you, Doctor,' said Coburg politely. 'Then we'll take them and get our forensic people to examine them before we return them to his family.'

'So, where to first?' asked Lampson as he headed towards Central London. 'The Yard, or Pimlico?'

'Pimlico, I think,' said Coburg. 'The sooner we let the widow know, the better. Even if it is bad news.'

Mrs Bothwell was alone when Coburg and Lampson arrived at the house in Pimlico.

'The children are at school,' she told them. 'I thought it was best to try and keep everything as normal as possible for them.' She regarded them in unhappy anticipation. 'Do you have any news?'

'I'm afraid we do,' said Coburg, as gently as he could. 'Your husband was found in the river at Shadwell Basin yesterday. He had no identification on him, so it was only today that the local police realised who he was. I'm very sorry to be the bearer of the bad news.'

Her eyes filled with tears, and as she wiped them, she said, 'I thought it must be the case. Bernard would never just have gone off without telling me.' She frowned, puzzled. 'What was he doing at Shadwell Basin?'

'We don't know that yet. We're beginning our investigation.'

'How did he die?' she asked. 'Did he fall in?'

'It seems that he was murdered. Someone stabbed him. I'm very sorry.'

'But . . . who would do a thing like that? Was it a robbery?'

'Possibly,' said Coburg. 'As I said, he had no form of identification on him, no wallet, which is why it's taken this long to let you know. It was the photograph you lent us that led us to him.' He took an envelope with the photograph of Bothwell from his pocket and handed it to her. 'I'm returning that photograph to you, as promised.'

'Can I see him?' she asked.

'In fact I was going to ask you if you would mind identifying him,' said Coburg. 'We usually need a close family member to do that.'

She nodded, as her tears began again. 'Yes,' she said in a small voice. 'Where is he?'

'At the London Hospital in Whitechapel,' said Coburg. 'I'll take you there. Tomorrow morning, if that's alright, to give you time to arrange things with your family. Do you have anyone to look after the children while you're at the London?'

'My neighbour's been very good, Mrs Purkiss. She's offered to do anything she can. I'll ask her.'

'In that case I'll call for you tomorrow morning at half past nine,' said Coburg. 'I do have some questions for you now, if you can cope with them. I'm sorry to ask them but we find the sooner we've got all the facts, the more chance we have of finding the culprit.'

She nodded. 'I understand.'

'Did he know anyone over at Shadwell?'

'Not as far as I know. Although it's not far from Whitechapel, and his sister's there.'

'I'm wondering how he would have got to Shadwell. Do you have a car?'

'No. If he went there I expect he went by bus. Bernard didn't drive.'

As they returned to their car, Coburg said, 'Right, there's a job for the local Shadwell bobbies. We'll get Sergeant Paulson to get his men to take the photo of Bothwell round the local bus garages and ask if any of their conductors recognise him as travelling on their bus last Friday. Personally, I doubt if we'll get anything, but we daren't leave any stone unturned.'

* * *

After they'd returned to Shadwell and asked Sergeant Paulson to distribute the photograph around the local bus companies, they returned to Scotland Yard. Lampson carried the box with Bothwell's still wet clothes to their office, while Coburg reported the latest events to Superintendent Allison.

'The King's valet has been found murdered?' asked Allison, as if unable to grasp the fact.

'Yes, sir. Stabbed in the heart. Body dumped in Shadwell Basin. We calculate he was killed and dumped in the water a week ago.'

'Has His Majesty been informed?'

'Not yet, sir. So far we've only informed Mr Bothwell's widow. I've made arrangements to take her to the London Hospital tomorrow morning to formally identify the body. My next immediate move will be to report this to the Prime Minister. He asked me to keep him informed and he will pass things on to His Majesty.'

'In that case you'd better do that,' said Allison. 'The sooner he knows, the better.'

Coburg returned to the office, where he found Lampson examining the dead man's wet clothes.

'They stink,' said Lampson, wrinkling his nose.

'I know, I could smell them in the car,' said Coburg. 'Have you gone through the pockets?'

'No. Dr McKay said the local police had already done that.'

'Looking for a wallet, or similar,' said Coburg. 'I wonder just how deeply they actually searched, considering the smell.'

He lifted the jacket from the box, spread it out on a desk and began to probe carefully into the damp clothes. He smiled as he pulled a sixpence out of one of the jacket pockets. 'Well, here's one thing they missed.' He put the small coin to one side, then continued to search through all the other jacket pockets. He then ran his finger around the jacket collar, and then the jacket's lining, before putting it aside.

He then picked up the trousers. They were still sodden, heavy with water. They also gave off a smell of excrement, the result of the man's bowels opening at the moment of death. He put his fingers into each of the pockets, one at a time, and then turned them carefully inside out.

'Hello, what have we here?' he said, curious.

Lampson looked as Coburg pulled a small ball of tightly screwed-up wet paper from the depths of one of the trousers' back pockets.

'Got a pair of tweezers?' asked Coburg.

Lampson went to his desk and took a pair of tweezers from the drawer, which he handed to Coburg. Tentatively, Coburg tried using the tweezers to separate the ball into its constituent parts, then he stopped.

'This is going to take a while,' he said. 'At least, to do it properly, without tearing the paper. The superintendent has instructed me to tell the Prime Minister that Bothwell's body has been found, and do it now, as a priority. Remembering how upset he got with me last time over it, I'd better make my way to Down Street.'

'Say the Prime Minister isn't there?'

'Then I'll leave a message asking him to call me. But at least I'll have made contact, which is what the superintendent ordered me to do.' He held out the tweezers to his sergeant. 'While I'm out, this is your job. To take this apart and find out what it is.'

Lampson took the tweezers and looked doubtfully at the wet ball of paper.

'What happens if I tear it? 'Cause it looks like it's wet all the way through.'

'Then I shall be displeased,' said Coburg. 'But I know you won't, because you're very good with things like this.'

The Watcher waited until the Bentley moved off before walking towards the police station. PC Bert Watts was standing watching the Bentley drive away.

'Who was that?' asked The Watcher. 'The Bentley. We don't see any of them round here.'

'Just a couple of government blokes,' said Watts.

'Oh yes? What are they doing down here?'

'It's the killings.'

'But what are they here for? From Scotland Yard?'

'Not as far as I know. Just government blokes.'

'Must be important, though, driving around in a Bentley.'

Watts shrugged. 'I didn't ask. Sergeant Harker just asked me to show them round Whitechapel. All their questions were about the two women who were killed.'

The Watcher nodded. 'That must be it, then. The killings.'

Watts made for the entrance to the police station. 'Anyway, that's my shift over for the day.'

So, thought The Watcher. *Top people investigating the killings, just as I thought. Not Scotland Yard, but higher up than that. Right, they definitely need to be interfered with.*

CHAPTER THIRTEEN

Coburg drove to Down Street, leaving Lampson working on the ball of wet paper, but found that Churchill wasn't there and they didn't know when he was expected. He left a message for him that said: *Sir. Valet found, dead. Please call me. DCI Coburg.*

Meanwhile, back at Scotland Yard, it took a very long time, the greatest amount of patience, and a steady pair of hands, but finally Lampson had teased the ball of wet paper apart with the tweezers. It turned out to be one small scrap of paper, still wet through, with neatly handwritten words in black ink, which had partially smudged due to the water. It looked to Lampson like the beginning of a letter.

He laid it carefully on the top of a radiator to dry, which would make it easier to handle, and to read.

By the time that Coburg returned, the paper had dried enough for the words to be read. It was fortunate that whoever wrote it had used black indelible ink, so it hadn't spread and become illegible. *Indelible ink*, he mused. *I've seen black indelible ink used recently.*

He read the note.

Dear David

I thank you for your letter, but I am sure you understand that what you ask is impossible at this present time. Contact with the person you mention is out of the question. The terms proposed cannot be entertained.

I remain, yours fraternally

Who was David? wondered Lampson. And who was writing to him? And who was the person mentioned with whom contact was out of the question?

He was just puzzling over these questions when the door opened and the chief inspector arrived.

'So, did you see Churchill?' asked Lampson.

'He was out. I left a message for him to call me. How did you get on with that ball of soggy paper?'

'Done,' said Lampson proudly. He pointed to the piece of paper laid on top of the radiator. 'Careful, though. It's still a bit damp, although not much.'

Coburg went to the piece of paper and looked at it, taking in the obscure message.

'It looks like the start of a letter,' said Lampson, 'but I don't know what it all means.'

'I think I might have an idea,' said Coburg, 'and if I'm right I think we've found the reason why Bernard Bothwell was killed.'

'For this?' said Lampson.

'For the moment I wouldn't say anything about this to anyone. If it's what I think it is, it could have dangerous consequences for anyone who knows about it.'

'How dangerous?'

'Very dangerous.'

Lampson backed away from the scrap of paper. 'In that case, I've never seen it.'

The telephone rang. Lampson picked it up.

'DCI Coburg's office.' He held the receiver towards Coburg. 'It's the Prime Minister's private secretary for you.'

'DCI Coburg,' said the chief inspector.

'The Prime Minister has returned to Down Street and received your message. He would appreciate it if you would come to see him as soon as you can.'

'Tell him I'm on my way,' said Coburg.

He hung up the receiver. He took an envelope from his desk, into which he slipped the now almost dried piece of paper.

'Right,' he said to Lampson. 'If anyone comes looking for me, I'll be at Down Street.'

This time Coburg was shown straight into Churchill's small office.

'You've found the valet,' said the Prime Minister.

'Yes, sir. The local police found his body in Shadwell Basin, after a man fishing there spotted something bulky floating in the water,' said Coburg. 'The body's currently at the London Hospital in Whitechapel. I've informed Mrs Bothwell about her husband's death. I'm taking her to the London first thing tomorrow morning for her to formally identify him.' He hesitated, then added, 'It won't be a good experience for her; Bothwell had been in the water for a week. But I have confidence that the doctor in charge there, Dr McKay, will make his face presentable.'

Churchill nodded, then asked, 'Did he have anything on him?'

'You're referring to the watch, sir,' said Coburg. 'No, sir, he didn't have the watch on him.'

'Don't prevaricate, man,' snapped Churchill impatiently. 'Did he have anything on him?'

'The local police reported that his pockets were empty.

However, when I examined his clothes properly today, I discovered something in one of his trouser pockets. It was a very small ball of soaking wet paper. I took it apart and found it was this.'

He passed the envelope to Churchill.

'Be careful with it, sir. It's still slightly damp, and fragile,' cautioned Coburg.

Churchill removed the piece of paper from the envelope. He read it, then asked, 'Have you read this?'

'I couldn't avoid reading it, sir.' He then quoted the words on it. '"Dear David, I thank you for your letter, but I am sure you understand that what you ask is impossible at this present time. Contact with the person you mention is out of the question. The terms proposed cannot be entertained. I remain, yours fraternally . . ."'

'The rest of it with the signature has been torn off,' said Churchill. 'So we don't know who wrote it.'

'The words "yours fraternally" suggest a brother,' said Coburg. 'The handwriting's similar to the note that came with the information His Majesty kindly sent me. As is the indelible ink that's been used, the same as in His Majesty's note to me. I think this is a handwritten draft prior to it being typed up.' He paused, then said, 'His Majesty's brother's name is David, isn't it? Although, while he was King, he was known as Edward.'

Churchill studied Coburg warily, then said, 'I could have you shot, you know.'

'You could, but I think Mrs Churchill might be upset. I've heard that she's a fan of my wife's music, and I expect the newspapers would express sympathy for Rosa.'

Churchill looked at Coburg, his face expressionless, his mouth tight. Then suddenly he relaxed and let out a chuckle.

'You're a difficult bugger, Coburg,' he said. He produced a cigar from a wooden box on his desk, which he offered to the chief inspector.

'No thank you, sir. I don't smoke.'

'Why not? Everyone else does.'

'I lost a lung during the First War, after being shot at the battle of Sambre-Oise. The surgeon advised me to look after the one I was left with.'

Churchill put the cigar away. 'Did your surgeon advise against brandy?'

'No, sir.'

'Good, because I think this occasion needs something.' From a lower drawer in his desk he produced a bottle of brandy and two glasses. He half-filled the glasses and pushed one across the desk to Coburg.

'*Santé*,' said Churchill, lifting his glass in a toast.

'*Santé*,' echoed Coburg, joining in with the French equivalent of 'Cheers'. It was a good French brandy.

'I have a tale to tell,' said Churchill, after he'd taken a mouthful of his drink. 'Once upon a time there were five brothers. There was also a sister, but as we're talking about the children of a king it's the boys we concentrate on. Their names were David, Albert, Henry, George and John. John, sadly, died young, leaving the other four. When the King died, David, the eldest, became King. You know where this is going, of course, so I'll cut to the nub of it. David fell in love with a woman who many thought was unsuitable. For one thing she was married, and for another she was American. I have nothing against Americans; my own mother was American. But to the powers that be she was deemed unsuitable as a Queen of England. Because they refused to allow David to marry her, he abdicated the throne and his younger brother, Albert, became King.'

'His Majesty George VI,' said Coburg.

'The royals have always had the practice of adopting a regal name.' Churchill nodded. 'David became Edward, Albert became George. David, as the eldest son, had been trained since birth to become King. Albert was not. It is my opinion he has made a great success of his reign.'

'I agree, sir,' said Coburg.

'The problem is that David, or the Duke of Windsor as he has now been titled, felt thwarted. He wanted the woman he loved, now his wife, to become Queen. He still would like that to happen.' Churchill tapped the handwritten letter. '"Contact with the person you mention is out of the question",' he read aloud. He looked at Coburg. 'What do you infer from that?'

'There are two possibilities to who is being referred to,' said Coburg. 'One is Mrs Simpson, now the Duchess of Windsor. The other is either a representative of Adolf Hitler, or Hitler himself.'

'And the most likely of those two possibilities?'

Coburg hesitated, then said, 'The second.' After a pause, he added, 'The watch was a ploy, wasn't it, sir?'

'Yes. It was my idea. His Majesty was unhappy with the deceit. He is the least deceitful man I've ever known. He does have a watch that was presented to him by his father of which he is very proud. It is currently securely locked away in his bedside cabinet.'

'So it was this handwritten letter you believed that Bothwell had and that you wished me to recover.'

'Yes. But we could not afford to inform you about it because of the contents. I assume you know that the Duke of Windsor has been in touch with Herr Hitler?'

'Yes, sir,' said Coburg. 'The tour of Germany he and the Duchess made was in most of the newspapers.'

'He claimed he was trying to arrange a peace treaty,' said Churchill. 'I have my own doubts about that.' Again, he tapped the letter. 'If this letter were to get out there would be hell to pay. Evidence of the brother of the King, the Governor of the Bahamas, corresponding with an enemy power. There would be calls for his arrest for treason.'

'Do you know why Bothwell had the letter, sir?'

'No,' said Churchill. 'All I know is that His Majesty contacted me and told me that his valet had disappeared, and so had the letter he'd drafted that he planned to give to his secretary to have typed, then sent in a diplomatic pouch to Washington, to be forwarded to the Duke in the Bahamas. That way it would ensure it would reach the Duke rather than be tangled up in the difficulties we often experience in sending post overseas in the current climate.'

'Where is the original letter sent to His Majesty by the Duke?'

'His Majesty still has it. His normal routine is to pass all correspondence on to his secretary, Sir Jasper Connor, along with his handwritten draft. The handwritten draft and a copy of the typed reply are then filed, attached to the original letter for reference.'

'Is Sir Jasper aware of the contents of the original letter?'

'According to His Majesty, no. The letter from the Duke of Windsor had "Confidential" written very clearly on the envelope, along with "For His Majesty's eyes only". The various royal crests on the envelope ensured that was adhered to.'

'Now Bothwell's body has turned up, and so has this letter, do you want me to investigate his murder, or will you be handing that on to Special Branch or one of the security services?' asked Coburg.

'I'm weighing that up,' said Churchill sourly. 'Unfortunately, apart from you, I don't know who to trust. Most of the people in the security services are a load of communists, especially MI6.'

'May I suggest Inspector Hibbert of MI5,' said Coburg. 'I've worked with him before on cases where our investigations crossed. He's no communist nor a communist sympathiser. He is a serious patriot.'

'How did you get on with him?'

'Very well,' said Coburg. He gave a wry smile. 'He can be quite cantankerous, but he's a damned good investigator.'

'Can he keep a secret?'

'Yes. Unlike some in the security services.'

Churchill nodded. 'You've got this far, Coburg. I'll let His Majesty know about Bothwell. I'll also say to him that I'd like you to investigate Bothwell's murder, working alongside Inspector Hibbert of MI5. But I need to assure him that there will be no mention of this letter getting out.'

'I can assure you of that from my perspective, sir.'

'Leave Hibbert to me. I'll meet him and sound him out. If he comes up to all the things you say about him, you and he will be working together.' He then looked pointedly at Coburg as he added in firm tones, 'I agreed you could tell your Sergeant Lampson about the watch, but this letter is a different matter. You are not to tell him about this, nor about your possible investigations into the Duke of Windsor. You will have MI5's Inspector Hibbert as a sounding board, and you may tell him about the letter. I may well do myself after I've met him and made up my mind about him. But no one else. If word of this leaked out it could cause a constitutional crisis, and we cannot afford another, especially at this time. Is that clear?'

'Yes, sir. Perfectly clear.'

CHAPTER FOURTEEN

'How did you get on? Did you see Churchill?' asked Lampson as Coburg entered the office.

'I did.'

'And?'

'Exactly as I thought. He considers that letter to be very dangerous. In fact he said he could have me shot for knowing about it.'

'I hope you told him I didn't know about it,' said Lampson hastily.

'I didn't need to. He told me very firmly that I wasn't to tell you about it.'

'And you haven't,' said Lampson pointedly. Then, curious, he asked, 'So what's going to happen now? About the dead bloke, Bothwell?'

'Churchill wants me to look into his murder, but in co-operation with Inspector Hibbert of MI5.'

'So I'm out of it?'

'I'm afraid so,' said Coburg apologetically.

'I'm not,' said Lampson. 'The last thing I want is to be caught up in something like this, where I could be shot for treason.'

'Don't worry, you're perfectly safe. As far as Churchill is concerned you never saw the letter and you don't know about it. Only I know about it. Although it looks as if Inspector

Hibbert is also going to be brought into it.'

'Does he know what he's letting himself in for?'

'He's MI5. This sort of thing is second nature to him. In the meantime, I suggest while I involve myself with this, you busy yourself looking into the Whitechapel killings.'

'Actually, I've been doing that while you were out.'

'Oh?'

'I've been finding out about Whitechapel Road station. It was opened in March 1884 as St Mary's Whitechapel. So it was open at the time the original Ripper was operating. Although none of the five women who were officially listed as the Ripper's victims were killed at the station, some of those who were believed to be victims of the Ripper, but survived, were attacked at the station. Remember Riley named a few. Well, I went back to the Black Museum and saw Mr Plomley and said we needed to check on something else, if he didn't mind. He looked like he minded, but he agreed I could go in.' Lampson grinned. 'Whatever his dad did, that must have been a big favour you did him. Anyway, I got the details about some of the other women who were attacked. and there were two at Whitechapel Road – or St Mary's as it was then.'

He checked his notebook and read the names and dates. '30th July 1888, a woman called Norah Pegg was attacked there, and on 20th August a woman named as Long Meg was attacked. They were both slashed with a knife, but because they didn't die they weren't counted as Ripper victims.'

'So it's possible that when Mary Ann Nichols was killed on 31st August, she might well have been the third victim, rather than the first,' said Coburg thoughtfully.

'And her body was found at the entrance to the stable yard at Buck's Row,' said Lampson. 'The thing is, Buck's Row doesn't exist anymore, as such. It's now called Durward Street. I checked some old maps of that part of London. It seems the name was changed in 1892 because of the murder of Mary Ann Nichols. Buck's Row had become so notorious that the council decided to change its name.'

'So you think the next attack will take place at Durward Street?'

'I don't know,' admitted Lampson. 'But it's a possibility. Of course, I could be reading too much into things.'

They were interrupted by the ringing of the telephone. Lampson picked it up.

'DCI Coburg's office.' He paused and looked at Coburg, then said, 'Yes, Inspector, he's here.' He held out the receiver towards Coburg. 'It's Inspector Hibbert for you.'

Coburg took the phone.

'Coburg,' he said.

'I've just come from seeing the Prime Minister,' said Hibbert. 'I think we should meet.'

'Shall I come to you, or you come here?'

'Neither,' said Hibbert. 'We want somewhere no one can listen in. Victoria Gardens on the Embankment, by the bandstand. There's a military band giving a concert there. They're always loud.'

'When's this concert on?'

'Now,' said Hibbert.

'In that case I'll see you there.' Coburg hung up.

'Things are moving,' he said. He got up. 'I'm off to Victoria Gardens on the Embankment. I suggest you go to Whitechapel and talk to Sergeant Harker. I can walk to the gardens, so you take the car.'

The Watcher had found the right people, a gang of local youths, too young for the army but too old for school. Tearaways.

Troublemakers. Usually to be found lounging on street corners on the lookout for things to steal. There were half a dozen of them, a motley assortment, some tall, some short, but all thin. Rationing and a lack of money did that. Their leader was a sixteen-year-old called Bazzer. Bright enough, but not *too* bright. Handy with his fists and boots, as were most of the others in the gang.

'Have you heard about the two old blokes going around our area?' The Watcher asked Bazzer.

Bazzer nodded. 'To do with the murders happening,' he said.

'That's just the story they've put out,' said The Watcher. 'I heard different.'

Bazzer and the other youths regarded The Watcher quizzically.

'The way I heard it is those two blokes, who look all very old-fashioned and English, are working for the Germans.'

'The Germans?!' exclaimed one of the youths in disbelief.

'In fact I don't think they're English at all,' continued The Watcher. 'I heard them talking to one another when they thought no one else was around. They were talking German.'

'So why haven't you said anything to anyone about it?' asked Bazzer suspiciously.

'I did, but they didn't believe me. These two blokes have conned the police. They've even been given a local copper to walk around with them.'

'Yes,' said another youth. 'We've seen him with 'em.'

'If what you say is true, why are the police cooperating with them?' asked Bazzer, still suspicious.

'They've got letters from the government saying they're from the Home Office here to investigate the murders, but I've been told they're forged.'

'Who by?' asked Bazzer. 'Who told you?'

'I can't tell you,' said The Watcher. 'But it's someone I trust.'

'So if they're Germans, why are they here?'

'They're here to report back to the Germans about how effective the air raids on Whitechapel are. The Germans want the proof up close. And, once they've seen for themselves how badly we've been hit here, they'll step it up even more.'

The youths looked at The Watcher, concerned.

'How sure are you about this?' asked Bazzer.

'Like I said, I got it from someone I can trust.'

'So why doesn't he do something? Get them arrested?'

'He can't. He says they're protected by someone higher up. This country's riddled with German spies and sympathisers.'

Bazzer thought it over, then said, 'We can do something about it.' He looked at his pals. 'Can't we, mates?'

There was a smattering of people in the chairs encircling the bandstand at the Victoria Gardens. A military band, resplendent in their ceremonial uniforms, played a selection of stirring martial tunes. Hibbert and Coburg had selected a couple of chairs that were set a distance back from the audience around the bandstand so they could still hear the music but not be overheard.

MI5's Inspector James Hibbert was a chunky man in his forties with a long experience of working for the intelligence service, which had made him suspicious and untrusting, even of some of his own colleagues.

'So it looks like you and me are in the firing line,' said Hibbert gloomily.

'What did the Prime Minister tell you?' asked Coburg.

'About this Bernard Bothwell going missing, and you finding him stabbed to death in Shadwell Basin. And him having something in his pocket of a sensitive nature. A matter of national security, he said.'

'Did he tell you what it was?'

Hibbert nodded. 'A letter. Or, rather, a handwritten draft of a letter.' He looked at Coburg. 'I'm guessing you know who wrote it, and who it was going to be sent to?'

'It was written by His Majesty and was addressed to his brother, the Duke of Windsor.'

'Yes,' said Hibbert unhappily. He let out a sigh. 'These are dark bloody waters. I don't like the fact that it's only you and I who are in the know. If things go wrong we know who'll get the blame, and it won't be the Prime Minister.'

'What can go wrong?' asked Coburg.

Hibbert gave a sarcastic laugh. 'You're joking!'

'No, seriously. All we've been asked to do is find out who killed Bothwell.'

'Which usually means finding out *why*. And it's the "why" that worries me. What are we going to uncover? Nothing healthy for us, I can bet. This is the King's brother we're talking about. Possible treason. And someone stabbed Bothwell to death. Someone who obviously knew what he had on him but they didn't find it. So who were they? Who were they working for? Our side, or the other side? And why did Bothwell have that letter on him? What was he doing at Shadwell? Was he taking that letter to someone? If so, who?' He looked at Coburg. 'Have you seen the original letter that Windsor sent to the King? The one he was replying to?'

'No,' said Coburg. 'Just the handwritten draft of the King's reply. But all the clues are there to tell us who he was writing to, and what about.'

'"Dear brother. No, I have no intention of meeting that evil bastard Hitler, so you can poke your suggestion up your arse. Yours sincerely",' said Hibbert sourly.

'Yes, that's the impression I got,' said Coburg. 'You've got a file on the Duke of Windsor, haven't you?'

'I've got a shelf-load of bloody box files on him,' said Hibbert sourly.

'I'd like to look at it.'

'Why?'

'Because I'm a detective. And the Prime Minister has asked us to work together. Whatever this is about, it involves the Duke of Windsor.'

'Who's currently in the Bahamas as governor,' said Hibbert.

'But he has friends here.'

'Influential friends,' said Hibbert warningly.

'I'm fully aware of that,' said Coburg. 'I want to know which of those friends also has links to Hitler and his crowd. This is connected to someone trying to arrange some sort of deal with the King and the Germans. And someone interfering with it.'

'That's just speculation,' said Hibbert.

'In view of the evidence, have you got anything better?'

'Evidence?' snorted Hibbert derisively. 'A scrap of wet paper!'

'But have you got anything that fits it better?' insisted Coburg.

'No,' admitted Hibbert.

'Then can we take a look at these box files you've got?' asked Coburg.

At Whitechapel police station, Lampson was in discussion with Sergeant Harker, setting out his theory about where the next murder might take place, based on the sequence of the original Ripper killings of Victorian times.

'It's only a thought,' said Lampson. 'I may be totally off beam.'

'It's a good thought,' said Harker. 'It might be worth stepping up the number of officers patrolling around Durward Street. To that end, I'll transfer some of the men keeping watch at Whitechapel station at night.'

'I'd hate for you to do that and something happen,' said Lampson uncertainly.

'The problem is we've only got so many men. I'll make sure the ones who do the duty at the air raid shelter are good men.'

'The trouble is we don't know when the killer's going to strike next,' said Lampson. 'It could be tonight, it could be next week.'

'I'll still keep up the patrols,' said Harker. He looked at Lampson thoughtfully. 'I've got the feeling it's someone who lives locally, rather than someone coming from outside. He seems to know the area, including being able to slip in and out of the station.'

'Yes, that makes sense,' said Lampson. 'The other thing to think about is who'd have the skill to cut his victims and rip out their organs the way he does? A surgeon? A butcher?'

'It needs to be someone with a knowledge of anatomy,' agreed Harker. 'And not just the knowledge. It's one thing to read about things; it's another to be able to do it. Maybe we should draw up a list of men living in the area who do those sorts of jobs. Surgeons. Slaughterers. Butchers.'

'It's a good thought,' said Lampson. 'This is where local knowledge comes in.'

'I might sit down with a man called Bert Watts,' said Harker. 'He's a constable here, been here for ever. He knows most people. We'll see what he can come up with.'

CHAPTER FIFTEEN

Coburg and Hibbert sat in Inspector Hibbert's office at MI5 looking at the files on the Duke and Duchess of Windsor. As Hibbert had said, there was a stack of them, and Coburg ruefully thought it would take days to go through them all properly.

'Here's something you might be interested in,' said Hibbert, handing a sheaf of papers to Coburg. 'They concern someone who I assume is a relative of yours, the Duke of Saxe-Coburg and Gotha. He's German. And a good friend of the Windsors.'

Coburg took the papers. The Duke of Saxe-Coburg was another of Queen Victoria's grandchildren. After Hitler launched an attempted coup in Germany in 1923, which failed, the Duke of Saxe-Coburg had hidden several of the plotters in his castles, earning him the eternal gratitude of Hitler. The Duke's aristocratic connections led to him making many visits to the stately homes of England between 1935 and 1939, including visits to the Duke of Windsor when he was King, as well as after his abdication. There were reports that via the Duke of Saxe-Coburg, Windsor was conducting negotiations with Hitler to conclude a peace treaty and form a new government in England. There were also reports of anti-Semitic outbursts by Windsor both from before the war and after it had begun.

Hibbert regarded Coburg quizzically. 'Well?' he demanded.

'If he is a relative of mine, which is possible, I've never met him or heard anything about him. My brother Magnus might know.' He gave a small smile to Hibbert. 'On the strength of this, I'm surprised you don't lock me up under suspicion of something.'

'If we locked up everyone because they had relatives on the other side, the House of Lords would be empty and the Tower of London would be full,' said Hibbert wryly.

He passed another sheet of paper to Coburg. 'This may interest you.'

Coburg looked at it. It was a typed report entitled *Wallis Simpson*. He read through it, then said in disturbed tones, 'According to this, Mrs Simpson was having an affair with Hitler's foreign secretary, Ribbentrop, when he was ambassador to London.'

'Yes,' said Hibbert.

'In 1936,' continued Coburg. 'At the same time as she was having an affair with the Duke of Windsor when he was King of England. The year he abdicated.'

'Yes,' said Hibbert again. 'She had a strong sexual appetite by all accounts. If you read through the rest, you'll see when she was in Washington in 1922 and married to her first husband, Earl Spencer, she had an affair with an Argentinian diplomat called Felipe de Espil. She later went to China where she met and had an affair with Mussolini's future son-in-law, Count Galeazzo Ciano. In 1927 she and her husband divorced and she met a man called Ernest Simpson, a former officer in the Coldstream Guards. Simpson was married and he divorced his wife in order to marry Wallis Spencer. In 1929, the now

Wallis Simpson was wiped out financially, like many others, by the Wall Street crash. She returned to England where she met Edward, the Prince of Wales, known to his family as David. He became obsessed with her and introduced her to his parents, King George V and Queen Mary. At this time she was also said to be having an affair with a man called Guy Trundle. By all accounts George V was outraged at the idea of his son, the heir to the throne, wanting this woman to be Queen of England.'

He pushed another single sheet of paper to Coburg. It was headed *Bahamas Associations*. It contained details of the Windsors' close association with a Swedish industrialist called Axel Wenner-Gren, who lived in Nassau and was a known Nazi sympathiser. According to this report, the Windsors spent a lot of time on Wenner-Gren's yacht. US Naval Intelligence suspected Wenner-Gren of using his yacht when he was in Mexico to refuel German U-boats in the Caribbean.

'Taken together, it's pretty much an indictment of the Duke and Duchess,' said Coburg. 'But is it treasonable?'

'Yes,' said Hibbert. 'Especially the business of the attempted peace treaty with Hitler. According to other reports, that would include the Duke becoming King again, and his wife as Queen. The present royal family would be exiled to Canada.'

'Would His Majesty have been informed of all of this?' asked Coburg, gesturing at the box files.

'Not everything, but most of it,' said Hibbert. 'Hence his reply to the Duke's letter turning down the idea of a meeting with Hitler.'

'That's the big question,' mused Coburg. 'Why did Bothwell have it? Did he take it for himself, or because someone asked him to. And why?'

'Money,' said Hibbert. 'Either he was going to sell it, or someone was paying him to get hold of it.'

'But who? Who would have known it existed? Only the King himself.'

'Trust me, from all my years at MI5, I've learnt there's nothing secret. Someone always knows. But it does narrow down the suspects.'

'We haven't got any suspects at the moment,' pointed out Coburg.

'We've got one: the valet himself for taking the note. But why? Either he took it to sell for himself, or someone paid him to take it. But what took him to Shadwell Basin? Was he supposed to hand it to someone there? And how did he get there? Did he own a car?'

'No. According to his wife he went everywhere by bus.'

'Are we sure he was killed there? Could he have been killed elsewhere and his body dumped?'

'It's possible. The problem is if that happened last Friday, there's been a week's worth of traffic coming and going from Shadwell Basin. Or there is another possibility. Shadwell Basin isn't far from Whitechapel. The valet's got a sister who lives in Whitechapel, who'd written to him asking for his help with her wayward daughter. She was hoping he'd call, but he didn't. Bothwell's wife told me she thought he might have gone to Whitechapel to see his sister, after she first reported him missing.'

'In what way was the daughter wayward?' asked Hibbert.

'Prostitution,' Coburg told him. 'In fact she was the second victim of the so-called New Ripper. Hacked to death at the old Whitechapel Road Tube station, which is now an air raid shelter.'

'It raises an interesting possibility,' mused Hibbert. 'Did she have a pimp who controlled her, who Bothwell confronted? Or maybe the pimp himself did her in to stop her talking to Bothwell. Which means finding out if she had a pimp, and if she did, who was he.'

'I'll go and talk to the girl's mother again,' said Coburg. 'See if she's got any names. On the other hand, if Bothwell's murder was connected to the letter he found, and it was someone in the Windsors' circle he was going to talk to, most of the people mentioned here as being close to the Windsors are outside Britain,' said Coburg. 'Bothwell was killed here. Have you got a list of people sympathetic to them in this country?'

Hibbert nodded and slid a brown paper folder across the table. The words *Very Top Secret* were stamped in big black letters on the cover.

Coburg opened it.

CHAPTER SIXTEEN

Saturday 5th April

When Coburg picked up Lampson from Somers Town the next morning, the sergeant's first question was, 'How did you get on with Inspector Hibbert yesterday?'

'Are you sure you want to know?' Coburg asked.

'Dangerous stuff?' asked Lampson.

'Very.'

'In that case, I never asked and you never answered.'

When they got to Scotland Yard, Coburg dropped Lampson off before heading for Pimlico to collect Mrs Bothwell and take her to Whitechapel.

Lampson had barely entered the office when the phone rang. It was Sergeant Harker.

'Is the chief inspector there?' he asked.

'He's out, over your way, at the London Hospital,' said Lampson. 'He's taken a woman to identify her dead husband. Can I help?'

'The killer's struck again, but got away.'

'In Durward Street?' asked Lampson.

'No, at the old Whitechapel Street station again, the air raid shelter. This time one of our officers interrupted him while he was in the middle of carving her up, so we've got a bit of a description. Unfortunately, the officer got stabbed.'

'How is he? Badly hurt?'

'Stabbed in the arm, so he'll be alright. But he was in a right mess. The killer tried to stab him again, but this time knocked him over and he fell into a pool of the victim's blood.'

'Who was he?'

'PC Wesley Dixon. You may remember him from when you came to look at the first victim.'

'Oh yes, a young man.'

'That's him.'

'Is he available for us to talk to?'

'Yes. The hospital stitched him up and sent him home, so at the moment he's off sick. If you come over I'll give you his address.'

'No problem. I'd better wait for the guv'nor to get back. For one thing, he's got the car, and the other is he'll want to be involved.'

'In that case be prepared for your guv'nor to be upset.'

'Why?'

'A local reporter, Charlie Brown, has done a piece in the *Whitechapel Chronicle*, front page, and he's quoting your boss. "'The Ripper's back' says Scotland Yard." He then goes on about his "exclusive interview" with Detective Chief Inspector Saxe-Coburg. I've got it here. I'll let you have it when you get here.'

'Nothing about the latest victim? Last night's?'

'No, but sure as shooting it'll be in the later edition that comes out at lunchtime, with a fuller story in tomorrow's morning edition.'

Coburg stood beside Mrs Bothwell, ready to catch her if she fainted, which sometimes happened, as Dr McKay peeled the sheet back from the dead man's face.

'Is that your husband?' he asked gently.

'Yes,' she said, her voice choked with grief.

Coburg nodded at McKay, who pulled the sheet back over Bothwell's face.

'Thank you, Doctor,' said Coburg. And he meant it. The doctor had been as good as his word, making the ruined face of the dead man presentable.

Coburg escorted Mrs Bothwell outside the mortuary and asked, 'Would you like a cup of tea? They have a cafeteria here at the hospital.'

'No thank you,' she replied. 'I think I'd rather get home.'

'Of course,' said Coburg. 'I'm sorry to put you through that, but we do need an identification from someone who knows the deceased. I'm afraid officialdom can be cruel.'

She merely nodded, lost in her own unhappy thoughts as they walked to the car. Once they were in the car and heading back towards Central London, Coburg asked, 'Did Bernard ever mention anything about the King's correspondence?'

She frowned, puzzled. 'In what way?'

'Well, had he ever mentioned any letters to you that the King had received, or was sending to people?'

'Good heavens, no. He never talked about the King's private business. He was very scrupulous about that.' Then she gave a sniff of disapproval. 'Not like some of the staff.'

'Oh?'

'Yes. Bernard used to get very upset about one or two of them who used to tip off the newspapers about what was happening. He thought it was a disgrace. He said people who did that should be let go.'

'Did he mention anyone in particular?'

'No, he disapproved of people telling tales, and that included himself. He was absolutely straight and honest, and he thought everyone else should be the same. Particularly when it came to people who worked at the Palace. He was very protective of the royal family.'

'Did he mention any particular newspapers?'

'No.' Then, after a thoughtful pause she added, 'He once came home angry and said a reporter had asked him if he had any stories about the royal family. This reporter said if he had it would be worth his while. There'd be a generous payment coming to him. Bernard said he was so angry he nearly hit the man, which was so unlike Bernard. By all accounts Bernard gave the man such a tongue-lashing that the man backed away from him and apologised, worried that Bernard might do him damage. Not that Bernard would have done. He was never given to violence of any sort. Anyway, as far as I know it never happened again. If it had, Bernard would have told me.'

'Did Bernard mention this reporter's name?'

'No.'

'Or the paper he worked for?'

Mrs Bothwell thought about it. 'I think it must have been the *Daily Reporter*. Because, after that happened, he said he never wanted that rag of a newspaper in the house ever. He was very firm about it.'

Magnus and Malcolm continued their tour of Whitechapel. Today they were without their guide, Bert Watts, but they had his list of suggested places he thought it was worth them looking at, including a former chapel, a former meat factory and a warehouse. The chapel and the meat factory both had subterranean areas that could accommodate people, and there was a possibility the warehouse could be strengthened internally. Malcolm had an open notebook in which he wrote comments about the premises they visited. Their previous visits had given them a total of six premises that Watts had told them had potential, and if the three they would be visiting today looked promising, that would make nine for them to propose to Churchill.

'Not bad,' said Malcolm as they made their way along a narrow street towards the former chapel.

The sound of running boots fast approaching behind them made them stop and turn, and the next second they were overwhelmed by a gang of men with scarves pulled up around their faces. Before Magnus and Malcolm could react and defend themselves, their attackers had leapt on them, fists and boots swinging. Magnus and Malcom, caught by surprise and by the sheer weight of numbers, found themselves unceremoniously pushed to the pavement while their attackers continued to lay into them.

'Get out of Whitechapel, you Nazi spies!' shouted one.

Magnus managed to grab hold of one of the boots swinging towards him and twisted it, and the attacker stumbled and fell, giving Magnus time to push himself up off the ground. Magnus looked to where Malcolm lay unconscious, blood coming from his nose and mouth. Magnus swung a punch into the face of another of the attackers, knocking him into the road, but before he could defend himself another onslaught was launched against him. Punches smashed into his body, sending him reeling. It was the shrill sound of a police whistle that brought his ordeal to a halt. Two policemen appeared running towards them, truncheons drawn, and the attackers turned and ran off, disappearing down the network of alleys and lanes.

The police officers pulled to a halt beside Magnus and the fallen Malcolm.

'What was that about?' asked one urgently.

'I've no idea,' said Magnus. He pointed at the unconscious figure of Malcolm lying on the pavement. 'But my friend's badly hurt. He needs an ambulance.'

The shrill sound of the police whistle had brought another constable running to the scene. One of the constables turned to the new arrival. 'Get back to the station and phone an ambulance. Tell them it's urgent!'

When Coburg got back to Scotland Yard, Lampson told him about the latest murder at Whitechapel Road.

'Not at Durward Road?'

'No,' said Lampson unhappily. 'Because of me there were fewer officers on duty at the air raid shelter. This is my fault.'

'Don't be ridiculous,' Coburg chided him. 'It was a good idea of yours, but it looks as if our killer isn't following the same timetable as the original. That's not your fault.' He headed for the door. 'Come on, let's get to Whitechapel. You can drive this time, although I suspect the car will be able to find its own way there pretty soon.'

As they headed for Whitechapel, Lampson asked, 'How was Mrs Bothwell?'

'Understandably upset. It's one thing being told your husband's dead; it's another to see him lying there. I'll say one thing for Dr McKay, he'd done a good job of making him presentable.'

When they got to Whitechapel they made for the police station, where Sergeant Harker was on duty.

'Another one, I understand,' said Coburg. 'But this time we've got a police constable as a witness.'

'PC Wesley Dixon. Unfortunately, he didn't get a good look at him, but we do have a description of sorts. I assume you'll want to talk to him?'

'I hear he got stabbed. Will he be in a fit state to talk?'

Harker nodded. 'It could have been a lot worse. He twisted to one side, so the knife went into his arm. It was only a small wound. The hospital stitched him up and he's at home.' He handed Coburg a slip of paper. 'Here's Dixon's address.'

'What about the victim?'

Harker consulted a sheet of paper with some handwritten notes on it. 'Marjorie Wethers. Aged forty. A widow. Her husband was killed firefighting during the early days of the Blitz.'

'Was she on the game before her husband died?'

'If she was, there's no record of it,' said Harker. He gave an unhappy sigh. 'Although, it's a familiar story. A bloke who's the only money earner for the household dies, leaving his widow broke.'

'Children?'

'Two. Both girls, aged twelve and ten.'

'Did they know what their mother did?'

'I haven't talked to the girls. I talked to Mrs Wethers's sister, Angela Scoular, who was in the air raid shelter with her at the start of last night. Mrs Scoular insists her sister wasn't a prostitute.'

'Maybe she wasn't. Maybe she was just in the wrong place at the wrong time.'

'Yes, well, I've got my men asking questions around the area about her. Until I hear to the contrary, I'm giving her the benefit of the doubt. An innocent woman murdered by this savage killer.' He reached under the counter and produced a newspaper, which he gave to Coburg. It was the *Whitechapel Chronicle* and on the front page, banner headlines proclaimed

Jack's back, says Scotland Yard. The New Ripper.
Exclusive interview with top cop DCI Saxe-Coburg.

There was a photograph of Coburg accompanying the article, which showed Coburg and Rosa on their wedding day outside the registry office, Lampson standing next to them. The caption read: *Aristo copper with his new wife, jazz singer Rosa Weeks.*

Coburg scowled. 'There was no need to bring my wife into this,' he said angrily.

'It's what Charlie Brown does,' said Harker wryly. 'Anything to push his profile.'

'I'll push his profile when I see him,' grunted Coburg menacingly.

'There's another thing that's happened,' said Harker, concerned. 'You know your brother and his pal were looking for prospective air raid shelters.'

'Yes.'

'Well, they were back here today, looking at places, and they were attacked.'

'Attacked?' repeated Coburg, shocked. 'Who by?'

'We don't know for sure, but we suspect a gang of youths.'

'Why did they attack them?'

'We're still not sure. Your brother said he thought he heard them shout out something about Nazi spies.'

'Nazi spies? That's ridiculous! Were they badly hurt?'

'Your brother got a few bruises, but I think it's his pride that was mostly hurt. His pal, however, was kicked unconscious. He's in the London Hospital. Your brother's there with him. One of my men went to the hospital with them in the ambulance to take statements from them and said that your brother's pal was still unconscious when he left.' He picked up the phone on his desk and said, 'I'll phone the hospital and see if there's any news.'

'Who called the ambulance?'

'I did, when one of the officers who'd intervened came and reported it.' He stopped and spoke into the receiver, talking to the operator. 'London Hospital, please. Sergeant Harker at Whitechapel police station calling.'

'We'll head there now,' Coburg told him. 'Knowing hospitals, by the time you get through on the phone, we'll be there.'

CHAPTER SEVENTEEN

When Coburg and Lampson arrived at the London Hospital, they were met by Magnus in the reception area.

'Edgar, thank God you've come!' exclaimed Magnus. 'They won't let me see Malcolm. They say it's outside visiting hours. Bloody petty bureaucrats!'

'Leave it to me,' said Coburg.

He left Lampson with Magnus and strode to the reception desk, where he showed his warrant card.

'Scotland Yard,' he said brusquely. 'This is urgent. Who's in charge here?'

'That would be the hospital administrator.'

'Get him,' snapped Coburg.

'He's not here today. It's a Saturday.'

'Then who is? I'm here with instructions from the Prime Minister.'

The receptionist gulped nervously, then reached for the telephone. She spoke quietly but urgently into it, then hung up.

'The senior surgeon's on his way,' she said. 'Sir William Price.'

Coburg waited and a few moments later a tall well-built man in his sixties appeared and approached Coburg. He looked seriously displeased at being summoned. *But not as seriously displeased as I am*, thought Coburg.

'The receptionist said something about Scotland Yard and the Prime Minister,' said Price.

Once again, Coburg produced his warrant card and showed it to the man.

'Detective Chief Inspector Saxe-Coburg from Scotland Yard,' he said. 'I am here on direct instructions from Winston Churchill himself. The Prime Minister sent two of his own personal staff here to Whitechapel on a research mission, my brother, the Earl of Dawlish, and his companion, Malcolm Grant. Both men were attacked today by a gang of thugs and Mr Grant was brought here unconscious. When my brother the Earl asked to see Mr Grant, he was barred from seeing him because it was outside visiting hours.

'Both men were here on an official government mission and are due to report their findings personally to the Prime Minister, but cannot because your staff have barred the Earl from seeing his companion and finding out how bad his injuries are. Unless that bar is lifted immediately there will be serious repercussions for this hospital.'

'You dare to threaten me?' demanded Price angrily.

'Yes,' said Coburg firmly. 'And any threats you believe are coming from me will pale by comparison with what Churchill himself will say to you if the Earl is prevented from seeing Mr Grant. A serious crime has been committed in a breach of national security and I have the power to arrest anyone who obstructs us and our investigation. That includes you, and as many of your staff as we can take to Scotland Yard, or the Tower of London.'

Price glared defiantly back at Coburg, but the detective inspector could see that he was torn by indecision between insisting that the hallowed strictures concerning visiting hours were adhered to, or to allow this unregulated breach of the rules. Finally, reluctantly and obviously unhappily, he said, 'Very well. I will accompany the Earl and yourself to the ward and explain the situation.'

'Along with my detective sergeant,' said Coburg, 'who is a crucial part of this investigation.'

Coburg raised a hand and gestured for Magnus and Lampson to join them.

'This is Sir William Price,' he told them. 'He has kindly agreed to escort us to Malcolm.'

'At last!' said Magnus. 'Thank you.'

Brendan Riley was sitting in the Plume of Feathers pub not far from the old St Mary's Underground station, sipping at a pint of bitter and reading the critical reviews of the latest productions in London's Theatreland – the business may have given him up, but he couldn't completely cut himself adrift from a profession he'd known and loved – when a shadow fell over his table. He looked up into the smiling face of Charlie Brown.

'Hello, Mr Riley.' Brown grinned. 'Long time no see. I wrote a piece about your Jack the Ripper tours before the war in the *Chronicle*, if you remember.'

'I do,' said Riley stiffly. 'I remember the tone of it was decidedly sarcastic. You claimed I made most of it up.'

'That wasn't me, that was my old editor,' said Riley, unabashed. 'But he's gone now and we've got a new one, who doesn't interfere in the artistic content in the same way his predecessor did.'

Riley looked at him in frank disbelief. 'Nonsense,' he said. 'All newspapers distort the truth for their own particular ends. I have read the *Chronicle* of late, and it seems to be no different from how it used to be under the previous editor.'

'It is,' insisted Brown. 'In fact, to show you how it's changed, I'm hoping to persuade him that we have a local expert on the Ripper killings who could write about them for us.'

'Who?' demanded Riley.

'You, of course, Mr Riley. There's no one who knows more about the original Ripper than you. And, as far as the New Ripper is concerned, you've had the personal experience of having been arrested on suspicion.'

'I was not arrested!' snapped Riley, full of righteous indignation. He rose to his feet and pointed an aggressive finger at Brown. 'And if you dare to suggest as such I will sue you for libel.'

'No, honestly!' said Brown urgently and defensively. 'I would never do that!'

'Then what are you suggesting?'

'A column we do together: "The New Ripper: an expert speaks". We talk about how you've studied the original Ripper murders and compare them with this latest lot. Find points of similarity.' He leant towards Riley and said in a low conspiratorial voice, 'You know they found items at the scenes of the recent murders that hark back to the original Jack.'

Riley looked at the reporter, obviously curious. 'No,' he said. 'What sort of items?'

'An old Victorian surgeon's case, complete with medical instruments at the first one. A leather apron at the second.'

'How do you know about this?' asked Riley.

Brown tapped the side of his nose and winked. 'The coppers who were on duty slipped me the information.'

'But there's been nothing about them in the newspapers. Not yours, not the nationals.'

'That's because I've been waiting to work out how to use the info to the best effect,' said Brown. He regarded Riley, putting on what he hoped came across as his sincere face. 'It could revive your career.'

'What career?'

'Your acting career. You had a reputation, Shakespeare, and all that. Get yourself famous again and they'll be after you to tread the boards. Especially if someone's putting on a revival of *Jack the Ripper*. Always been very popular, that play. And to have an acknowledged expert in the cast – possibly even playing Sherlock Holmes himself . . .' Brown left the sentence unfinished, leaving the thought to sit in Riley's brain. *Vanity*, Brown thought. *No actor could resist this.*

Coburg and Lampson stood by Malcolm's hospital bed, making notes as Malcolm and Magnus gave their reports of what had happened to them. It was Magnus doing most of the talking; Malcolm was still quite groggy. All of this was happening under the disapproving eyes of the nursing staff, and every now and then the ward sister came over to tell them to keep their voices down. 'There are very sick people here, you know. Thanks to Sir Willam you've been allowed in outside of visiting hours.'

Coburg was tempted to ask sarcastically if, during visiting hours, the very sick people were still on the ward, or were they removed. Then he decided against it.

'There were five of them,' said Magnus. 'They had scarves pulled up over the lower parts of their faces, so we couldn't describe them.'

'They were young, though,' put in Malcom groggily.

'Yes,' agreed Magnus. 'It was in the way they moved. Almost

dancing about. Fortunately, we managed to land a punch or two, so some of them will have the marks to show. Bruises. Black eyes. That sort of thing.'

'And they called you Nazis,' said Coburg.

'Nazi *spies*,' clarified Magnus.

'What gave them that idea?' asked Coburg.

'Who knows?' said Magnus. 'People everywhere have got more and more suspicious of strangers since this war started. People see spies everywhere.'

Lampson nudged Coburg. 'Sister Frankenstein is coming over again,' he muttered.

Coburg looked at the ward sister as she appeared beside them.

'I need to know how much longer you will be here?' she demanded. 'This really is very disruptive to my staff.'

'I believe we're virtually finished, Sister,' said Coburg. 'We have the descriptions of the people who carried out this attack. We also need to know when you consider Mr Grant might be able to leave and return home.'

'That will be decided by Sir William or one of the other doctors,' she said primly. 'Although, in my opinion, that will not happen until tomorrow at the earliest. The safety of our patients is paramount here.'

'Of course,' said Coburg. 'You think there might be complications?'

She hesitated, then said, 'That is for a doctor to decide.' Then, reluctantly she added, 'So far there do not appear to be any complications, but one can never be sure in a case involving concussion.'

'In that case, we'll leave you,' said Coburg. He tapped Magnus on the shoulder. 'I suggest we let Malcolm get some rest and return tomorrow, when we can hopefully take him home.'

'We don't know if he will be leaving tomorrow,' said the sister, determined to assert her authority.

'In that case we'll telephone first to find out his situation,' said Coburg, adding pointedly, 'As I informed Sir William, the Prime Minister himself has asked to be kept personally informed about Mr Grant's condition and I'm sure he will be arranging to collect Mr Grant when you give permission for him to leave.'

'When the supervising *doctor* gives permission,' she corrected him.

'Of course,' said Coburg. 'I expect the Prime Minister's office will be telephoning tomorrow for an update.'

Magnus held out his hand towards Malcolm, who shook it. 'Keep well, old chap,' he said. 'I'll see you tomorrow.'

'How are you going to get home?' asked Malcolm. 'You know what you're like in London traffic.'

'We'll arrange that,' Coburg assured him.

Magnus waited until they were out of the ward before demanding of his younger brother, 'What on earth did you mean by saying Winston would be phoning here tomorrow?'

'I said that the Prime Minister's *office* would be telephoning,' Coburg corrected him. 'That will be me.' He looked at Lampson. 'Would you mind driving His Grace home in his Bentley, Ted? After what happened, we can't take the chance of leaving the car unattended in Whitechapel overnight.'

Lampson grinned. 'Drive a Bentley? It'll be my pleasure, Your Grace.'

'There's no need for all this "Your Grace" stuff, Ted,' said Magnus. 'My younger brother's just being sarcastic. Magnus will do fine.'

CHAPTER EIGHTEEN

Coburg drove the three of them to where Magnus's Bentley was parked close to the police station. Luckily, it was untouched. He told Lampson he'd see him as usual in Somers Town on the Monday morning, and assured Magnus that he'd telephone him as soon as he'd talked to the hospital to check on Malcolm in the morning.

After Lampson and Magnus had driven off, Coburg considered going to report to Sergeant Harker what had happened at the hospital, then decided instead to call on PC Dixon and get his eyewitness report on what had happened the previous night.

PC Dixon lived with his widowed mother in a terraced house in the centre of Whitechapel. Mrs Dixon, a middle-aged woman with a sad face, led them into the small but immaculately tidy living room, where Wesley Dixon sat in shirtsleeves in an armchair reading the local newspaper. Coburg introduced himself.

'Yes, we met before,' said Dixon. 'The first one.'

'I remember,' said Coburg. He sat down. 'How's the arm?' he asked.

'It hurts a bit, but it could have been a lot worse.' He showed them where his upper arm had been bandaged at the hospital, a thick crepe bandage wrapping his upper arm from shoulder to elbow. 'It looks worse than it is, the amount of bandage they used,' he said. 'But they said they wanted to make sure no infection got in the wound.'

Coburg noticed a family photo on the sideboard and got up to look at it. It showed a woman, obviously Mrs Dixon, and three men, one older, the other two very young.

'That's Dad and my brother William, with me and Mum,' explained Dixon. 'Dad and William were killed fire-watching. They were on the roof of a building that took a direct hit.'

Coburg turned to Mrs Dixon and said sympathetically, 'I'm very sorry for your loss, Mrs Dixon.'

'Derek and William died doing what they could to save others. At least I've got Wesley. Some women have got no one.' She looked at her son and the detective. 'I'll leave you together to talk.'

After she'd gone, Coburg said to Dixon, 'Can you tell me exactly what happened?'

'Well, for a start me and the other officers on duty had done what Sergeant Harker told us to do if we spotted any women who were known to be prostitutes,' said Dixon. 'We took turns in one of us taking them to the station to lock them up overnight. The trouble is, you miss a few with the large crowd that gathers in the shelter, and it's such a big place with all those nooks and crannies in the tunnels. Anyway, somebody told me they'd seen this woman going off with this man, heading towards the tunnels. So I went that way. It was the same part of the tunnel where the last two bodies were found. As I entered the alcove I switched on my torch because it was dark, and there he was.'

'There was no light in the alcove? No torch on, no lamp?'

Dixon shook his head. 'No, but the thing is if he'd been there a while, there was some light that trickled through and your eyes adjust to it so you can see well enough.'

'What was he doing?'

'He was bent over a body lying on the ground. Her skirt was up over her waist. He was holding a knife and cutting her.'

'Did you see what he looked like?'

'Not properly. He had this sort of hood over his head, which shielded his face, and he turned away from me. I was going to shout for help, but suddenly he spun round and charged at me, pointing the knife straight at me. I dodged to one side and felt it go in my arm. I was trying to get hold of my truncheon to belt him, but he hit me and I fell over, right on the woman's body. I saw him rush off, but when I tried to get up I slipped in the blood.' He shook his head unhappily at the hideous memory. 'There was so much blood.'

'But you saw him?'

'Not his face. Just his back.'

'What was he wearing?'

'A long coat. It looked like a waterproof. To be honest, it looked like the waterproofs we're issued with.'

'Was he tall? Short?'

'Tall. Taller than me, anyway.'

'And he took the knife with him?'

'He must have done because we couldn't find it. I got up and ran out of the tunnel and shouted "Help! Murder!" and one of the other officers came running.'

'The name of this other officer?'

'Tony Cartright. He took one look at me and said "My God, what happened?" He saw the blood all over me and thought it was me who'd been murdered. Or, almost murdered. I pointed the body out to him and told him I'd been stabbed in the arm, but I was alright really. The blood was from where I'd fallen over on the dead woman.

'Then other officers arrived and I told them about the tall man wearing the hood and the long waterproof, and they set to searching the shelter and the tunnels, looking for him. But he'd disappeared.'

'And somebody definitely told you they'd seen this woman going off with a man towards the tunnels?'

'Yes.'

'Do you know who it was who said that to you?'

'No. It was no one I knew.'

'The reason I ask is because the dead woman's sister told Sergeant Harker that her sister wasn't a prostitute. And he could find no record of her ever being charged as such.'

Dixon looked uncomfortable. 'Well, she must have been. What else was she doing going off with the bloke?'

'A good point,' said Coburg. 'Anyway, we've asked Sergeant Harker to look into the situation, see if he can find any evidence against her.'

Now it was time to check in with Sergeant Harker at Whitechapel police station, decided Coburg.

'How was your brother and his pal?' was Harker's greeting as Coburg walked in.

'My brother's fine. As you suggested, mainly it was his pride that was hurt. The hospital are keeping Malcolm in for observation. He wasn't happy about that, but a kick to the head can have problems that aren't at first apparent, so I'm glad the hospital insisted.'

'You were lucky they let you visit him. They are very strict on visiting hours. I know when my wife was in there, they kept me out, along with everyone else, until the magic hour.'

'I used the Prime Minister's name to force entry. They didn't like it, but they didn't want Churchill descending on them and tearing them to shreds.'

'Is that what you threatened them with?'

'Among other things. Including having them all locked up in the Tower of London.'

Harker chuckled. 'I shall have to remember that for the future.'

'I think it'll only work if Churchill is really involved. Anyway, after that I went to see PC Dixon.'

'A brave bloke, and lucky in this case. Going up against someone armed with a knife who carves his victims up.' Harker sorted through some papers on his desk and handed a page to Coburg. 'This came from Dr Webb, his report on the latest victim.'

Coburg studied it. 'Stabbed in the heart with the same sort of blade as the first two victims. He agrees with Dr McKay it could be a bayonet.'

'Which suggests an ex-soldier,' said Harker. 'Plenty of men brought back souvenirs from the war.'

'Dr Webb says that the evisceration wasn't completed. The organs had been removed but left with the body.'

'Because Wesley Dixon turned up and disturbed him,' said Harker. 'Dixon was lucky the bloke didn't finish him off. But I suppose he was desperate to get away in case anyone else turned up. Where there's one copper there's always another.'

'Dixon said there was a search made for the weapons and clothing.'

'Yes. One of the officers came to my house and knocked me up. I was asleep. It was one o'clock in the morning. I got dressed and came here, and got my men to go round every part of the shelter and the tunnel searching, doing it in pairs for safety. They questioned everybody to see if they'd seen this tall bloke wearing a hood and a long waterproof, but no one had. At first I thought he might have dumped the coat and the hood and the knife.'

'Were they found?'

Harker shook his head. 'No. And a proper search was done, so Lord knows what he did with them. All I can think is he had his own way in and out of the tunnels. There's nooks and crannies all over the place, and ways in and out.'

'Another thing has come up about Sarah Mars,' said Coburg. 'Do you know if she had a pimp, or at least a minder of some sort?'

Harker frowned thoughtfully. 'If she had I never heard it mentioned. Why?'

'We're looking into the murder of her uncle, whose body was fished out of Shadwell Basin the other day. He'd been stabbed in the heart. His wife and sister said he was thinking of coming to Whitechapel to have a word with Sarah and try and sort her out.'

'And you're thinking that if he did, he might have run into her pimp and had a confrontation with him?'

'It's a thought,' said Coburg. 'But we've got nothing to base it on. I thought I'd go and have a word with Ethel Mars and see if she knew of any bloke Sarah was involved with in that way.'

'If she does give you anything, I'd be interested to hear about it,' said Harker. 'It's always good to know about people we need to keep an eye on.'

'If we get anything, you'll be the first to know,' said Coburg. 'Getting back to the attack on my brother and Malcolm, any idea who did it, and why? They recall someone shouting about them being Nazi spies, but where did they get that idea from?'

'Who knows? There are different gangs that hang around the streets. We're going to pull some in and quiz them.'

CHAPTER NINETEEN

Coburg's next call was to Ethel Mars, whose haggard expression showed she was still mourning her murdered daughter.

'I'm really sorry about Sarah, Mrs Mars. A terrible thing to happen to her.'

'I warned her,' said Mrs Mars. 'But she kept saying she'd be alright.'

'Did she give any reason why she thought she'd be alright? Did she have anyone looking out for her?'

'A pimp, you mean?' she said disgustedly.

'It's a horrible thing to ask, but we need to know if she had,' said Coburg. 'I don't know if your sister-in-law's been in touch?'

'Jean?' She shook her head. 'No. Why? Has Bernard been found?'

'Yesterday,' said Coburg. 'I'm afraid he was found dead in Shadwell Basin. I took her to the London Hospital to identify his body this morning. I'm sure she'll be in touch with you about it when she's had time to recover from the shock.'

Mrs Mars shook her head sadly. 'Poor Jean. She was always a sensitive soul. And poor Bernard. Shadwell Basin, you say?'

'Yes.'

'What was he doing there? Did he drown?'

'I'm afraid to tell you he was murdered. He was stabbed. We believe it happened last Friday.'

'At Shadwell Basin?' she asked, even more bewildered.

'It occurred to us he might have been coming to Whitechapel to see you in answer to your letter about Sarah.'

'But Shadwell Basin isn't Whitechapel.'

'But it's near enough, especially if he was coming from Pimlico.'

She looked at him thoughtfully. 'You're asking me if Sarah had a pimp. You think, if she had, Bernard might have found out who it was and confronted him?'

'We don't know. At the moment we're clutching at straws.'

Mrs Mars shook her head. 'As far as I know, she never had anyone acting like that for her. She was too independent. Which was one of her troubles.' She fell silent, obviously thinking, then she said, 'There was one bloke who came round bothering her, said he could fix her up with clients. He told her he'd get her good prices. Decent blokes, he told her.' She gave a bitter laugh that was part scorn, part disgust. 'Sarah told him where to get off, and quite right, too. I wanted her to give it up; this bloke wanted her to do more of it.'

'Who was this man?'

'Benny Jimpson.'

'Does he live in Whitechapel?'

'Yeah. I'm not sure where, but he's always around. Dresses flash. Horrible, he is. Greasy sort.'

'Thank you, Mrs Mars. You've been very helpful.'

'D'you think it was him who killed Sarah? 'Cos she wouldn't let him do business with her?'

'At this moment, we're just speculating. Groping around

in the dark. But we're doing our best to catch whoever killed Sarah, I promise you.'

Time for one more visit before I return home, decided Coburg.

Sergeant Harker was surprised to see the chief inspector returning so soon.

'Has something happened?' he asked.

'Do you know someone called Benny Jimpson?' asked Coburg, returning one question with another.

Harker scowled. 'That scum.'

'I see that you do,' said Coburg. 'I've just talked to Ethel Mars and she told me that this Benny Jimpson was putting pressure on Sarah to try and get her to work for him. Sarah said a very firm no.'

Harker looked doubtful. 'I can't see Jimpson wanting to bump off prostitutes. They're his business.'

'No, but I can see him having a confrontation with Sarah's uncle. Does Jimpson carry a knife?'

'Yes. We took it off him and cautioned him about it, but he said he needed it for protection, so I have no doubt he got himself another. Do you want us to have a word with him?'

Coburg thought it over. 'If you would,' he said. 'I suppose it should be me, or maybe Sergeant Paulson at Shadwell station, but you know Jimpson. If you think there's anything there, we'll come in and have a second go at him.'

'Will do,' said Harker.

After Lampson had delivered Magnus to his flat, he caught the bus to Somers Town. He found that Terry was busy getting his kit ready for the next day's football match against Warren Street

Boys, cleaning his boots and even ironing his shirt and shorts.

'I could have done that for you,' Eve said to him.

'I thought I'd do it because you've only got one arm at the moment,' said Terry. 'And ironing needs two arms, otherwise you end up with creases. And Dad showed me how to iron things properly.'

'Alright, but in future I can do it,' Eve told him.

'Are you okay to go to the match tomorrow?' Lampson asked Eve, concerned. 'It'll be uneven ground, and remember what the doctor said. You don't want to fall over and make everything worse again.'

'I'll be fine,' said Eve. 'I'm not going to give up the chance to support Terry. And don't worry, I'll take my stick, even though it makes me look like a frail and wobbly old woman.'

'You don't look old,' protested Lampson.

'But I do look frail and wobbly?'

Lampson dodged the question. 'You look beautiful to me,' he said.

'Ha!' said Eve disparagingly. She looked at Terry, who gave a grin and chuckled quietly.

At their flat in Piccadilly, Coburg and Rosa were tucking into a shepherd's pie that she'd made – or, at least, one whose filling contained mainly vegetables with gravy.

'You've done wonders with this,' complimented Coburg.

'I was fortunate that Mr Warren decided to give me the day off so I could practise for the broadcast on Tuesday.'

'So, instead of practising you made this shepherd's pie,' said Coburg, happily eating.

'I can do more than one thing at a time,' said Rosa. 'Anyway, how was your day?'

'Malcolm and Magnus got attacked by some thugs while they were in Whitechapel.'

'What?' said Rosa, shocked. 'Why?'

'That's what I'd like to know,' said Coburg. 'The thugs who did it shouted at them that they were Nazi spies.'

'Nazi spies? Magnus and Malcolm?'

'I know,' said Coburg.

'Were they badly hurt?'

'Malcolm was. He ended up in hospital. He's still there. Ted Lampson drove Magnus home in his Bentley.'

'I bet Ted enjoyed that.' Rosa smiled.

'He did indeed,' said Coburg. 'I've left it at that, if Malcolm's able to leave hospital tomorrow, we'll pick him up. Is that alright with you?'

'Of course. You seem to be spending a lot of time in Whitechapel.'

'I am,' agreed Coburg. 'Three murders there, and I'm sure it's also connected to the King's valet. His body was pulled out of a river quite near Whitechapel.'

'With the attacks happening on Magnus and Malcolm, I think you ought to be careful while you're there.'

'I am, I assure you,' said Coburg.

CHAPTER TWENTY

Sunday 6th April

Coburg's first telephone call on the Sunday morning was to the London Hospital to see if Malcolm was being allowed home. After holding on for some ten minutes, he was informed that the doctors were still doing their rounds at the moment, and advised to call again in a couple of hours.

He hung up and told Rosa gloomily, 'Call again in a couple of hours.'

'So the magic words "Scotland Yard Detective Chief Inspector" didn't work this time,' said Rosa.

'Apparently not,' sighed Coburg. 'We'll try again later.'

In Whitechapel, Benny Jimpson was worried. He owed Big Jimmy Custer fifty quid and he hadn't got it, and Big Jimmy wasn't one to be sympathetic to people who owed him money. Big Jimmy had a habit of breaking things when people upset him: thumbs, fingers, arms. Alright, Jimpson had his knife, a big clasp knife, but it wouldn't be much of a defence against Big Jimmy. Knives didn't scare Big Jimmy; he'd been struck with them often enough. He usually just swatted the knife away and then proceeded to bash whoever had been holding it, making sure they suffered even more for daring to pull a knife on him.

No, the only thing that could stop him getting a beating from Big Jimmy was cash – ideally fifty quid, but at least something as a part-payment. Thirty quid might do it. Maybe even twenty. But right now, all Jimpson had was four pounds in change, which was weighing his trousers down as a lot of it was copper.

Sandra Hancock owed him money. Fifteen quid. The last time she'd worked for him she'd had four punters, each of whom had paid her rather than him, and then the cheating cow had gone off after the last one before Jimpson could get hold of her. She'd been supposed to see him and give him the cash, but she'd done a runner. Right, it was time to find her and get the dosh off her. And if she tried it on, saying she didn't have it, he'd show her his knife. That should do the trick.

Ted and Eve Lampson stood with Lampson's parents, Bert and Ada, at the side of the football pitch on the public park, shouting approval whenever one of the Somers Town Boys team did something good, like block a shot headed goalwards, or booted the ball up towards the Warren Street team's half for Terry, the Somers Town centre forward, to chase. So far the match had been pretty even, with both teams playing well, and the score at one-all.

'Someone said to me there's talk of this turning into an official Junior League next season,' said Bert Lampson. 'If it does, are you and Eve going to be able to cope with it?'

'Who said about that?' asked Lampson.

'Jerry Punt. He's got the sports shop in Camden High Street.'

'No one's mentioned anything about this to me,' said Lampson. He turned to Eve. 'Have you heard anything about them making a proper league about the local teams?'

'No,' said Eve. 'But it's a good idea.'

Just then, there was the sound of angry yells from the Warren Street supporters and shouts of 'Send him off, ref!'

The culprit had been Terry, who'd gone for a sliding tackle on the Warren Street forward and the studs of Terry's boot had caught the boy on the ankle, who rolled on the floor in agony. Terry went to the fallen boy and offered his hand in apology, but the boy slapped it away angrily.

'Send him off!' shouted a man near to the Lampson. 'Dirty play!'

'He didn't mean it,' defended Bert Lampson. 'The ground's slippery. He slid more than he meant to.'

The man shook his head. 'Don't give me that,' he retorted scornfully. 'He's a dirty player.'

'You're talking about my grandson,' snapped Bert.

'I don't care who he is, he's a dirty player,' said the man.

On the pitch, the incident had escalated. Some of the Warren Street team had gathered round Terry and were pushing and shoving him, while Terry's teammates came to his aid, grabbing at the Warren Street boys to pull them off Terry.

The referee intervened, separating the warring teams and ordering the players away from one another. The boy Terry had tackled was on his feet, but having to be helped off the pitch, two boys supporting his weight while he limped and hopped out of play. The referee had also taken the decision to send Terry off, pointing him towards the touchline, to equal the number of players each side was left with. Terry, looking upset, joined his family by the side of the pitch.

'I didn't do it deliberately,' he protested. 'The ground was slippery.'

'We know that,' said Bert Lampson. 'But if that referee lets that boy back on, we'll make sure he lets you back on as well. Fair's fair.'

Ada Lampson gestured to her son and Eve that she had something to say to them. Leaving Terry with his grandfather, the couple joined Ada.

'I know that boy that Terry tackled,' she said quietly, watching out for the man who'd spoken up against Terry in case the man could hear her. 'His name's Derek Weems, and he's a nasty piece of work. He shoplifts and steals. Mrs Wagstaff, who's got the greengrocer's, told me. Weems has got a pal called Jed Barnes. That's him there, the one he's talking to now. They're always in trouble. They pick on other kids.'

'Terry can handle himself,' said her son.

'Yes, but not when there's two of them,' said Ada. 'That's how those two work. They pick on someone and get them on their own and beat 'em up. Tell Terry to keep a watch out for them. I've seen the way they're looking at him.'

'We will,' Lampson promised her. 'Ah, it looks like the ref's letting them back on.'

The referee, indeed, had looked at Derek Weems and seen that he seemed to have recovered, so he waved both him and Terry back on the pitch. As the two boys ran back on, Weems came up to Terry and waved a bunched fist at him, menacingly, before joining his own side.

'See what I mean?' said Ada.

It was at the third time of trying that Coburg was finally informed by the London Hospital that Mr Grant was ready to leave hospital.

'In that case I'll send a police car to collect him,' said Coburg.

163

He hung up and then telephoned Magnus to tell him the good news.

'Excellent,' said Magnus. 'I'll arrange a taxi for him.'

'No need,' said Coburg. 'Rosa and I will pick him up and bring him to the flat.'

When they got to the London Hospital, Malcolm was full of complaints.

'There was no need to keep me there as long as they did,' he said, annoyed. 'I was perfectly recovered yesterday afternoon.'

'The trouble is, you never know with concussion,' said Rosa. 'I've seen it happen with some of the people we've picked up in our ambulance. They insist they're perfectly alright, and suddenly they collapse.'

'I *was* alright,' insisted Malcolm. 'I survived the trenches in the First War. I know what it feels like to be badly hurt.'

He continued in this vein the whole journey back to the flat, moaning about the ward sister, who he described as a dictator, and the hospital porters who he thought were idiots. 'Incapable of using a wheelchair properly.'

It was Magnus who changed the tone of the conversation once they were at the flat by asking Rosa about her radio show.

'It's a live show and it'll be broadcast on Tuesday at half past seven,' Rosa told them. 'Vera Lynn, and Flanagan and Allen will be guests on it.'

'Flanagan and Allen.' Magnus chuckled. 'It's a pity you're not having the rest of the Crazy Gang. They are wonderful!'

'They are rubbish!' snorted Malcolm. 'Comedy of the lowest order.'

'Nonsense!' said Magnus indignantly. 'But then you have no appreciation of humour.'

'Good humour I can appreciate,' retorted Malcolm. 'The Crazy Gang are just knockabout clowns.' He looked at Rosa. 'Though I appreciate Flanagan and Allen, especially their singing. It's just that when they're put together with Nervo and Knox, Naughton and Gold and "Monsewer" Eddie Gray . . .'

'They are hilarious!' said Magnus firmly.

'Huh!' said Malcolm disparagingly. 'But what else can you expect from a man who thinks that George Formby is funny?'

'He is funny,' said Magnus. 'He makes me laugh out loud.'

'He is moronic,' argued Malcolm. 'Another knockabout so-called comedian.'

'There's nothing wrong with knockabout,' said Coburg. 'Look at Laurel and Hardy.'

'Ah, now you're talking,' agreed Malcolm. 'The masters of comedy.'

In Whitechapel, a beat constable doing his rounds came upon Bazzer Jenkinson and his gang lounging on a street corner. Aware of the reports on the attack on Magnus and Malcolm, and that Magnus had managed to get a few punches in, he was intrigued to see that three of the youths had bruises on their faces.

'Been in a fight?' he asked.

'Us?' said Bazzer. 'We don't get in fights.'

'So where did the bruises come from?'

'Boxing practice,' said Bazzer.

'Boxing practice? You're taking up boxing?'

'Yeah,' said Bazzer. 'It's a manly sport.'

In Somers Town, the football match had ended in a one-all draw. Derek Weems and Jed Barnes sat in the back yard at

Derek's house after the game, talking about it.

'We would have won if that Terry Lampson hadn't fouled you the way he did,' said Barnes.

'I know,' said Weems angrily. 'The ref shouldn't have let him back on the pitch.' He sat on a wooden crate, simmering with anger. 'We ought to have our own back on him.'

Barnes looked doubtful. 'He's a bit tasty with his fists,' he commented.

'Yeah, but if we get him when he's on his own we can do him easy enough.'

'I don't know,' said Barnes. 'I've heard he took on two kids at once at his school and beat them.'

'Then we make it three of us,' said Weems. 'Jack Carter will join us. We'll grab him when he's walking home from school. I know which way he goes, and he's usually on his own. You and Jack hold him, and I'll give him a smacking he won't forget. That'll teach him.'

Barnes nodded. 'Yeah,' he said. 'When do we do it?'

'Tomorrow, after school. That way he'll know why we're doing it.'

CHAPTER TWENTY-ONE

Monday 7th April

When Coburg picked Lampson up, he elected to remain in the driver's seat, rather than handing over to Lampson.

'After I've dropped you off at the Yard I need to go and see Inspector Hibbert at MI5,' he explained.

'That's fine by me,' said Lampson. 'I'm very happy not to know anything about it.'

'If Superintendent Allison asks for me, you can tell him where I've gone, and that it's to do with the King's valet. That should keep him happy. How was your weekend? Another football match?'

'The last of the season,' said Lampson. 'It was a draw.'

'How's Eve coping with it?' asked Coburg. 'Will it be much longer before she's fit enough to get back to her old life?'

'The doctor says she's nearly there, but she's got to be careful she doesn't fall and damage anything. So she's got a walking stick to make sure she doesn't fall, which annoys her a lot. She hates it.' He gave a sigh. 'The other thing is, I wish Terry wouldn't call her Eve. We're married now. I'd like him to call her Mum, make it sound like we're really a family.'

'It must be strange for him,' said Coburg. 'After all, he never knew his mother. For his family, all he's known is you and your parents.'

'Yes, but I don't want her to feel excluded.'

'I'm sure she doesn't. She strikes me as a very strong woman. Look at the way she recovered from the accident.'

'It wasn't an accident.' Lampson scowled. 'That scum ran her down deliberately.'

'Because he thought she was you,' said Coburg. 'Anyway, that's behind you all now.'

'I still wish Terry would call her Mum.'

'It'll happen,' said Coburg. 'So long as you don't push it.'

'That's what Eve says,' said Lampson.

They pulled up outside at the Yard and Lampson got out.

'If you need me, you know where I'll be,' said Coburg.

'MI5.' Lampson nodded. 'But I don't need to know the details.'

At Whitechapel police station, Sergeant Harker listened to the constable as he mentioned his encounter with Bazzer Jenkinson and his gang.

'Bruises?' said Harker.

'On a couple of their faces. They claimed they'd been practising boxing.'

'Sounds to me like someone else was doing some boxing with them,' said Harker thoughtfully. 'The Earl said he got in a few blows.'

'That's why I've been keeping my eyes open,' said the constable. 'You reckon they were the ones who beat up those two blokes?'

'It's certainly a possibility,' said Harker. 'Well done, Constable.'

'What do you want me to do, Sarge?'

'Round up a couple of uniforms and take a van and bring them in.'

At MI5's office, Inspector Hibbert looked at Coburg, puzzlement on his face.

'You don't think Bothwell took the letter to make money from it?' he asked.

'No,' said Coburg.

'Then why did he have it?'

'I think he took it off the person who had stolen it, and possibly whoever that was had him killed to ensure his silence.'

'How do you come to that conclusion?'

Coburg told him what Mrs Bothwell had told him about the reporter offering the valet good money for any inside information from the palace.

'I'd been weighing up the idea that Bothwell may have gone to Whitechapel to confront a man who may have been trying to pimp for his niece, Sarah. Someone called Benny Jimpson. But Mrs Bothwell insisted that Bothwell wasn't a violent man in any way.'

'Of course she'd say that. She was his wife.'

'True, and I'm yet to talk to this Benny Jimpson. But I think it's more likely that Bothwell went to Shadwell to recover the letter.'

'Then why was it still in his pocket? Surely whoever killed him would have taken it back?'

'Perhaps the person who killed him wasn't the same person who had the letter. Think of this as a possible scenario: Bothwell discovers that someone inside the palace has taken the letter.

Instead of reporting it to the palace authorities, he goes after them.'

'Why?'

'Who knows? Perhaps he doesn't want to get them in trouble. He recovers the letter. The person he recovers it from tells someone else that Bothwell has taken the letter. Maybe this other person is the one who was behind the letter being taken.'

'This is starting to get very complicated,' said Hibbert doubtfully.

'Say the person behind taking the letter doesn't themselves work at the palace, but they have a relative who does. Their mother, sister, aunt.'

'A woman?'

'It's speculation, but the fact that Bothwell wants to protect them suggests that to me.'

'He's kind to women?'

'Why not? Bothwell goes to Shadwell and persuades the woman who took it to give him the letter back. He promises he'll make sure it's returned and she won't get into trouble. Soon after, she tells the person who persuaded her to get hold of the letter that Bothwell's taken it. He goes after Bothwell . . .'

'*He?* Not a woman this time?'

'No. A man. Possibly a relative or a lover. He goes after Bothwell and catches him at Shadwell Basin. He forces him at knifepoint to turn out his pockets, hence there was no wallet found on Bothwell. But Bothwell scrunches the letter into a tiny ball and forces it deep into his pocket. He tells the man he hasn't got it. The man doesn't believe him; he knows he has. Maybe there's a struggle, maybe there isn't. The long and the short of it is that Bothwell ends up stabbed in the heart and topples into the water.'

Hibbert regarded Coburg, suspicion writ large on his face. 'You ever thought of writing crime fiction?' he asked. 'This is just fantasy.'

'It's possible,' said Coburg. 'It fits the facts.'

'There are no facts,' said Hibbert impatiently. 'Not in your version. We know that Bothwell had the letter on him. Fact. He was stabbed to death. Fact. His body was hauled out of the water at Shadwell Basin. Fact. We don't know how or why he went to Shadwell.'

'He was an honest man,' insisted Coburg. 'He didn't steal the letter.'

'That's what his wife said. I don't believe it,' retorted Hibbert.

'Then what's your theory of what happened? If he took it to make money, why was the letter still on him when he died? And scrunched up the way it was?'

'I don't know,' admitted Hibbert in exasperation.

'The key is this reporter who tried to bribe him for information about the goings-on at the palace,' said Coburg.

'Who may not even exist,' said Hibbert.

'You think his wife made this reporter up?' asked Coburg. 'Does that sound likely?'

'Alright, no,' said Hibbert reluctantly. 'Maybe Bothwell made him up.'

'Why?' asked Coburg.

Hibbert fell into a thoughtful silence, then said, 'Alright, maybe the reporter was true. But we know nothing about him. We don't even know which newspaper he was working for.'

'Mrs Bothwell thinks it must have been the *Daily Reporter*.'

'That rag!' said Hibbert in disgust. 'That scandal sheet!' Once again he fell silent, and Coburg could see his mind was actively weighing all this up.

'Say it's true,' he said at last. 'Say this fantastic idea for some novel you've come up with really happened.'

'You're starting to come round to the idea?' said Coburg.

'Maybe,' said Hibbert. 'But even if we find out who this reporter is, how does that help?'

'He may have asked the same of other people at the palace. Or, if it wasn't him, it shows there are reporters operating who want any palace inside stories and are prepared to pay for them. So we question the reporters who handle royal stories for the papers and find out if any of them were offered a piece of a letter.'

'Like anyone's going to admit it,' scoffed Hibbert.

'Have you got a better idea?' asked Coburg.

'No,' admitted Hibbert reluctantly. 'Alright, it's far-fetched, but I'll admit it's possible. But how do we dive into it, without upsetting Their Majesties?'

'Sir Jasper Connor,' said Coburg. 'The King's private secretary. He must know what goes on with the staff. Who's likely to sell stories to the papers and who isn't.'

'I've met Sir Jasper,' said Hibbert thoughtfully. 'He plays things close to his chest.'

'I'm sure he does, but in this particular case I'm sure he'll see the necessity of opening up to us. Or, if not to us, to the Prime Minister.'

'Bring Churchill in?'

'He brought us in. He's our big gun.'

Hibbert nodded thoughtfully. 'Alright,' he said. 'But we'll start by talking to Sir Jasper. Both of us. You and I together. Then, if we don't get what we want from him, we bring in Churchill.'

Sergeant Harker walked into the detention area, which contained three cells, in reality little more than cages with metal bars from floor to ceiling. One was empty. In the middle one, the sullen figure of Benny Jimpson slouched on the cell's wooden bench. The gang of five youths the constables had brought in occupied the larger cell, and they crammed together on the two benches.

'On your feet!' snapped Harker.

The youths looked at one another, uncertainly, then shot questioning looks at their leader, Barry Jenkinson.

'I said on your feet!' barked Harker. 'Now! The lot of you! Jump to it!'

Two of the youths did jump to it, standing up and to attention. The other three pushed themselves up reluctantly.

'What's this about?' asked one of the boys.

'The two men you attacked,' said Harker. 'You got that badly wrong.'

'We didn't attack anyone,' protested Jenkinson.

'No? Where did your bruises come from?'

'I've already said, we were practising boxing,' said Jenkinson defiantly.

Harker gave a sarcastic laugh. 'Let's see if Scotland Yard believe that,' he said.

At the mention of Scotland Yard, the boys looked at one another, worried.

'Scotland Yard?' said Jenkinson in disbelief. 'You're making it up.'

Harker shook his head. 'You picked on the wrong men to attack. They're from the government doing important work in this area.'

'That's rubbish,' snorted Jenkinson.

'Is it?' said Harker. 'You'll find out right enough when Scotland Yard arrive to deal with you.'

'Ain't you going to let us go?' appealed another of the youths. 'We didn't do nothing bad.'

Harker shook his head. 'You're going nowhere, not until Scotland Yard have talked to you. And even then, you'll be lucky if you don't get locked away for a long time. You're in deep trouble.'

With that, the sergeant walked out of the detention area, pulling the door shut after him. The worried boys looked at Jenkinson.

'We ought to tell them why we did it,' said one. 'About them being Nazi spies. We were being patriotic. They ought to give us a medal.'

Jenkinson shook his head. 'No,' he said. 'We say nothing. This is just a con to get us to admit we did it. We're admitting nothing. Providing we all stay quiet, they've got nothing on us. We tell the same story we told the coppers: it was boxing practice. We had nothing to do with attacking them blokes.' He looked menacingly at the other four. 'Have you got that? No one admits anything. If any of you do, you'll have me to deal with.'

CHAPTER TWENTY-TWO

In the office of the King's private secretary at Buckingham Palace, Sir Jasper Connor looked at the two inspectors, Coburg and Hibbert, and asked doubtfully, 'Do you have any reason for doubting that Bothwell took the handwritten note from the King's bedside table?'

'Call it more an assessment of his character,' said Coburg. 'It's my belief that the draft of His Majesty's letter was taken by another member of the staff.'

'To what purpose?' asked Connor.

'For money. Selling it to a newspaper. Some of the rags are always after stories about the royal family. Do you know of anyone on the staff who might be amenable to selling stories concerning the palace?'

'Absolutely not,' said Connor, obviously highly affronted. 'Such a suggestion is outrageous and totally not in keeping with the palace staff's behaviour.'

'Be that as it may,' said Coburg, 'it is a line of enquiry I shall be pursuing. In my opinion, the person I'm thinking of either lives in the East End, or was doing it on behalf of someone who lives there, possibly in the Shadwell area. I believe that Bernard Bothwell discovered who'd taken it, and went to Shadwell to recover it. He managed to recover it and, because he realised he was in danger, he screwed it up and stuffed it deep into his trouser pocket to hide it. However, he was killed and his body thrown into Shadwell Basin.'

Connor looked at Hibbert. 'Do you share the chief inspector's belief?' he asked.

'It makes more sense than the idea that Bothwell took it himself. All the evidence is that he was honest and absolutely loyal to Their Majesties.'

'But if he knew who'd taken it, why didn't he contact the police, or the palace authorities and report it? The palace has its own security structure; Bothwell would have known that.'

'We can only assume it was to protect the person who'd taken it,' said Coburg. 'In other words, someone he was friends with. What we're looking for is someone on the staff who either lives at Shadwell, or has family or friends who do. If not Shadwell, then somewhere near to it in the East End. Whitechapel, for example. Bothwell came from Whitechapel originally.'

Connor gave a heavy sigh and said, 'Do you know how many people are on the staff at Buckingham Palace?'

'No,' admitted Hibbert. 'Quite a lot, I would imagine.'

'Eight hundred,' said Connor.

Hibbert and Coburg exchanged looks of surprise.

'Eight hundred?' repeated Hibbert.

'There are seven hundred and seventy-five rooms at Buckingham Palace, including state rooms, fifty-two royal and guest bedrooms, a hundred and eighty-eight staff bedrooms, ninety-two offices and seventy-eight bathrooms. That requires a lot of housekeeping staff, cleaners, maids and such. Footmen. Drivers. There are twenty chefs to cater for everyone. As well as the housekeeping staff there are private secretaries, government liaison officers, media representatives. Most people are unaware that twice a year, when the clocks go back or forwards, it takes a team of horologists more than thirty hours to change the time on hundreds of clocks at the palace. Then of course Their Majesties have their own personal staff: valets for His Majesty, dressers for the Queen. There are gardeners for the outside areas. What you're asking for – personal details of every member of staff, their friends and families, their associations with certain districts – is a huge task.'

'I believe we can reduce that greatly,' said Coburg. 'We're looking for someone who would have had access to the King's private quarters. Cleaners, obviously. Footmen. Possibly members of the secretarial team. Maids. Servants bringing messages or refreshments. If you can let us have details for those members of staff, with their addresses and as much information about them as you can, I'm sure between us Inspector Hibbert and I can check if they've got contacts in the East End.'

Hibbert looked as if he was about to protest at this, then thought better of it and nodded. 'Absolutely,' he said. 'We can do that.'

'Very well,' said Connor. 'I'll get one of my staff on to it.'

As Coburg and Hibbert left the palace, Hibbert said in astonishment, 'Eight hundred staff!'

'It's a big house,' commented Coburg.

'Yes, but eight hundred!'

'I think it'll be a good idea to let Churchill know what we've asked Sir Jasper for,' said Coburg. 'For two reasons: one, it lets him know we're doing something. And two, if Churchill passes it on to the King, he'll make sure that Connor gets on with it.'

'You realise, if you're wrong about Bothwell going after the letter, we're going to look pretty stupid,' said Hibbert.

'Yes,' said Coburg. 'Which was why I said it was *my* belief. If it turns out I'm wrong, you can say it wasn't your idea.'

'Too late for that,' said Hibbert gloomily. 'I've said I supported it.' He looked at Coburg and said, 'Sir Jasper didn't give much credence to your idea that someone on the palace staff might be selling information about the royals.'

'That's understandable,' said Coburg. 'He's got his position and the staff at the palace to protect. So, I'm going to try another tack. I'm going to make contact with some reporters I know and ask them who they get their royal stories from.'

'I doubt if they'll tell you,' said Hibbert.

'Oh, they will,' said Coburg confidently. 'In the meantime I'm heading back to Scotland Yard and seeing how my sergeant has got on with the New Ripper.'

'That's a tacky title,' said Hibbert.

'I know. And I also intend to have a word with the tacky local reporter who came up with it.'

As Coburg arrived in the office, Lampson was just hanging up the phone.

'That's timely, guv,' he said. 'Joe Harker from Whitechapel was just on the blower. He's got sone news.'

'About what?'

'Two things: the killings of the prostitutes, and the attack on your brother and Malcolm.'

'Did he say if he was going to be at the station?'

'I'm sure he is. Joe usually stays at his post, unless something special comes up.'

Coburg picked up the phone and asked the operator to connect him with Whitechapel police station. Sergeant Harker answered it.

'DCI Coburg,' said Coburg. 'Ted said you'd just called with news about the killings, and the attack on Magnus and Malcolm.'

'I did,' said Harker. 'The killings, first. It may be sheer coincidence but we've got Benny Jimpson here in the cells. He threatened one of his girls with a knife, demanding money from her. She kicked him in the balls and his screams brought one of our coppers running.'

'Excellent. And Magnus and Malcolm?'

'I've had my blokes checking on the local gangs, and one of them noticed that some of the local tearaways who are part of Bazzer Jenkinson's gang had bruises on their faces. I remember your brother said he'd got in a couple of good punches, so we brought them in for questioning. There are five of them. They all deny they had anything to do with it, of course, but I wondered if you wanted to talk to them. A detective chief inspector from Scotland Yard will have more impact on them than a local sergeant who they're familiar with.'

'Yes, please. And if it is them, I know Magnus will want to say thank you to the officer who apprehended them.' He looked at his watch. 'Will it be alright if we come over now? We can question this gang, as well as Jimpson, while we're there.'

'That's fine by me.'

Sergeant Harker smiled in welcome as Coburg and Lampson walked into Whitechapel police station.

'We've got them all ready for you, under lock and key,' he

said. 'Bazzer Jenkinson and his gang of teenage hooligans, and Benny Jimpson. Who do you want first?'

'We'll start with the gang. Who are they?'

'Their leader is Barry Jenkinson, known as Bazzer. The others are Tommy Duggan, Arnold Kemp, Shug Pirie and Jerry Trump. They're all under eighteen, hence none of them have been called up. My guess is even if they were, they'd dodge out of it.'

'Who's the weakest?' asked Coburg. 'In every gang there's one who's weaker than the others.'

'Jerry Trump,' said Harker. 'He's fifteen, the smallest of the gang and likes to strut around and act big, but he's really just a kid. Scares easily, which is why he hangs around with Bazzer and his gang.'

'Are they in separate cells?' asked Coburg.

Harker chuckled. 'Come off it, Chief Inspector. You've been here before. This ain't the Ritz. We've bunged all of the gang in one cell. Benny Jimpson's in another. That leaves one other cell free.'

'But in the same place?'

Harker nodded.

'Pity,' said Coburg. 'Someone like this Jerry Trump, a cell can be an intimidating place to be questioned. We'll just have to talk to him in the interview room where I saw Brendan Riley. But put handcuffs on him. That'll unsettle him.'

Coburg and Lampson settled themselves in the interview room and shortly after two uniformed officers brought in a short, thin and very nervous boy of about fifteen who looked at them warily as the uniforms pushed him down onto a hard wooden chair at the bare wooden table. The two uniformed officers moved back, but remained intimidatingly close to the boy.

Coburg and Lampson glowered at the boy, but remained silent for a few minutes, their hard looks boring into Trump's eyes. Under their gaze, Jerry Trump shifted nervously on the chair, his handcuffed hands resting on the table.

'Sit still!' snapped Coburg.

Trump seemed to wither before their eyes, shrinking down.

'What's your name?' barked Coburg harshly.

'J-Jerry,' stammered Trump.

'Jerry what?'

'Jerry, *sir*,' said Trump apologetically.

Coburg glared at the boy, while Lampson did his best not to smile at the tough act his boss was putting on, so unlike his usual style, and the effect it was having on the boy.

'I meant, what's your surname?' said Coburg curtly.

'Trump, sir, Jerry Trump.'

'Well, Jerry Trump, you and the gang you were with are going to be charged with the attempted murder of those men you attacked.'

'We didn't attack anyone!'

'Oh, please, don't insult my intelligence,' Coburg scoffed. 'You were identified.'

'Who by?'

'The men you attacked. One was kicked unconscious and it was thought he was going to die, so that would have been murder. But he's recovering. And both him and the other man have given good descriptions of you and your pals.'

'It wasn't us,' said Trump, but Coburg could see his lips trembling and his hands shaking.

Coburg leant forward and growled. 'Yes, it was. And you're

all going to prison. You're lucky, being the youngest, I expect you'll just go to a young offenders' institution. But those are hard places, trust me. Why did you attack them?'

'We didn't.'

Coburg gave a weary sigh, and now he relented sightly from his hard-man pose. It was time to reel Trump in if he was going to get the confession he wanted. It was time to become Mr Gently Sympathetic.

'Look, Jerry, we can do this the easy way, or the hard way. The hard way is where you say you didn't do it, even though we've got witnesses who identify you, and so you get put in prison on remand, and then you go to court and spend days in the dock, before a judge decides whether or not to keep you in prison until you're eighteen, when you can be hanged.'

'You can't hang me!' burst out the terrified Trump, and his handcuffed hands began scrabbling desperately at the wooden tabletop.

'Have you ever seen anyone hanged, Jerry? I have, and it's not a pretty sight. If you're lucky and the hangman's done his job properly in fixing the rope, your neck breaks and you die quickly. But sometimes he hasn't, and I've known prisoners dangling while their neck is stretched and they choke, and in the end someone has to hang on to their legs to haul them down so they die. A really painful death. And, of course, they mess themselves.'

'They won't hang me!' said Trump, and he began to cry.

'Not if you tell the truth,' said Coburg. 'Why did you and the others attack the two men?'

'I don't know,' mumbled Trump, wiping his eyes and nose with the back of his jacket sleeve.

'You called them Nazi spies. Neither are Nazis or spies. They're both old soldiers who fought bravely in the last war. What made you think they were Nazi spies?'

'Someone must have said something,' mumbled Trump.

'Who?'

'I don't know.'

'In that case you'll stay here until you remember,' said Coburg.

'I can't!' appealed Trump. 'I can't stay locked up in a cell. What about my mum? What will she say?'

'She'll say you were an idiot to listen to other people and you deserve everything you're going to get,' said Coburg. He looked at the two uniformed officers. 'Keep an eye on him,' he said. 'Sergeant Lampson and I are going to talk to Sergeant Harker.'

With that, Coburg and Lampson left the interview room. Trump followed their exit with terrified eyes, then looked nervously at the two uniformed officers.

'I need to go to the toilet,' he appealed.

CHAPTER TWENTY-THREE

Brendan Riley entered the offices of the *Whitechapel Chronicle* and asked if it was possible to talk to the editor.

'Is it still Mr Cuthbertson?' he asked the receptionist, recalling the name from the time the *Chronicle* had first given his Jack the Ripper tours a mention in their pages.

'No. Mr Cuthbertson retired,' she told him. 'The editor's Mr Jack Phelps. He took over nine months ago.'

'In that case, could you ask Mr Phelps if he could spare me a moment. My name's Brendan Riley and I have a matter I'd like to discuss with him that I believe may be to our mutual advantage.'

The receptionist picked up the telephone and made a brief call, then she said to Riley, 'Mr Phelps says he'll be right out.'

'Excellent.' Riley beamed.

There was the briefest of pauses before Phelps appeared in the reception area. He was a tall, thin, harassed-looking man in his thirties with a sallow face, bags under his eyes, and thinning hair that he had attempted to comb over the top of his skull to hide his baldness. He wore shirtsleeves, with a pair of braces stretching over his shoulders.

'Mr Phelps,' said Riley, proffering his hand for the editor to shake, which he did. 'I'm Brendan Riley. I hope my name may be familiar to you.'

Phelps looked at Riley, puzzled. 'I'm sorry, Mr Riley, I'm sure it should be, but for the moment I can't place it.'

'Charlie Brown,' said Riley. 'Your reporter. He came to see me.'

'Oh?'

'Yes, about the killings that have been taking place here. He made me an interesting offer, for me to co-write a series of articles with him for your newspaper in which I could bring my expert knowledge to bear.'

'Your expert knowledge?' queried Phelps.

'I used to run walking tours of Whitechapel, before the bombing raids interrupted them, about the original Jack the Ripper, showing people the sites where the murders took place, along with the awful details of each of the killings. Gruesome, I know, but the public seemed to like it. Which is why I assume your Mr Brown is interested in me writing these articles with him. Now it's not that I don't trust Mr Brown's veracity, but – as I've had previous experience of Mr Brown – I thought it advisable to check with you, the editor, that this idea has your approval and authority.'

Phelps looked at Riley, obviously uncomfortable. 'I'm afraid to say, Mr Riley, that this is the first I've heard of this.'

'So, he hasn't approached you with this idea, nor you with him?'

'No. I'm sure it's a very good idea, but as a small local paper we are on a tight budget and we can't afford to pay local contributors.'

'So, if I did this collaboration with Mr Brown, my name would not appear with a credit in your pages.'

'I'm afraid not. Only people who are on the payroll receive

185

a contributor's credit. That's the policy of the paper's owners.'

Riley thanked Phelps for clarifying the situation, then left the newspaper's offices. Outwardly he seemed calm, but inside he was seething. That bastard Charlie Brown! He'd cheated him, conned him into getting him to provide copy for his column for nothing, on a promise of resurrecting his theatrical career. A promise that was a lie.

As Riley walked along the street he remembered with rising anger the negative comments Brown had made about his Ripper Walking Tours, describing them as a desperate throw of the dice from a failed second-rate so-called actor. When he'd read those words, Riley had been tempted to confront Brown and challenge him to a duel. Or, if not a duel, to kill him. He'd tried to seek Brown out, but the reporter had made sure he avoided him. In the end, Riley had decided that making a fuss about it would only draw attention to the hatchet job that Brown had done on him in the paper. At the moment it was just a piece in the *Whitechapel Chronicle*, hardly something that would be read in other richer areas, where most of his clients had been drawn from. But it still stung. And now this, the blatant lie, only exposed as such because Riley had checked out the newspaper's editor.

Brown was a lying duplicitous louse. The lowest of the low. He needed to be taught a lesson. A serious lesson. A grim smile appeared on Riley's face. Brown wanted to find out about the Ripper? Riley would show him.

CHAPTER TWENTY-FOUR

Harker listened as Coburg detailed the result of their interview with Jerry Trump.

'Young Trump as good as admitted he and the gang attacked Magnus and Malcolm, but he won't say who told them they were Nazi spies. He's terrified.'

'And I think I know why,' said Harker. 'Jenkinson rules that pea-brained mob by fear. Trump is terrified of what Jenkinson will do to him.'

Coburg thought about it, then asked, 'You said you had a cell free. Could you put Trump in it? My thinking is when they see he's been put in another cell it will make the others think he's told us what happened, but they won't be able to get at him.'

'You think this business of whoever told them that your brother and his pal were Nazi spies is important?'

'I do. Someone told the gang that story to make Magnus and Malcolm targets, to stop them. But why? Not to stop them selecting suitable places for air raid shelters, because no one except you and Bert Watts knew that was why they were here. So it's something else. Something that's going on that someone doesn't want Magnus and Malcolm poking their noses into.'

'But what?'

Coburg shrugged. 'The trouble is, in Whitechapel it seems to me there's always something crooked going on. Dodgy activities that people want to hide. Magnus and Malcolm look like government types, so maybe someone thinks they're here to investigate one of the many frauds that take place. Tax fraud. Black-market diesel and petrol. Ration-book fraud. There are so many. But I think it's to do with the false story that was put out about what they were doing here.'

'Them looking into the murders?'

'Yes. It was a clever idea, but I'm now thinking that the person behind the murders may have got nervous when they heard it. Ted and I have just been talking about it.'

'I think the guv'nor's right,' added Lampson. 'We reckon the murderer spun that tale about them being Nazi spies, to make sure they were attacked in an effort to scare them off.'

Harker nodded. 'When you put it like that, it makes sense. So, if we can get the name of the person who told Jenkinson's gang about them being Nazi spies, we may well have our murderer.'

'And hopefully we'll get that name from Jerry Trump. In the meantime, once Trump's been moved to the spare cell, Ted and I will return to the interview room and await the pleasure of Benny Jimpson's company.'

Mrs Dixon answered the knock on her door and opened it to find Charlie Brown smiling cheerfully at her.

'Mrs Dixon?' he asked, taking off his hat and tipping it to her. 'Cheerful Charlie Brown from the *Whitechapel Chronicle*. Is your son Wesley in? My editor wants me to do an interview with him for the paper. He's a hero, after all. Wounded in the line of duty.'

She regarded him doubtfully, then said, 'I'll see if he's available to talk to you. He's still recovering.'

She shut the door. Brown waited. As he looked at the number on the door, a memory was jogged from almost a year ago. Dixon. But not Wesley Dixon. Another name. He struggled to search his memory for the story, but for the moment it eluded him. The door opened and Mrs Dixon looked out at him.

'He'll see you,' she said. 'But don't tire him. He's been through an ordeal.'

'No problem,' said Brown.

He followed her through to the living room where Wesley Dixon was sitting on a settee. Dixon got up as Brown entered and the two men shook hands.

'Charlie Brown,' said Brown as Dixon sat down on the settee, and gestured for Brown to take an armchair. 'Cheerful Charlie Brown, most people call me. I like to keep people's sprits up, especially at a time like this.' He took out his notebook and a pencil. 'The thing is, Wesley, you're a hero. A real hero. And the only one to actually lay eyes on the New Ripper.'

'I never saw him enough to describe him,' said Wesley uncertainly. 'Like I said to the Scotland Yard men who came to talk to me, he was wearing a long coat with a hood, and it was dark in the tunnel.'

'Scotland Yard.' Brown nodded. 'Would that be DCI Saxe-Coburg?'

'It was.' Dixon nodded.

'The top man,' said Brown. 'They must think you're important.'

'I was only doing my job,' said Dixon. 'That's what I told them.'

Brown strolled over to the sideboard and looked at the photographs on display. He pointed at the one of Wesley with his parents and brother. 'Family photograph, eh?'

'Yes. That's me with my mum and dad and my brother William. My dad and William were killed fire-watching.'

'Were they?' said Brown thoughtfully. 'I remember your dad was, because I wrote about it, but your brother William was different, surely.'

'No!' said Dixon firmly.

'I'm sure it was,' said Brown. 'I was at the hospital when he died. Tragic, it was. A real decent young man. Awful way to go.'

'You're mistaken,' said Dixon.

'I don't think I am, Wesley,' said Brown, his voice loaded with sympathy. 'I've got a good memory for things like that. I mean, we never said in the paper what it was, out of deference to your mum. It wouldn't have been fair. But . . .'

Dixon got to his feet and glared at Brown, pointing firmly at the door. 'Out,' he said.

'But I haven't finished yet,' appealed Brown.

'Oh yes you have,' said Dixon. 'I want you out of this house and I don't want you coming back.'

'There's no need to be like that,' protested Brown. 'All I said was . . .'

'I know what you said and I won't have it said in this house. William died fire-watching, and if you write anything different you'll have me to deal with.'

Brown forced a smile. 'Alright, I get it. I'll say thank you for your time, PC Dixon, and wish you a speedy recovery.'

With that, Brown got up and made for the door. 'Give my regards to your mother,' he said, then left.

For their interview with Jimpson, Coburg had decided on a different tack.

'You take Jimpson,' he told Lampson. 'I've got the feeling he may not be intimidated by some posh-sounding detective inspector from Scotland Yard, but someone with a similar accent to his might make him less confident of being able to lie his way out of this.'

'The North London accent is different from the East End one,' said Lampson.

'You know what I mean,' said Coburg. 'I'll just sit in silence and glower like a toff, and sneer at everything he says to unsettle him.'

Coburg moved his chair slightly away from the table, leaving Lampson facing the empty chair on the other side. Consequently, when Jimpson was shown into the room by a constable, he looked at the two detectives uncertainly, unsure which one he would be questioned by. Lampson solved matters for him, pointing to the empty chair and grunting 'Sit.'

Jimpson sat.

'I'm Detective Sergeant Lampson from Scotland Yard. This is Detective Chief Inspector Saxe-Coburg. We're here to question you about the attack you launched against a woman called Sandra Hancock.'

'I never did!' protested Jimpson.

'That's not what she says. According to her, you tried to carve her up. Just like this bloke here in Whitechapel they're calling the New Ripper.'

'That's rubbish and you know it,' snorted Jimpson.

'No, I don't,' said Lampson. 'You took a knife to her.'

'I was never going to cut her, just threaten her. She owed me money. She'd taken money from a punter and kept it. She's supposed to give it to me first, then I take my cut and give her what she's due.'

'So you admit to living off the proceeds of immoral earnings,' said Lampson. 'Which is a criminal offence and will land you in jail for some years.'

'Oh come off it!' scoffed Jimpson. 'Everyone does it!'

'And those who are caught go to jail,' said Lampson.

'Look, it ain't like that,' said Jimpson. 'I'm really acting as her agent. Just like if she was an actress or a musician, or one of them sort. They all have agents who arrange the money and look after them.'

'Their professions are legitimate. Prostitution is illegal.'

'Only because there's some sort of discrimination. Admit it, it's been going on for ever; that's why they call it the oldest profession. The ancient Romans had it.'

'Well, we're not in ancient Rome, we're in England and it's illegal. So you're a criminal. And threatening someone with a knife is a criminal act. So you're in deep trouble on two counts.'

'What about her and her criminal act!' protested Jimpson. 'She kicked me in the balls. I bet I can't have children now. Why hasn't she been arrested and charged?'

'Self-defence,' said Lampson. 'She was protecting herself. Is that what happened with Sarah Mars?'

'Is what, what happened with Sarah Mars?' demanded Jimpson defensively.

'You put pressure on her to let you be her pimp. She refused, so you threatened her with your knife. Only it went too far. You killed her.'

'I never touched her!' protested Jimpson.

'But you tried to get her to work for you?'

'Wrong way round,' said Jimpson. 'It'd be me working for her. I'd be the one doing all the grafting, arranging good blokes for her, checking them out, making sure she was safe.'

Lampson shook his head in disapproval. 'You're a piece of work, you are. Pretending it's all for the girls' own good. You make me sick.'

'I've never harmed anyone,' insisted Jimpson.

'Really? Where were you on the nights of 30th March, and 1st and 4th of April?'

Jimpson stared at him, bewildered. 'How can I be expected to remember? Why?'

'Those were the nights the three women were knifed and carved up at Whitechapel air raid shelter.'

Jimpson shook his head. 'I wasn't there any of those nights.'

'Where were you?'

'I was in my mum's cellar.'

'Your mum's cellar?'

Jimpson nodded. 'She gets nervous with the bombing, so I go along to her house and keep her company. She's got a cellar and she goes there when the warning goes off.'

'So that's where you were on those nights? At your mum's in her cellar?'

'Yes.'

'Anyone else with you?'

'Her mum and dad, my grandparents. They're old. Their house hasn't got a cellar; it's got an attic. That's the way it works in their street. Alternate attics and cellars.'

Lampson slid a writing pad across the table to Jimpson.

'Write down their addresses,' he said. 'And their names. Are they on the phone?'

'No,' said Jimpson, beginning to write. 'Hardly anyone's got a phone in Whitechapel. Too expensive.'

'Well, what do you think of him?' Coburg asked Lampson after Jimpson had been returned to the cell.

'I think he's scum,' said Lampson. He gave a sigh. 'But I don't think he's our killer, not if his alibi holds up.'

'I'll ask Sergeant Harker to send one of his men round to Jimpson's mother to check it out.' Coburg nodded.

A constable appeared and said, 'Sergeant Harker said you might want Jenkinson and the rest of his gang next.'

'Yes, please, Constable.'

'Do you want to see them in their cell, or in here?'

'In here, I think,' said Coburg. 'Let's leave Jerry Trump to stew in the cell on his own. And bring in any of your fellow officers who might be free along with the gang. Nothing like a bit of pressure to sharpen their minds.'

'What minds?' said the constable sarcastically.

'I like that constable,' said Lampson, after the officer had left.

'So do I,' agreed Coburg.

The door of the interview room opened and the four youths filed in, accompanied by three uniformed constables. One of the constables dragged three additional chairs to the table.

'Sit,' snapped Coburg.

The boys sat. Three of them looked distinctly uncomfortable

and uneasy. The fourth, obviously the leader, Barry 'Bazzer' Jenkinson, wore a sneering defiant look on his face. Coburg looked at the notes he'd been given by Sergeant Harker.

'Duggan?' he asked.

A red-headed boy nodded.

'I want words, not nods,' snapped Coburg. 'Duggan?'

'Yes,' said Duggan.

'Yes, *sir*,' Coburg corrected him.

He then proceeded with the other names, as if reading a register at school.

'Kemp?' he barked.

A slightly older boy said, 'Yes, sir.'

'Pirie?'

Another boy responded with 'Yes, sir.'

Coburg fixed a steely look on the last remaining one. 'Jenkinson?'

Jenkinson hesitated, then sneered, 'Yes.'

Coburg kept his hard glare on Jenkinson, until he reluctantly added an uncomfortable, 'sir.'

'So, who told you the two blokes you beat up were Nazi spies?' asked Coburg.

'What two blokes?' asked Jenkinson cockily.

'Including the one you tried to kick to death,' said Coburg. 'At the moment he's still hanging on, but if he dies it'll be murder.'

'We're saying nothing,' said Jenkinson, and he folded his arms across his chest and looked at the two detectives defiantly.

'You don't need to,' said Coburg with a knowing smile. 'We've already got the evidence we need to hang you all.'

'Hang us?!' said Kemp, shocked.

'Why is Jerry being kept separate?' blurted out Pirie.

'Shut up!' snapped Jenkinson. 'I said we don't talk to them.'

'I don't think they're going to listen to you any more, Jenkinson,' said Coburg. 'It's amazing what looking at the reality of a hangman's noose does to some people. You may be happy to hang, but I don't think all your comrades feel the same.'

'Jerry's talked!' burst out Duggan. 'He's told!'

'Shut up!' shouted Jenkinson in fury.

Coburg looked at the boys and laughed.

'Temper, temper,' he said genially. 'We don't want you dying of a heart attack before we've had a chance to hang you.'

'You can't hang us!' shouted Pirie desperately.

Coburg looked at the waiting constables.

'You can take them back to their cell,' he told them.

'Come on, you lot, up,' snapped one of the constables.

The boys stood up and tried to put on a swagger, but even Jenkinson didn't seem so confident. The constables ushered the gang towards the door, but before they got there one of them turned and said, 'You can't hang us! It won't be allowed!'

Coburg's response was to laugh. 'Keep believing that,' he said. 'I bet you'll still be saying that when they slip the nooses over your heads and tighten them around your necks.'

The constables ushered the gang out and pulled the door shut after them.

'I think you've got them rattled, guv,' said Lampson.

'Let's hope they're rattled enough that one breaks ranks and tells us who started this business about Magnus and Malcolm being Nazi spies,' said Coburg thoughtfully.

CHAPTER TWENTY-FIVE

Janet Trump was leaving the police station when The Watcher stopped her in the street.

'What's happening, Mrs Trump?' asked The Watcher. 'You don't look happy.'

'Nor would you be,' said Mrs Trump angrily. 'That idiot son of mine, Jerry. He lets himself be led. Always in trouble.'

'What is it this time?'

'It's that Barry Jenkinson. Bazzer, they call him. My Jerry thinks the sun shines out of him, even though he's always getting him in trouble.'

'What happened?' pressed The Watcher.

'Bazzer and his stupid gang, including my Jerry, attacked a couple of blokes.'

'Why did they do that?'

'According to Sergeant Harker, someone had told Bazzer these blokes were Nazi spies. In fact they weren't spies at all. It seems they were in Whitechapel working for the government.'

'Doing what?'

'I don't know,' said Mrs Trump crossly. 'All I know is, because of that my Jerry is in a police cell.'

'What about the others?'

'They're all in the cells,' said Mrs Trump. 'Most of 'em are used to it, but not my Jerry. He's always been more of a nervous type, never been in a cell before. He's delicate, you see.'

'I'm sure they'll let him go.'

'I'm not so sure,' said Mrs Trump doubtfully. 'The police want to know who said these two blokes were Nazi spies. Trouble is, Bazzer's got a tight hold on all of 'em except for my Jerry. He's told 'em to say nothing. Told them the police can't hold 'em for ever; they'll have to let them go after twenty-four hours. Bazzer says he's no grass and he won't have any snitches in his gang.'

'So it'll be alright,' said The Watcher.

'No it won't,' said Mrs Trump. 'My Jerry won't be able to cope with being locked up overnight. I'm going in there to get him out.'

'How?'

'I'll tell him to tell Sergeant Harker who it was who said about them blokes being Nazi spies. And if Jerry don't, he'll be in trouble from me.'

The Watcher nodded. 'Quite right, Mrs Trump.' Then The Watcher hesitated a moment, before saying, 'Although, I hope you don't mind my interfering, but I've got a suggestion. Based on the fact that I had a similar problem some time ago with mine. Like Jerry, they were locked up in a police cell because they wouldn't tell who'd done something, for which they'd got the blame. They didn't want to be thought of as a grass, see. So what I suggested to the police was I took mine home with me and gave them a good talking-to until I got a promise they'd say who it was.'

'And did they?'

'They did, but not until the following morning.'

'And did you take them back to the police station?'

'I did. But the trick was not to pressure them to say anything at first when I brought them home. Leave it until the morning. That's what I did. It was much easier.'

Mrs Trump nodded thoughtfully. 'That makes sense to me. But do you think Sergeant Harker will agree to let Jerry go before he's said who it was?'

'I'm sure he will if he thinks about it. If he wants Jerry to give him the names of whoever it was, Jerry needs to be away from Bazzer and the others in the gang. As long as he's in a cell with them he won't talk. I'm sure Sergeant Harker will let him go if you promise to bring Jerry back tomorrow when he'll say the name. He's very approachable, is Sergeant Harker.'

'Yes, he is,' agreed Mrs Trump.

Eve was still concerned about the way the two boys had looked at Terry, especially after what Ada Lampson had said about them. She looked at the clock. Terry would be leaving school shortly and setting out on his way home. The one thing she didn't want to do was have Terry think she was out near the school to escort him home, as if he was still a little kid. That really would drive a wedge between them.

She put on her coat, then took her walking stick from the rack.

From the cover of an alleyway off the main road that led to Terry's school, Derek Weems, Jed Barnes and their friend Jack Carter watched. Most of the other kids had already left, and Terry was just saying goodbye to his friends who lived in the opposite direction from him.

'Here he comes.' Weems grinned, and he took a hand-made

cosh from his pocket, a thick sock filled with sand and ball-bearings.

'You sure he'll come this way?' asked Carter.

'Certain.' Weems nodded. 'I checked it out. This is the way he walks home.'

Terry was just passing the end of the alleyway, when suddenly two boys stepped out and grabbed him by the arms. He recognised them as from the Warren Street Boys club, Jed Barnes and Jack Carter. Then he saw Derek Weems appear, a smug smirk on his face and banging a small lethal-looking cosh into his palm of his hand.

'Well, well, look who's here,' sneered Weems. 'The dirty fouling player who needs to be taught a lesson.' And he swung the cosh menacingly. 'Hold him tight, boys, we don't want him slipping away before we give him what we owe him.'

Terry felt the grips of the two boys tighten painfully on his arms, twisting them up behind his back. Weems swung the cosh back, ready to bring it down on Terry's face, when a woman's angry voice shouted out, 'Oi! You lot! What do you think you're doing?'

The boys swung round, startled at this interruption, and saw a woman moving intently towards them. Although she was using a walking stick, there was no mistaking the look on her face. This was no frail, weak woman, realised Weems.

'We're only paying him back for the nasty tackle he did on me yesterday at the football,' said Weems defensively.

'Well, it may interest you to know that that's my son you've got there, and if you don't release him, you and I are going to have trouble.'

Weems sneered. 'A mummy's boy, eh.'

Eve shook her head. 'Far from it. If you want to settle this, that's fine by me. But not three against one. Nor with a cosh. If you want to fight him, by all means, but you do it one at a time. Fists only.'

Derek, Jed and Jack looked at one another, uncertainly, and Jed and Jack let go of Terry's arms.

'Is that alright with you, Terry?' asked Eve. 'Can you take on all three?'

Terry looked at Eve in surprise, then nodded, and stepped towards the boys, his fists at the ready.

'Who's first?' he demanded.

The three boys backed away from him.

'That ain't fair,' complained Barnes. 'She's got a stick she can hit us with.'

Eve put her stick down on the ground. 'Now I haven't,' she said.

Terry stood, fists raised, ready for action.

'Come on,' he said. 'Which one of you is going to be first?'

Jed shook his head. 'Not me,' he said.

'Nor me,' said Derek.

Jack Carter also shook his head.

'In that case,' said Eve, 'you'd better clear off.' She bent down and lifted her walking stick from the ground and pointed it at the three. 'And if you pick on my boy again like this, three against one, you'll have me to deal with as well.'

The boys looked uneasily at Terry, and at Eve, and then retreated slowly a short distance, before turning and hurrying away.

Terry looked at Eve. 'Would you have really let me fight them?' he asked.

'I thought you'd prefer that to me getting involved,' said Eve. 'Or was I wrong?'

'No,' said Terry. 'You were right. Now they know I can stand up for myself.'

'I've always known that,' said Eve.

'Yes, but now they know it, too,' said Terry. He looked at Eve, curious. 'How come you were here when it happened?'

'I didn't come to meet you from school, if that's what you're asking,' lied Eve. 'The doctor told me I need to exercise my arm to help it heal, so I go out for a walk now and then. It just happened today I walked this way.' She looked at Terry. 'Shall we go home? I got a cake at the baker's we can have with a cup of tea, and you can tell me how school was today.'

'It was boring,' said Terry as they set off. Then he stopped and looked at Eve and said, 'I'm glad you were here.'

'So am I,' said Eve. 'Come on, let's get home and have some cake.'

Bazzer Jenkinson and his gang sat on the hard wooden benches in their cell and looked across the detention area at the two smaller cells on the other side. In one, a man who Bazzer recognised as Benny Jimpson was asleep on a bench. In the other the disconsolate figure of Jerry Trump sat slumped on a bench, his head down, avoiding eye contact with his gangmates.

'Why have they put Jerry in a cell on his own?' asked Tommy Duggan.

'He must've talked,' whispered Shug Pirie. 'They think we're going to beat him up because of it.'

'Are we, Bazzer?' asked Arnold Kemp. 'Are we going to beat him up?'

'I'll decide if we beat him up,' said Bazzer curtly. 'Now shut up talking about it. He can hear us.'

'Will they hang us?' came the plaintive wail from Kemp.

'Shut up,' snapped Jenkinson.

The door to the detention area opened and Sergeant Harker walked in and went to the cell where Jerry Trump sat slumped in misery. Harker took a key and opened the cell door.

'Out you come, Jerry,' he said. 'Your mum's here to take you home.'

At these words, Trump leapt off the bench and was about to run towards the door, when he stopped.

'Good,' he said, doing his best to put on a swagger.

The rest of his gang looked at him through the bars of their cell, unconcealed venom obvious on their expressions.

'I told you,' muttered Pirie. Suddenly he called out, 'Grass! Snake!'

'Shut up!' barked Harker.

He led Jerry Trump out of the detention area, locking the door behind him. The gang members looked at Jenkinson.

'What do we do?' asked Duggan.

'We shut up, that's what we do,' snapped Jenkinson tersely.

Sergeant Harker had sent one of his men round to Benny Jimpson's house to check whether it contained a cellar.

'It does,' Harker told Coburg and Lampson. 'And Mrs Jimpson swears that Benny was with her and her parents in it during the air raids.'

'Think she's telling the truth?' asked Coburg.

Harker nodded. 'I've known her years. She's loyal to her rotten son, but she wouldn't lie to keep him out of jail if he'd done something bad.'

'Okay,' said Coburg. 'Give him a caution and kick him out. You'll need the cell space.'

'So we hang on to Jenkinson and his gang?'

'For the moment. I still need to know who told them Magnus and Malcolm were Nazi spies.'

'With a bit of luck, we might have the answer shortly,' said Harker. 'I've just had Jerry Trump's mother come in. She said if I let her take him home, she'd do her best to make sure he gave me the answer we're after. I thought it was worth the risk. Jerry's not likely to run away; he's too scared for that. She said she'll bring him back in the morning.'

Coburg nodded. 'Yes. Get him away from the rest of the gang. Hopefully, you'll get the answer.'

'I'll phone you as soon as I've spoken to him tomorrow,' said Harker.

As Coburg and Lampson made for their car, Coburg asked, 'What did you think of Sergeant Harker's decision?'

'I approve,' said Lampson. 'Trump's mother is more likely to get the information from him than anyone else. Working-class mothers are among the most terrifying people on the planet. They rule the roost.'

'You sound like you're talking from experience,' said Coburg, amused.

'You've met my mum,' said Lampson pointedly.

'Yes, good point,' said Coburg.

When Coburg and Lampson got back to the Yard, Coburg telephoned a reporter, Justin Penrose, he knew who worked at *The Times*, covering royal events.

'Justin, I'm trying to identify a reporter who might have offered money to staff at Buckingham Palace in exchange for stories about the royals,' he said.

'Well, it's not me,' said Penrose, slightly indignant.

'No, I never thought it was,' said Coburg. 'But you know the other royal reporters. For example, someone mentioned the *Daily Reporter*. They cover royal stories.'

'The *Daily Reporter* isn't a proper newspaper,' snorted Penrose disparagingly. 'It's a scandal sheet.'

'Exactly,' said Coburg. 'Do you know who their royal correspondent is?'

'I'd hardly call him a royal correspondent,' said Penrose. 'He deals with everything where there's shady business to be done: politicians, show business, sport, anywhere where there's evidence of chicanery, or bribery and corruption.'

'Including Buckingham Palace?'

Penrose sounded uncomfortable. 'Anywhere there's power and money is a target for him.'

'Who is he?'

'His name's Edward Crosby. An awful man. Which is a pity. He comes from a good family. Well-educated. Public school. Gone to the bad. The ideal person to earn his living muck-raking for a rag like the *Daily Reporter*.'

In the middle of washing up, Janet Trump looked at the clock on the kitchen wall. Jerry had been gone for an hour. Where could he be? He'd gone out to the shop to get himself some sweets. She felt he deserved it after being locked up. And with sweets in his pocket he was more likely to tell her the name of whoever it was who'd got him in trouble. Nazis spies, indeed!

At least she knew he wasn't getting into any trouble with that Barry Jenkinson and his gang; all of them were still locked up in the cells at the police station. None of their parents had turned up to try and get them out like she had, just left them. That was because she was the only one who cared enough about her boy to try and keep him on the straight and narrow.

A loud banging on her street door made her jump, then she calmed down. It must be Jerry, having forgotten his key. He was a stupid boy. No, she swiftly corrected herself, not stupid. He was just badly led by others, and forgetful.

She dried her hands and hurried to open the front door, just as the loud banging on it started up again. The caller was Norman Payne, who had the ironmongers next to the sweet shop. He looked in a state.

'Mrs Trump!' he said, agitated. 'Something's happened to your Jerry. I found him on the pavement outside my shop. He's in a bad way. I've called an ambulance and I waited until they arrived before I hurried over.'

'What's wrong with him?' he asked urgently. 'Was it an accident?'

'I don't know,' said Payne. 'All I saw was him bleeding. There was blood on the front of his jacket.'

'Where is he?' asked Mrs Trump, taking her coat from the stand in the hall and pulling it on.

'The London,' said Payne. 'I've got my van here. I'll take you there.'

At Scotland Yard, Coburg called the number he'd been given for Edward Crosby at the *Reporter*. The man's voice that answered was very much as Coburg had expected after the warning from

Justin Penrose, a superior, slightly louche, languid upper-class drawl. After introducing himself, Coburg asked, 'Did you ever meet or talk to a man called Bernard Bothwell?'

There was a silence, then Coburg heard Crosby repeating the name slowly. Finally, he said, 'No, not that I'm aware of. Who is he?'

'He was a valet at Buckingham Palace.'

'Really. Whose valet?'

'To be honest, Mr Crosby, that's doesn't really matter.'

'Oh, but it does,' said Crosby. 'Anything that happens inside the palace is interesting to me.'

'Yes, so I understand. I've been informed that you offered Mr Bothwell money in exchange for inside information about life at the palace.'

Crosby chuckled. 'If I may have, that's not illegal. It's par for the course in the newspaper world. But, I repeat, I'm not aware of this Bernard Bothwell.'

'The palace is one of your areas of speciality, I believe,' said Coburg.

'It is,' agreed Crosby. 'My editor felt, with my background and contacts, it was perfect for me.' Then he said, 'You were at Eton, weren't you? You must have lots of contacts in the royal circle. And in the world of politics. I was at Harrow so I've got my share of reliable people I can talk to. You must have lots of stories that would be of interest to the public.'

'I'm not for sale, Mr Crosby,' said Coburg, and hung up.

CHAPTER TWENTY-SIX

Edward Crosby was a regular visitor to the stables at Buckingham Palace. His press pass, along with his public-school accent, and his easy-going air of authority got him access. Providing he didn't attempt to enter the actual palace, of course. Not that he needed to; his main source of information was Jumpy Watson, a groom who looked after the horses. If there was anyone else on the palace staff who it was worth him talking to, a pound note slipped into Watson's hand led to a place and time that would be arranged for Crosby to meet that someone.

Watson looked at Crosby with a welcoming smile, because a visit from the journalist usually meant money.

'Do you know a man called Bernard Bothwell?' asked Crosby. 'He's one of the King's valets, I understand.'

'The one who got murdered?'

'Murdered?' repeated Crosby, pleasantly surprised. If that was true, this was turning out to be a major story. He could see the headline, with his name as the all-important byline. *Murder at Buckingham Palace by Edward Crosby. King's valet slain.* 'How was he murdered?' Crosby asked.

'I don't know the exact details,' said Jumpy. 'All I know is there was a lot of talk about this valet going missing, and a week later he turns up dead.'

'Who does know the details?' asked Crosby. 'It's worth money.'

'The police do,' said Jumpy. 'There was a Scotland Yard detective here to see Sir Jasper Connor, the King's private secretary.'

'Who in the police? What was the name of this detective from Scotland Yard?' asked Crosby, although he was fairly sure he already knew the answer: Detective Chief Inspector Saxe-Coburg.

'How much is it worth?' asked Jumpy.

Crosby weighed it up. He wanted to keep Jumpy happy, but he didn't want to just throw good money away. He needed to talk to someone in the King's inner circle, rather than the groom. The trouble was, most of the people in the King's inner circle usually refused to have anything to do with people from the *Reporter*.

He handed the groom a ten-shilling note. 'This is on account,' he said. 'If you can put me in touch with anyone who knew Bothwell, there'll be at least a pound. Maybe more, depending on what they can tell me. Do you happen to know if he lived in? Most servants do.'

'No,' said Watson. 'He lived out.'

'Where?'

Watson thought, then he said, 'What's it worth?'

Crosby chuckled and produced another ten-shilling note.

'This is getting very expensive,' he said.

'Good information always is,' said Watson, taking the note. 'Pimlico, I believe.'

'Where in Pimlico?'

Watson shrugged. 'No idea,' he said. 'But I could find out.'

Crosby chuckled again. 'You could, but I can't afford it,' he said.

He waved the groom goodbye and made his way out of the palace grounds and towards the nearest public telephone box, where he looked up Bernard Bothwell in the directory. There were three subscribers listed, all called B. Bothwell, but only one in Pimlico. He made a note of the address and set off for Pimlico.

Dr McKay and Sergeant Harker stood in the mortuary at the London Hospital looking at the dead body of Jerry Trump. He'd been brought straight to the mortuary once the ambulance drivers realised he was dead.

'Stabbed in the heart,' said McKay. 'And I'd swear it was the same weapon that was used to kill those women in the air raid shelter. A bayonet.'

'You sure?' asked Harker.

'I'll know for certain once I've opened him up, but I'd put money on it. And I'm not a betting man.' He shook his head in despair. 'What's happening in this place? That's five murders so far if you count the dead man pulled out of Shadwell Basin. Although he was killed with a different kind of knife. But the three women at the air raid shelter and now this boy were definitely killed with the same weapon.'

'I only let Jerry go earlier today,' said Harker sadly. 'He would have been safer if I'd kept him locked up.'

'What was he at the station for?' asked McKay.

'He and the rest of a gang attacked two men who were in Whitechapel on a fact-finding mission,' said Harker.

'Attacked?' asked McKay. 'What sort of fact-finding were they doing?'

'Officially, I'm not supposed to say,' said McKay, 'but I don't suppose you're involved in property development.'

McKay gave a harsh laugh.

'Chance would be a fine thing,' he said.

'They were checking out sites for possible air raid shelters.'

'And some thugs attacked them?' said McKay in bewilderment. 'My God, the people in this area are madder than I thought.'

'They thought they were Nazi spies,' said Harker.

'What on earth gave them that idea?'

'Someone told them.' He looked down at the body of Jerry Trump. 'This boy was supposed to be coming to the station tomorrow to tell me who it was.'

McKay gave a snort. 'It's a pity you didn't hang on to him until he told you.'

'His mother appealed to me. Said he'd be more likely to tell me in the morning if I let him go home today.'

'One of these over-protective mothers, eh,' said McKay in disapproval. 'At least you've got the rest of the gang in jail. It sounds to me like whoever said to them about Nazi spies wanted to shut him up before he talked to you. So lean on the bastards, that's my advice. Tell them if they don't tell you who it was, one of them could be next.'

Crosby pressed the doorbell of the neat suburban house in Pimlico and waited. The door was opened by a respectably dressed middle-aged woman, who Crosby assumed to be Mrs Bothwell. Just to make sure, he put on his best accent and most ingratiating manner and asked, 'Forgive me for intruding, but am I addressing Mrs Bothwell?'

Jean Bothwell regarded Crosby warily.

'Yes,' she said.

'Please allow me to offer my deepest sympathy on the loss of your husband.'

She looked at him, suspiciously. 'You knew my husband?'

'Not personally,' said Crosby. 'I'm a journalist with the *Daily Reporter* newspaper . . .'

Even as he said it, he saw the flush of anger cross her face, and the sudden awful realisation hit him that he *had* met Bernard Bothwell before. He'd forgotten his name. He'd been told by Jumpy Watson that the man worked for the King and might be worth tapping up. So, Crosby had accosted him and made the usual offer, and been verbally assaulted by the man in the most vile terms.

Damn, he thought. Swiftly, he began to lie.

'Firstly, I must apologise for the dreadful way in which someone on my newspaper acted when he saw your husband some time ago. I understand he offered money for information about His Majesty. When I heard about this I made the strongest possible complaint to the editor, and I insisted the man be sacked. Which happened. So, this morning when I heard about the tragic death of your husband, naturally my first thought was to call and explain what had happened before, and assure you that nothing like that would ever happen again involving the *Daily Reporter*. I just thought your husband's passing deserved a proper mention, out of respect for him. Would you mind if I asked you some question about him? It won't take long, I promise.'

Jean Bothwell studied the man. For all his good manners, his ingratiating style, his obvious upper-class speech and bearing, there was something she didn't trust about him.

'I'm sorry,' she said. 'It's all too fresh for me. I can't talk now.'

'I understand,' said Crosby, laying on the sympathy with a trowel. He produced a business card, which he handed to her. 'This is my card. Edward Crosby, with my contact details. Perhaps, when you are ready, you can contact me. Our readers will be eager to hear your husband's story, and I promise you whatever I write will be done very respectfully, and you will have the last word on whether or not you want it to appear in print. Your feelings are paramount.'

She nodded, put the card in her pocket, then closed the door.

So far so good, thought Crosby. *At least she didn't slam the door in my face.* But he was still mentally kicking himself for having forgotten his earlier confrontation with Bothwell.

In the office at Scotland Yard, Sergeant Lampson picked up the ringing telephone.

'DCI Coburg's phone,' he said. 'Sergeant Lampson speaking.'

'Sergeant Lampson,' said a woman's voice. 'This is Mrs Bothwell. Your inspector and you called to see me following the tragic death of my husband.'

'Yes, Mrs Bothwell, I remember you,' said Lampson. 'Once again, we are both very sorry for your loss. What can I do for you?'

'Is the inspector there?'

'I'm afraid he isn't, he's out at the moment, but he's asked me to take any messages and pass them on. Which I will do, I promise.'

'I'm calling because I've just had a visit from a man called Edward Crosby who works for the *Daily Reporter* newspaper. I'm fairly sure he's the man who upset Bernard some time ago.'

She then told Lampson the details of their conversation. 'I'm suspicious of what he's after,' she said. 'I thought the inspector ought to know.'

'And I'll make sure he does,' said Lampson.

He hung up and asked the operator to put him through to Whitechapel police station.

Coburg parked outside the offices of the *Whitechapel Chronicle* and strode into the reception area.

'I'd like to talk to Mr Charles Brown,' he said to the receptionist.

'You and everyone else,' she replied with a sigh. 'He hasn't been in and there's messages waiting for him. I tried phoning him at home but the operator says there's no answer. Which isn't like him. He likes to keep in touch in case anyone wants him. He's always keen to get a story.'

'Does he live locally?'

'Yes. He prides himself on being the Whitechapel reporter for Whitechapel people.'

'Perhaps you can give me his address.'

She shook her head. 'Sorry, it's against the rules. Some people have been known to get upset with some of the things Charlie and our other people write, and might go round and punch them. The editor says we've got to protect our staff.'

Coburg produced his warrant card and held it out for her to look at.

'DCI Coburg from Scotland Yard,' he said. 'Can you ask

your editor if I can talk to him?'

She nodded and picked up the phone. She dialled a single number, then said, 'Mr Phelps, it's reception. There's a detective chief inspector from Scotland Yard would like to have a word with you.' There was a brief pause while she listened to the editor ask something, then she said, 'I think it's about Charlie Brown. No, he hasn't been in yet, nor phoned. Alright, I'll tell him.'

She hung up the phone, then said, 'Mr Phelps is on his way.'

Phelps appeared at the desk a few moments later. Despite a wary look in his eyes, he held out his hand towards Coburg. *A defensive action*, thought Coburg, shaking it.

'Jack Phelps, Chief Inspector,' said Phelps. 'I'm the editor. Janice said you're enquiring after Charlie Brown.'

'Yes, I need to talk to him about one of his reports in your paper, but I understand he isn't here and you haven't heard from him, so I need his address.'

Phelps regarded Coburg, then said, 'Saxe-Coburg. The aristo cop. Charlie put your photo in his piece about the New Ripper. You and your missus. Rosa Weeks. Tell her I love her stuff. She's a great piano player, and she sings like a dream.'

'I will. Now, can you let me have Charlie Brown's address?'

'Why?' asked Phelps guardedly.

'Because he's got information that could help us in a murder enquiry we're conducting, and I need to talk to him urgently.'

'You're not upset with what he wrote about you? You did give him an exclusive interview? At Scotland Yard, as he said?'

Yes, I am upset, thought Coburg. *And when I see him I*

shall tell him so. But right now, he needed Phelps to give him Brown's address.

'Yes,' said Coburg. 'I just need to talk to him. I believe he may have vital information. My concern is that, as he hasn't reported in, and he isn't answering his phone, he may be lying ill at home.'

'Yes, the same thought struck me,' said Phelps.

He took a piece of paper from the reception desk and wrote the address down.

'Do you know Whitechapel?' he asked.

'I can find my way around it,' replied Coburg.

'It might help if I send Ben, the office boy, with you. He knows where Charlie lives; he's taken messages to him often enough. It's in a cul-de-sac and not easy to find.'

'That would be very kind,' said Coburg.

Phelps went to a door at the back of the reception desk, opened it and hollered 'Ben!'

A short boy of about fifteen with a mop of fair hair appeared. 'Yes, Mr Phelps?'

Phelps gestured at Coburg. 'This is a detective chief inspector from Scotland Yard. He wants to call on Charlie Brown at his house. I want you to show him where it is.'

'Yes, sir.' He looked at Coburg. 'Do you have a car, or do we walk?'

'How far is it?' asked Coburg.

'Not far, but it's easier by car.'

'In that case my car's outside.'

Ben followed Coburg out and his eyes lit up when he saw the police car.

'I've never been in a police car!' he said excitedly.

'Let's hope you don't make a habit of it,' said Coburg.

They got in the car and Coburg followed the boy's directions. Soon they were entering a short cul-de-sac of terraced houses.

'This is it,' said Ben. 'Cheerful Charlie's that one in the middle, number 8.'

'Stay here and look after the car,' said Coburg.

He got out and walked up the short pathway to the front door of number 8. He knocked. When there was no answer, he knocked again. When there was still no response, he pushed open the letterbox and peered into the passageway of the house. The body of a man was lying there. Although Coburg couldn't see the face, the shape of the body convinced him it was Charlie Brown.

He returned to the car and asked the office boy, 'Do the office keep copies of reporters' keys? You know, in case they lock themselves out.'

'Yes,' said Ben. 'How did you know?'

'Just a guess,' said Coburg.

He drove back to the newspaper's office and asked for Mr Phelps.

'Did you find him?' asked Phelps.

'Yes,' said Coburg.

'How was he?'

Coburg looked at Ben, then said, 'You can go now, Ben. Thanks for your help.'

'Don't you want me to come back with you?'

'No thanks. You've been very helpful.'

The boy hesitated, apparently hoping that Coburg would change his mind and ask him to stay, but when it was obvious that wasn't going to happen, Ben reluctantly made for the door behind the reception area into the offices.

'What's happened?' asked Phelps, aware that something wasn't right.

'There's a dead body in the passageway of Charlie Brown's house. I think it's Brown, but I couldn't see his face. I understand you've got a key to his house. I need you to come with me and take a look., For one thing, if it is Brown, you'll be able to identify him.'

'I'm not very good with dead bodies,' said Phelps.

'No one is,' said Coburg. 'But, if he is dead, as his boss you'll need to know. Unless you can suggest anyone else who knew him who can come with me.'

'No, I'll come,' said Phelps. 'I'll just get my jacket.'

A short time later they returned to the house, where Phelps used the spare key to open the front door.

'Yes, that's Charlie.' Phelps shuddered, recoiling from the portly body lying on the red passageway carpet. Blood from a wound in his chest had spilt out and mixed with the colour of the carpet.

'It looks like he was stabbed in the heart,' said Coburg. 'Death will have been instantaneous.'

Phelps looked down at Brown's dead body, bewildered.

'What happens now?' he asked.

'I want you to go back to your office and telephone Sergeant Harker at Whitechapel police station. Tell him what's happened, and that I'm here waiting for him. Tell him we need the duty medic to come and do the examination. I'll meet them all when they arrive. I'll keep the spare key because we'll need to lock up afterwards.'

'Right.' Phelps nodded.

'And after that, I want you to make a list of everyone Brown talked to about any stories he's been working on lately.'

'I think it's been mainly about the New Ripper.'

'Then list all of them, and check in case he was working on anything else. Also, I want a list of people who didn't like him, and anyone he's upset lately.'

Which would include me, he thought ruefully.

In his basement flat in Notting Hill, Wally Dawes ran through the numbers they'd be doing at Maida Vale the following day. He used brushes to soften the sound; no sense in upsetting his upstairs neighbours. The last thing he needed was complaints against him just when he was about to finally get a major break. Not just a live radio broadcast, but accompanying big stars like Vera Lynn and Flanagan and Allen. This was moving into the big time. He'd been in the big time before when he was with Joe Loss, but somehow things hadn't gone the way he'd hoped. All that would change with this broadcast. The audience for music on the radio was in the millions. And this time he'd be part of a trio with Rosa and Eric, not just an anonymous musician, lost in a large orchestra.

In his head he heard Rosa's piano and Eric's double bass, and he added trills and pops, complementing their playing and giving the sound the depth that only a full kit could provide.

He stroked the skins with his brushes, and then did a rapid drum roll using the whole kit, drums and cymbals. Yes, that would be the perfect thing tomorrow.

CHAPTER TWENTY-SEVEN

The body of Charlie Brown was taken out on a stretcher by the ambulance men and was now on its way to the London Hospital. Dr Webb had made his preliminary examination, confirming what Coburg had already deduced, that Brown had been stabbed in the heart.

'The reports from you and Dr McKay suggest that most of the other victims were stabbed by a bayonet, or similar sort of weapon, whereas Mr Bothwell was stabbed in the heart with a carving knife. So, which sort of weapon was used to kill Mr Brown, a bayonet or a knife?'

'You're weighing up which group of victims Mr Brown falls into,' said Webb thoughtfully. 'As soon as I get him to the London, I'll open him up as a matter of urgency and let you know.'

He nodded to Coburg and Sergeant Harker and left the house.

'Second one today!' said Harker sourly.

Coburg looked at him quizzically.

'Jerry Trump,' said Harker.

'Jerry Trump?' said Coburg, stunned.

'Stabbed in the heart as he was coming out of a sweet shop. According to Dr McKay it was the same weapon that killed the women. What do you want me to do with the rest of the gang?'

'Hang on to them,' said Coburg. 'We need that information about who suggested Magnus and Malcolm were Nazi spies. It seems to me Trump was very likely killed to stop him talking. If I'm right, we need to keep the others in the cell for their own safety.'

I knew it was connected to the business of 'the Nazi spies', thought Coburg. Someone had been determined to stop Jerry Trump telling who had said it to the gang. Somehow, they had to get the gang members to give up the identity of the person who'd said it to them.

Sergeant Harker had been studying the door jambs and the lock.

'This wasn't a break-in,' he said.

'No, which means Brown opened the door to his killer,' said Coburg. 'From the fact that Brown was killed in the passageway, my guess is that the killer struck almost as soon as the door was opened. It's backed up by the fact he was stabbed in the heart, which indicates he didn't have time to turn and run away.'

'Brown must have known his killer, to open the door to him,' said Harker. 'He was a careful chap. He knew he'd upset a lot of people, and here in Whitechapel, people who get upset are liable to settle it with their fists, rather than words.' He indicated the safety chain attached to the door jamb. 'I know for a fact he kept that safety chain on if he didn't know the person calling, just in case.'

'Right,' said Coburg, 'I'm going to talk to Mr Phelps, the editor of the *Whitechapel Chronicle*. I'm hoping he'll have the list of people who Brown had upset recently ready.'

'If the killer was someone he knew he'd upset, he wouldn't have opened the door to them,' pointed out Harker.

'True,' said Coburg. 'Unless it was someone he wasn't aware

he'd upset. In my experience, that happens all the time.'

'By the way, I was coming to find you, anyway,' said Harker. 'Ted Lampson phoned with a message for you. Mrs Bothwell's been in touch with him.'

'What about?'

'She had a visit from some reporter called Edward Crosby, from a paper called the *Daily Reporter*. If you can call it a newspaper,' he added scornfully. 'She's suspicious of him.'

'I'm not surprised,' said Coburg. He walked to the telephone, lifted the receiver and asked the operator to connect him with DCI Coburg's office at Scotland Yard. When Lampson answered, he said, 'Ted, I got your message about Mrs Bothwell and Edward Crosby. Can you phone her back and tell her it's all in hand, and not to have anything to do with him. Tell her I'll be in touch soon and explain everything.'

'Right, guv,' said Lampson. 'How are things in Whitechapel?'

'Two more dead bodies,' said Coburg. 'One's a teenage tearaway. The other one is Cheerful Charlie Brown. Both stabbed to death.'

'Bloody hell, guv. Whitechapel is getting more dangerous by the day. You ought to get out of there.'

'I will. I've got one more call to make, to the editor of the *Whitechapel Chronicle*, hoping to get a list of suspects. I suggest you head home. I'll see you as usual in Somers Town in the morning.'

When he got to the *Whitechapel Chronicle*, Coburg learnt that Jack Phelps was in his office.

'I'll take you in to him,' the receptionist told him. 'I know he was looking for you. He asked me to check your number at Scotland Yard.'

She took Coburg to the editor's office. Phelps smiled when he saw Coburg walk in.

'Ah, Chief Inspector,' said Phelps. 'I was about to call you, but I didn't know if you were still in Whitechapel or if you'd returned to Scotland Yard. I've done that list you requested. People who'd had run-ins recently with Charlie Brown.'

'Thank you,' said Coburg.

He sat down, took up the list of names Phelps passed to him and ran his eye down it. He noticed it was quite a short list, so obviously Brown hadn't been too offensive to most people.

'There's someone here called Fred Chalk,' he said. 'Who's he?'

'He's the son of Billy Chalk, a local butcher. He works for his dad. Because he's involved with food production, so he's got exemption from the call-up.'

'What did he row with Brown about?'

'Well, that's a bit strange,' said Phelps. 'Billy Chalk is a communist. Arch-communist, I might say. Hates the Tories, and thinks we should get rid of the royal family.'

'Like they did in Russia?'

'No. He doesn't think they should be killed, just retired and have to work for a living like everyone else. Anyway, whenever there was a story that involved the royals, or the Tories, Billy was always good for a comment slagging them off. Like when Buckingham Palace was bombed, Charlie went to see Billy and asked didn't he have sympathy for them, now they'd suffered like the people of the East End.' Phelps chuckled. 'That was like a red rag to a bull as far as Billy was concerned. Billy gave Charlie a long rant about how privileged the royals were, and asked how many of them had been killed, compared to the thousands of East Enders who'd died in the air raids. And that's just one example. Billy felt really strongly about it. So much so that he set up a petition in his butcher's shop demanding more air raid shelters for Whitechapel and Stepney, and he asked all his customers to sign it.'

'And did they?'

'Oh yes. He sent it to Herbert Morrison, the Home Secretary.'

'Morrison? Not the Prime Minister?'

Phelps shook his head. 'Morrison's Labour Party. Billy can't stand the Tories, and he especially can't stand Churchill. Every time anyone said how Churchill was a hero, he'd talk about how he'd ordered the killings of striking miners in Tonypandy. He hates Churchill. Like I say, usually he could be counted on for a rant against Churchill and the royal family, but a few days ago Charlie went to the butcher's shop to ask the Chalks for their opinion about something to do with the royal family, and Fred was there, and Fred threw him out of the shop. Charlie tried again when he'd seen that Billy had come in, but as soon as Charlie started talking about the royals, *Billy* threw him out. He even threatened Charlie with his butcher's chopper!'

'What did Charlie want to talk to him about?'

'Something to do with the Duke of Windsor. It wasn't even about the King and Queen and the two princesses.'

Coburg continued looking down the list. 'I see you've got Brendan Riley's name here.'

'Yes. Riley came to see me. Apparently, Brown had promised him a co-writing credit on a story he was doing about the New Ripper. I had to tell Riley that Brown had no right to tell him that; we couldn't do that at the *Chronicle*.'

'How did Riley take it?'

Phelps looked uncomfortable. 'He seemed alright with it, but there was something in his manner, in his eyes, that made me realise he was actually furious about it.'

'Did you confront Brown about it?'

'No. Riley only came here his morning and Brown hasn't been in today. Even if he had been, Brown can be a difficult person to deal with. He always puts on this agreeable personality, Cheerful Charlie Brown, set on pleasing everyone. He would have just denied he'd said anything like that to Riley, claim that Riley had got the wrong impression.'

Coburg continued checking the list. 'You've put PC Dixon down.'

'Yes. Charlie didn't say what it was about. He just said he'd been to talk to Dixon about his heroic action in tackling the New Ripper after the last killing, and Dixon had told him to leave. Quite abruptly.'

'He didn't say why?'

'No. But I got the impression that Charlie was keeping something back. He sometimes did that if he felt a story was stirring and he didn't want anyone else to get hold of it.'

The telephone on Phelps's desk rang.

'Jack Phelps,' he said. Then he looked at Coburg and said, 'Yes, he's here.' He held out the receiver towards Coburg. 'It's for you. Dr Webb at the London Hospital.'

Coburg took the phone.

'DCI Coburg,' he said.

'I wasn't sure where you were, so I phoned Sergeant Harker at the police station,' said Webb. 'He told me you'd gone to see the editor at the *Chronicle*. I can report that Brown was stabbed with a bayonet.'

'Not a knife?'

'No. I asked Dr McKay to have a look, and he agrees.'

'So whoever killed Charlie Brown also killed the women at Whitechapel and Jerry Trump.'

'That's how both Dr McKay and I see it,' said Webb.

Coburg hung up the phone.

'Information?' asked Phelps.

'But not for publication,' said Coburg. 'However, I promise you, you'll be the first to know when it can be released.' He picked up the list of names. 'Thank you for this, Mr Phelps. I'll be in touch.'

As he left the newspaper offices, he pondered over what Dr Webb had told him. Three prostitutes, a teenage thug and a local newspaper reporter, all killed by the same person. What was the connection?

Instead of going straight home, Coburg made for Scotland Yard, where he telephoned Inspector Hibbert.

'We've got a problem,' he said.

'What sort of problem?'

'An inquisitive journalist called Edward Crosby, who writes for the *Daily Reporter*. He's been round to Mrs Bothwell's house asking about her husband.'

'From the *Daily Reporter*? That scurrilous rag? How did he find out about her husband being murdered?'

'I was given Crosby's name as someone who rakes up muck from palace sources. I thought he might have been the reporter who was after the stolen piece of paper.'

'I don't believe it!' burst out Hibbert. '*You* told him about Bothwell being murdered?'

'No,' said Coburg. 'I was just trying to find out if he had contacts at the palace who he got information from, and if so, who they were.'

'So you threw in Bothwell's name!' said Hibbert in disgust.

'Yes, alright, I was clumsy,' admitted Coburg.

'Worse than that,' said Hibbert. 'My God, Coburg, I thought you had more sense than that.'

'Yes, I should have been cleverer about it,' admitted Coburg. 'The thing is, Crosby's obviously trying to get a story out of this. Some real headline-grabber in which he'll reveal the King's valet has been murdered.'

'Not on my watch he won't,' growled Hibbert.

'What do you want me to do?' asked Coburg.

'Nothing,' grunted Hibbert. 'You've done enough landing us in this situation. The palace and Churchill will go ballistic if this appears in a rag like the *Reporter*. Or any paper, come to that.'

'I know,' groaned Coburg.

'Leave it to me,' said Hibbert. 'I'll stop the story coming out.'

'How?'

'If necessary I'll kill this bloody reporter.'

'Inspector . . .' began Coburg, but Hibbert had already hung up. *Damn*, thought Coburg.

At their flat, as Rosa waited for Coburg to arrive home, she received a telephone call from John Fawcett.

'I'm afraid I've got some bad news, Rosa,' said Fawcett. 'Bud Flanagan has lost his voice. Laryngitis. Chesney has offered to do it on his own, but he's not particularly happy about it. I can understand that because it's the harmonies of the two voices, the musical contrapuntal aspect, if you will, that gives their songs their essence. There is the possibility of replacing them with another guest, but it's very short notice and I'm not sure who might be available. It would need to be someone whose songs you're familiar with.'

'That shouldn't be a problem. If they're doing popular songs, I know many of them, and I can work out an accompaniment for those I'm not familiar with.'

'Could I ask you to join me tomorrow morning at Maida Vale? Say at ten o'clock. I hope I'll have been able to arrange someone else by then, and that will give you time to go through the numbers they'll be doing with them, before we start the rehearsal in the afternoon.'

'Of course,' said Rosa.

'I'll telephone Eric and Wally and get them to come in earlier for the same reason,' said Fawcett. 'I'll tell them eleven to give you time to talk to Chesney.'

'In that case I'll see you at Maida Vale at ten tomorrow,' said Rosa.

'What's happened?' asked Coburg, walking into the living room as she hung up and catching her concerned expression.

'That was John Fawcett, my producer,' she said. 'Bud Flanagan has laryngitis. He can't sing tomorrow. Mr Fawcett said that Chesney Allen says he'll do it on his own, but he's not happy about it. So Mr Fawcett is going to see if he can find someone else to fill in as a replacement for them.'

'That's a blow,' said Coburg. 'I was looking forward to seeing Flanagan and Allen.'

'The trouble is, most of the listeners will be looking forward to hearing them as well,' groaned Rosa. 'It's in the *Radio Times*.'

'I wonder who he'll get,' mused Coburg. 'Someone good, I hope.'

'That's the problem; at this short notice it could well be

someone who's available rather than someone who's good. The best people are usually booked up weeks ahead.'

In Somers Town, the day's work over, Lampson, Eve and Terry were relaxing with cups of cocoa before bed. While Eve read a book, Lampson and his son were in the closing stages of a game of draughts.

'I wonder how much longer we'll be able to drink cocoa like this,' said Lampson.

'Why?' asked Terry.

'Because the bloke who runs the canteen at Scotland Yard reckons there are plans to ration chocolate and other sweets,' said Lampson.

'Ration sweets!' said Terry, shocked.

'There's not enough sugar in the country,' said Lampson. 'At least, that's what he said.'

'How long's this war going to go on, Dad?' asked Terry, plaintively.

'Who knows, son?' said Lampson. 'When it started they said it would be over by Christmas, 1939. Here we are in 1941 and no sign of it ending.'

'Ah-ha!' said Terry suddenly in delight. With a deft move he took four of his father's pieces, clearing the board. 'I win!'

'You do, indeed,' said Lampson with a grin. 'Well done, son.' He looked at the clock. 'Just in time for bed, as well.'

'Can I take my comic up?'

'Alright,' said Lampson. 'But don't read for too long.'

'Right-ho,' said Terry.

At the door he stopped and said, 'Goodnight, Dad. Goodnight, Mum.' Then he headed up the stairs.

Lampson looked at Eve in pleased surprise, and mouthed 'Mum?'

'I told you he'd say it when he was ready,' said Eve.

Edward Crosby held Dolores del Rio in his arms and kissed her. It had been a superb evening of glorious sex, two bottles of good red wine, and very little chatter. Dolores was a wonderful companion, but her primary language was Portuguese with only occasional general phrases in English entering her speech. Not that Crosby cared about that; he had more than enough of people who wanted to talk to him, usually about themselves, which Crosby found boring. What Crosby thrived on was salacious gossip, the stories he picked up and usually repackaged for his columns in the *Reporter*. And, if a story was particularly juicy, there was always the possibility of offering the subject the opportunity for it *not* to appear in print, for a price, of course. But all that was business. The evening with Dolores had been pleasure, and it left him with a warm glow as he descended the stairs from her flat and made his way out into the street and towards where he had parked his car. He looked at his watch. There was just time to get back to his own flat, and the basement air raid shelter beneath, before the night's air raids began.

As he approached his car he became aware of two men walking along with him, one on either side of him. He stopped and turned to the one on his right, a tall man with a sour expression on his face.

'If this is a mugging, I'm afraid you're going to be disappointed,' he said. 'I don't have my wallet with me, and the small amount of change I had I've left with a friend just now.'

The tall man looked at the man on Crosby's other side, who suddenly took hold of Crosby's arm in a very firm grip.

'Ow!' complained Crosby. 'I'm sure whatever you're after can be settled without recourse to violence.'

'That depends on you,' said the tall man.

Crosby stopped and gestured at his car. 'This is my car,' he said.

'I know,' said the tall man. 'But you'll be travelling with us in ours.'

'Why?' demanded Crosby. 'Who are you?'

'We are MI5.'

'MI5?' echoed Crosby in surprise. 'What do MI5 want with me?'

'At the moment, silence,' said the tall man. He nodded towards the man firmly holding Crosby's arm, and Crosby found himself being propelled forward towards a black car parked immediately behind Crosby's own car. The doors of this car opened and a stocky man wearing an overcoat got out.

'What about my car?' demanded Crosby.

'For now, your car is the last thing you need to be worried about,' said the stocky man.

With that, Crosby found himself being shoved into the black car.

'Where are we going?' demanded Crosby anxiously.

There was no answer. Instead he found himself squashed between the two men in the rear seat of the car. There was a metallic click, and he looked down to find a pair of handcuffs had been fixed to his left wrist and he was now attached by them to the wrist of the stocky man.

'Shouldn't I have a lawyer?' asked Crosby.

Still there was no answer. Instead the car started up and moved off.

CHAPTER TWENTY-EIGHT

Tuesday 8th April

Lampson was still full of delight the next morning when Coburg picked him up.

'Terry called Eve "Mum",' he told him happily as they drove along.

'I said it was only a matter of time,' said Coburg.

As they drove to the Yard, Coburg admitted to Lampson his mistake over talking to Edward Crosby. 'I'm afraid I cocked up,' he said unhappily.

'How dangerous is this Edward Crosby, guv?' asked Lampson.

'For me and my reputation, very dangerous. Certainly, as far as Inspector Hibbert is concerned.'

Coburg told Lampson about Trump's murder, and his conviction it was connected to the person who'd said that Magnus and Malcolm were Nazi spies.

'We need to get that information,' he said. 'Who said it to the gang.'

'The trouble is, they've clammed up tight,' said Lampson.

'Then it's up to me to unclam them,' said Coburg determinedly. 'I'll be at Whitechapel if anything comes up.'

* * *

Rosa arrived early at Maida Vale and learnt that John Fawcett was in his office on the telephone. Still trying to get someone to replace Bud Flanagan, she thought. She walked through the underground corridors and then into the studio-cum-theatre, where she was surprised to find both the tall elegant figure of Chesney Allen and his chunky partner, Bud Flanagan, already on the stage, waiting.

'Ah, Rosa Weeks!' Chesney Allen beamed. 'We meet at last!'

He and Flanagan jumped down from the low stage and came forward to greet her, and hands were shaken all round in introduction, although Rosa noticed that it was Allen who did the talking.

'This is so wonderful for me,' said Rosa enthusiastically, adding, her voice showing her concern, 'But I heard you had laryngitis, Mr Flanagan.'

'Mr Flanagan?' Allen chuckled. 'Bud and Chesney, please. We're both really looking forward to this show. But you're right, Bud has lost his voice, but he was determined to come and appear. The audience will expect it.'

Flanagan mimed enforced silence, pointing at his throat and opening his mouth with no sound.

'A friend of ours has offered to step in and take Bud's place as far as the singing is concerned,' said Allen.

Flanagan nodded.

'Who?' asked Rosa.

'*Moi !*' shouted a cockney voice. Rosa turned and saw the inimitable figure of comedian Eddie Gray in his 'Monsewer' role, complete with bulbous drooping moustache and a pair of steel-rimmed spectacles, walking down the sloping aisle between the seats towards them. 'I thought I'd put the stage outfit on already.' He grinned and came forward, hand outstretched towards Rosa. 'Rosa Weeks, I presume.' As Rosa shook his hand, he said, 'I saw you at Blackpool before the war. It was at the Hippodrome. Fantastic! I said then "Some day I'm going to have to meet this woman. Do an act with her."'

Bud Flanagan held up his hand to get everyone's attention, then did a quick soft-shoe shuffle.

'As Bud has just shown, there's no reason he can't perform. Yes, his voice has gone so he can't sing, but the idea is he does the dance routine with me, and Eddie, and Eddie and I sing. Will that be alright with you, Rosa?'

'Alright?' said Rosa, delighted. 'It will be wonderful! The audience are going to lap this up!'

Edward Crosby stood at the window of the small room looking down on Tower Green, with its neatly mown lawn and trees that separated the old Tudor houses from the ancient tower where he was presently confined, with a sense of wonder and awe. He was actually in the Tower of London! A prisoner in the tower! But why?

He'd been given no information the previous evening, except that the men who'd picked him up and brought him here had been MI5. He'd been doubtful about that until they drove into the Tower itself.

Once inside the tower he'd been escorted by the silent men up an ancient winding staircase and then put into this room, not much larger than a box room. Fortunately, a toilet and washbasin had been added since medieval times. Food had also been provided in the form of a bowl of soup in the evening, and then this morning some toast with what looked like pâté, although the taste confirmed it was actually fish paste. Cups of tea and glasses of water had also been provided, but no information. No reason why he had been brought here. In fact no one had said anything to him at all since he'd arrived. Why the vow of silence? he wondered. Had he fallen into the clutches of some sub-sect of Trappist monks?

The sound of a key being turned in the lock made him turn towards the door, and the stocky man from the previous evening entered. He was still wearing his long overcoat.

The stocky man walked to the bare wooden table and the two chairs beside it. He sat down on one of the chairs and rapped on the table to get Crosby's attention, and pointed to the other chair.

'Sit,' he said curtly.

At least we'll be talking, thought Crosby as he walked to the chair and sat.

'My name is Inspector Hibbert from MI5,' said the stocky man. 'You are Edward Crosby.'

'I am,' agreed Crosby. 'But why am I here? Why the Tower of London?'

'We bring people who are a risk to national security here,' said Hibbert.

'Why am I a risk to national security?' asked Crosby.

'Tell me about Bernard Bothwell,' said Hibbert.

'Who?' asked Crosby, putting on an air of innocence.

Hibbert stared grimly at him.

'If you're going to take that attitude you'll be here for the rest of your life,' he stated sourly. 'You've been asking about Bernard Bothwell. Why? Who is he, and what do you know about him?'

'I assume you know who he is, otherwise I wouldn't be here,' said Crosby.

'Tell me anyway.'

'He's the King's valet. Or one of them. He was murdered.'

'Did you murder him?'

'No, of course not!'

'Who did?'

Crosby looked at Hibbert, bewildered. 'How do I know? That's why I was asking about him.'

'How did you know he'd been murdered?'

'Someone told me.'

'Who?'

'You know a newspaperman never reveals his sources,' said Crosby.

'He does if he wants to get out of here alive,' snapped Hibbert.

'Alive?' said Crosby, shocked.

'The penalty for treason is death,' said Hibbert. 'Carried out here within the precincts of the tower.'

Crosby looked at Hibbert, stunned.

'What's this about treason?' he demanded.

'Gaining information about the royal family for the benefit of a foreign power, to be used against this country,' said Hibbert. 'Now, who told you he'd been murdered?'

'A groom at the palace.'

'Buckingham Palace?'

'What other palaces are there?' retorted Crosby.

'Plenty,' said Hibbert. 'So, a groom at Buckingham Palace told you that Bernard Bothwell had been murdered?'

'Yes.'

'What's the name of the groom?'

'Jumpy Watson.'

'Jumpy?'

Crosby shrugged. 'It's what he's called. I doubt if it's his real name, but that's the name everyone knows him by.'

'Did you approach this Jumpy about it, or did he approach you?'

'I approached him.'

'Why?'

'Because Bothwell's name came up when I was talking to someone.'

'Who were you talking to?'

'A Scotland Yard chief inspector called Edgar Saxe-Coburg.'

'Did he approach you or did you approach him?'

'He approached me. He asked if I knew anyone called Bernard Bothwell. I told him I didn't.'

'And then?'

'And then . . . nothing. He didn't tell me why he wanted to know. All he said was he'd been told I'd offered this Bernard Bothwell money for any stories he could tell me about what went on at the palace. That got me interested. It meant that this Bothwell worked at the palace in some capacity. So I went to talk to someone I knew who worked at the palace to see what he knew.'

'This Jumpy Watson?'

'Yes.'

'What did he tell you?'

'Like I told you: just that this guy had been murdered and he was the King's valet. To a reporter, that's gold dust.'

'Or a long prison sentence,' said Hibbert.

At Whitechapel police station, Coburg and Harker pressurised the gang to try and get one of them to tell them who'd told them that Magnus and Malcolm were Nazi spies; but not one would to talk.

'They're scared of Bazzer,' said Harker afterwards. 'Also they're worried if they talk, they may get what Jerry Trump got.'

At Maida Vale, Rosa and Eric ran through the numbers they were scheduled to do on the show while they waited for Wally to appear.

'I've got a bad feeling about this,' said Eric unhappily. 'I hope he didn't get caught up in another air raid last night.'

'I don't think there were any in Notting Hill,' said Rosa. 'Unless he's moved.'

John Fawcett appeared and walked down the sloping aisle towards the stage, and Rosa and Eric stopped playing and looked at him expectantly.

'I've been trying to get hold of Wally, but without success,' he told them. 'There's no answer to his home phone and his agent says she hasn't heard from him. If he doesn't appear in the next fifteen minutes, I'm going to have to arrange for someone else.'

'Who?' asked Rosa. 'It's a bit short notice to get anyone good.'

A man's voice calling out a rather plaintive 'Hello' was heard from just outside the theatre, then the figure of Wally appeared.

'Thank God,' muttered Fawcett. 'He's here.'

'I wouldn't thank God just yet,' murmured Rosa warily, as Wally stepped unsteadily forward.

'I've got my kit in a taxi outside,' called Wally. 'I'll need help bringing it in.'

He did a wobbly walk forward, but as soon as his feet touched the slope of the aisle he stumbled and tumbled forward, crashing into a row of seats.

'My God, he's drunk!' exclaimed Fawcett, horrified.

'I'm afraid so,' said Rosa sadly. 'It's my fault, Mr Fawcett. You had your doubts but I was the one who said he'd be alright.' She shook her head unhappily, then hurried towards the fallen drummer, John Fawcett close behind her.

'I seem to have had a bit of an accident,' slurred Wally as he attempted to push himself up off the floor, but instead fell forward, his face thumping against the carpet, hard enough to start his nose bleeding. Rosa took a handkerchief from her pocket and began to dab the blood from Wally's upper lip.

'I'll be fine,' protested Wally.

'No you won't,' snapped Fawcett. 'I can't take the risk of you appearing on a live broadcast in this state. I'll get someone to take you back to your taxi and you can go home.'

'No!' pleaded Wally. 'I need this job!'

But Fawcett had already left, in a hurry to find a pair of commissionaires. Rosa looked sympathetically down at the fallen Wally. 'What happened, Wally?' she asked.

Wally looked at her, his face a picture of misery. 'I don't know,' he said. 'I just thought of the audience here in the theatre, and then the audience at home who'd be listening.' He looked at her, aghast at the thought. 'Millions of them, Rosa. Millions! And I couldn't bear it. So I thought a little drink would buck me up. Make me feel better about it.'

He looked at her, and then his face crumpled and he began to cry. 'It's not good, is it?'

Rosa shook her head sadly. 'No, Wally. I'm afraid it isn't.'

'I can try,' he pleaded. 'Pour some coffee down me. I'll be alright.'

'We can't trust you, Wally. *I* can't trust you.' Then an idea struck her, and she said, 'But we can still get something out of this for you. Your drum kit.'

'What about it?'

'You said it's in the taxi outside.'

He nodded.

'We'll hire it from you. For the day. At least you'll get some money. And it'll be here for you to collect tomorrow. When you're feeling up to it.'

'What are you going to do with it?' he asked.

'At the moment, I don't know,' Rosa admitted.

'I don't want just anyone playing it,' said Wally, obviously pained at the idea. 'They could damage it.'

'I promise they won't,' said Rosa. 'I'll look after your kit for you.'

John Fawcett reappeared accompanied by two burly-looking uniformed commissionaires.

'I need you men to take Mr Dawes to the taxi that's waiting for him outside,' Fawcett told them. 'I think it will be best if you carry him out.'

As the men moved to take hold of Wally, Rosa spoke up and told them, 'But can you bring in the drum kit you'll find in the taxi?'

Fawcett looked at her, puzzled. 'Why?' he asked.

'I have an idea,' said Rosa.

Fawcett hesitated, then nodded. 'Fine,' he said. 'Bring the drum kit in here and put it on the stage.'

The commissionaires lifted Wally up and then carried him

unceremoniously out of the theatre, one holding his legs, the other bearing the weight of his upper body.

Fawcett looked enquiringly at Rosa. 'What's your idea?' he asked.

'While Eddie Gray and Chesney do the song and dance routine, Bud plays drums.'

'Bud?'

'He wrote "Underneath the Arches", so he's got a musical ear. And I'm sure he used to play drums before the war.'

Fawcett thought about it, then said, 'Yes, I believe he did. But will he?'

'I'm sure he will, if you ask him. He's an old trouper.'

Just then there was a babble of voices from outside, and then in walked the whole of the Crazy Gang. Fawcett stared at them.

'We heard that Bud has lost his voice,' said Nervo, 'and I said to Jimmy, "This is a miracle! Bud not able to talk? I need to see and hear this for myself before I believe it."'

'So we all decided to come down here and see for ourselves,' said Knox.

'And, since we're here, we thought we'd help our old mate out. He can do his what some people call a dance routine with Chesney, while we sing along.'

'Like a chorus,' added Naughton. And he called out 'One, two, three,' and Rosa was treated to the whole Crazy Gang suddenly singing, in perfect unison.

Awkwardly, John Fawcett told them, 'It's a wonderful idea, gentlemen, but I'm afraid there's no money left in the budget.'

'That's alright,' said Nervo. 'We'll share whatever you were paying Bud. After all, he can't talk so he'll not complain.'

Flanagan looked at Fawcett with a look of mock-anguish appeal and pulled his trouser pockets inside out to show he had no money.

'By the way,' asked Eddie Gray, 'who was that bloke we saw being carried out just now?'

'That was our drummer,' said Rosa ruefully.

'Bloody hell!' said Gray. 'Bud loses his voice, and now the drummer gets carried out. It's like one of them bloomin' Agatha Christie books. Who's gonna be next to go?'

There was a thump, and they looked round to see Naughton lying on the floor, clutching his throat and gasping dramatically.

Jimmy Gold gave a deep heartfelt sigh and announced, 'This show's in big trouble! It needs us.'

CHAPTER TWENTY-NINE

Coburg arrived back at Scotland Yard and heard from Lampson that there had been no repercussions following Edward Crosby's interjection.

'Nothing from Inspector Hibbert?' asked Coburg.

'No,' said Lampson.

'It doesn't mean it's not the same killer,' said Lampson.

'True,' said Coburg. He showed Lampson the list Jack Phelps had given him. 'I meant to show this to you before. This is a list of people Brown had upset recently. I'd like to compare it with the list of workers that Sir Jasper Connor gave us, see if there are any names the same.'

Lampson took the list and ran his eye down it. 'There's one name here that's the same,' he said. 'Chalk.' He picked up the list Sir Jasper had given them. 'I've been studying the list while you were out. There's a woman on it called Maud Chalk who lives in Whitechapel. She's one of the cleaners.' He looked enquiringly at Coburg. 'Think they might be related?'

'Possibly,' said Coburg. 'Although Chalk is a common enough name. But there's a Whitechapel connection that might make it worth looking into her.'

He picked up the phone and asked the operator to get him Sir Jasper Connor at Buckingham Palace.

'Sir Jasper,' he said when he was put through. 'There's a woman on the list you gave us called Maud Chalk, one of the cleaners.'

'Yes?' questioned Connor warily.

'Do you know her?'

'Not personally,' said Connor. 'I checked the list of employees against the requirements you gave me. She was the only one with an address in Whitechapel, which is why I included her.'

'Is she at the palace at the moment?'

'I couldn't say. I'd need to check with the head of housekeeping. Why?'

'At the moment it's just something we need to check with her. We'll be talking to others on the list, but we thought we'd start with her because she lives in Whitechapel.'

'As I said, I'll need to check with the head of housekeeping. If she is still at the palace, do you want to come here and talk to her?'

'Possibly, providing that doesn't cause problems.'

'Of course. I'll check and phone you back.'

It was five minutes before Sir Jasper returned Coburg's call.

'Miss Chalk left the palace two hours ago,' he told the DCI. 'She was on an early shift.'

'Thank you,' said Coburg.

He called Inspector Hibbert at MI5, and luckily the inspector was in his office.

'We may have a lead on the Bernard Bothwell murder,' he said. 'That list of employees that Sir Jasper gave us, there's a woman on it called Maud Chalk. One of the cleaners. She lives in Whitechapel.'

'And?'

'There's a man called Billy Chalk who's a butcher in Whitechapel. Could there be a connection?'

'Chalk's a pretty common name,' observed Hibbert.

'True. But I think it's worth having a word with her. After all, she works at the palace and lives in Whitechapel, not far from Shadwell Basin.'

There was a brief silence while Hibbert thought this over, then he said, 'It's a bit thin, but we've got nothing else. Yes, alright. Where is she at the moment?'

'According to the palace, she's gone home.'

'I suggest we bring her in to Scotland Yard to talk to her,' said Hibbert. 'If she's anything like most ordinary people, the idea of being questioned in Scotland Yard is unsettling. With something like this we need her to feel ill at ease.'

'And if it turns out she's not involved?' asked Coburg.

'We release her. No harm done,' said Hibbert. 'I'll pick you up at the Yard. Oh, and we've picked up that reporter bloke, Edward Crosby. He's currently in the Tower of London, so he won't be causing any trouble.'

Coburg replaced the receiver and filled Lampson in on what was happening.

'Do you want me to come with you?' asked Lampson.

'I think Inspector Hibbert and I should be enough to bring her in.' Coburg smiled.

'That's a relief,' said Lampson. 'I must admit, guv, this business makes me uneasy.'

At the Maida Vale studios, Rosa had managed to put a telephone call through to Magnus's flat.

'Magnus,' she said, 'I have to tell you, we've got the whole of the Crazy Gang here in the studio, and they're going to appear together on my show tonight. If you can get to the Maida Vale studios for half past five, I'll see if I can arrange a seat for you.'

'Rosa. That is so kind of you!' said Magnus, delighted. 'And if you can't, I'll be happy to stand at the back.'

Maud Chalk was a small, thin, nervous-looking woman who became even more jittery when the two men who called at her small terraced house in Whitechapel introduced themselves as DCI Coburg from Scotland Yard and Inspector Hibbert from MI5.

'MI5?' she gasped. 'What have MI5 got to do with me?'

'We just need to ask you some questions,' said Coburg.

She stepped back from the door. 'You'd better come in,' she said.

'Not here,' said Coburg. 'We need to talk to you at Scotland Yard.'

'Scotland Yard?' she said, horrified. 'I'm not going to Scotland Yard!'

'I'm afraid you have to,' said Coburg. 'If you refuse we will have to call a WPC to accompany you, and bring you in by force if necessary.'

'But I haven't done anything!' she burst out, and the note of sheer desperation in her voice caused Coburg and Hibbert to exchange meaningful looks. This woman, they knew, was frightened.

'In that case, you have nothing to fear,' said Hibbert. He pointed at the car where his driver sat waiting.

Maud Chalk stood studying the car, the two men, and then reluctantly took her coat from the coat rack.

CHAPTER THIRTY

In the bare interview room in the basement of Scotland Yard, Coburg and Hibbert sat side by side at the wooden table, facing Maud Chalk. A uniformed woman police constable stood on guard immediately behind her.

'Don't I have to have a lawyer with me?' Maud Chalk asked, again the same note of desperation in her voice.

'No. You're not being charged with anything,' said Coburg. 'At the moment we just have to ask you some questions.'

'What about?'

'About Bernard Bothwell. Do you have a relative called Billy who has a butcher's shop in Whitechapel?'

She didn't answer and her face paled. Coburg was sure she was shaking beneath her uniform.

'Billy Chalk?' he asked again.

She gulped, then said in a voice so low they could barely hear, 'He's my brother.'

Coburg looked at Hibbert, who asked the next question. 'Did he ask you to look for anything in the King's private quarters?'

'No,' she said quickly. Too quickly, thought Coburg.

'What about his son, Fred. Your nephew?'

This time she didn't answer; she dropped her gaze from theirs down to her lap.

'You took something.'

'It wasn't anything worth anything,' she said defensively. 'I didn't steal anything.'

'A piece of paper,' continued Coburg.

She lifted her head and looked at them defiantly. 'That's all it was. A scrap of paper. It didn't look important, just a few words scribbled on it.'

'Why did you take it?'

She hesitated, then said awkwardly, 'Fred asked me.'

'For that piece of paper?'

'No, not that specific piece of paper. He said he was interested in anything with the King's handwriting on.'

'So you looked in the bedside table drawer while you were cleaning?'

'It wasn't like it was valuable,' she said defiantly.

'It was valuable enough to get a man killed,' said Hibbert. 'You knew the King's valet, Bernard Bothwell?'

She gulped nervously. 'I knew him to see, but not to speak to.'

'He was murdered because you took it. That makes you an accessory to murder.' He leant forward towards her and added in menacing tones, 'That's a hanging offence. You could hang.'

'No!' she screamed.

'Yes,' said Hibbert firmly.

She began to sob, great wailing sobs that shook her body. The two men exchanged looks, and Hibbert nodded to Coburg as if to say, *Over to you.*

Coburg waited until her sobbing had subsided, then said gently, 'But if you tell us everything that happened, there may well be a way out for you. From the beginning.'

They waited until she'd managed to bring her sobbing under control, then Coburg gently nudged her to tell her story by saying, 'Tell us about your brother, Billy.'

'He's a communist,' she began, falteringly.

'How does he feel about the royal family?'

'He thinks they should be kicked out of Buckingham Palace, and all their other palaces, and the buildings given over to ordinary people to live in. Like they did in Russia. He's always talking about Russia and how they got things right.'

'How did he feel when you got a job at Buckingham Palace?'

'At first he was angry, telling me I was a lackey. But then he said maybe it was a good thing; I could keep him informed of what they were up to so he could use it for propaganda for the cause. That's what he called it, the cause for working people, the poor and the underprivileged.'

'And did you?'

'Not really, because I didn't know anything. I was a cleaner. I never had anything to do with the actual royal family.'

'But you cleaned their quarters.'

'No. Usually I cleaned the rooms the staff lived in. There's a team of us who do it. Lots of teams, because there are so many rooms.'

'So how did you come to be doing the King's private rooms?'

'The woman who usually does it was ill, so they said could I do it because I'd done such a good job on the staff quarters.'

'You must have felt pleased.'

'I was. It was like a promotion. No more money, but it felt important.'

'And you told Billy?'

She hesitated, then said awkwardly, 'No. I thought he might

get angry with me. But I had to tell someone, so I told Fred. Fred and I have always got on. In a way, I was like his second mum. Billy's wife, Gladys, Fred's mum, died soon after he was born, so Billy had to bring Fred up on his own. Lots of people told him it would be better if he gave him up for adoption, but Billy wouldn't hear of it. So I stepped in and did what I could.'

'What did Fred say when you told him about doing the King's rooms?'

She looked uncomfortable. 'Well, he got excited.'

'Excited? For you?'

'No. For his dad. I was a bit surprised. I always knew that Fred supported the communists; growing up with his dad telling him all about Russia, he couldn't be anything else. But I didn't think he was as mad about it as his dad, not as fierce. Fred said I might be able to find some stuff when I was cleaning that would help his dad.'

'Help him, how?'

'If I found anything that Billy could pass on to the papers to back up his view that the royal family were corrupt. Like I said, Billy was very strong on wanting to get rid of the royal family. He blamed the papers for praising them all over the place. He said if the public knew the truth about how the royals lorded it up in luxury while the ordinary people starved, there'd soon be a move to get rid of them. He was especially angry about how thousands were dying from the bombing here in the East End while the royals were safe and sound in Buckingham Palace and Windsor Castle. He put a petition in his butcher's shop asking people to sign it to get more and better air raid shelters for Whitechapel and Stepney. Loads of people signed it. He had a lot of support.'

'So Fred asked you to poke around in the King's rooms?'

'I only had the bedroom to do. Someone else did the living area.'

'And you found something.'

She nodded. 'Fred had said anything that had handwriting on it would be good. Anyway, I opened the drawer of the bedside table, and there was the little piece of paper with handwriting on it. I knew the King had written it because I'd seen his writing on other things. It didn't look important; it was more of a note than anything else.'

'Did you read it?'

'Not as such. I read the opening words, then didn't bother with the rest. It didn't look that important, nothing secret or important as such, but I thought it would keep Fred happy.'

'You didn't think the King would notice it had gone?'

'No. I didn't think about it. I knew the King and Queen were going to be at Windsor that night. They often went to Windsor to spend time with the two princesses, Elizabeth and Margaret. So I didn't think the King would notice it had gone, and if he did he wouldn't know it was me who'd taken it.'

'So how did Bothwell know you'd taken it?'

'He'd seen me leave the room and then gone in to check something. There was a pair of cufflinks in the drawer on top of the piece of paper; he may have gone to get them. If he knew the cufflinks were in the drawer, he'd have seen the piece of paper they were on, and that it was now gone.'

'Did he come looking for you?'

'He may have done, but I'd left. My shift ended after I'd done the King's bedroom, and I wanted to get that piece of paper to Fred as soon as I could. I didn't want it on me.'

'So you took it to Fred?'

'I did.'

'Was Billy there?'

'No, he was out delivering. So I gave the piece of paper to Fred and then went home.'

'I assume Bernard Bothwell confronted you about the piece of paper,' said Coburg.

There was a pause, then she said, 'Yes,' lowering her eyes from their gaze.

'When was that?'

'The following morning.'

'What day was that?'

'Friday. He was waiting for me when I arrived at the palace to start work. He told me he'd seen me leave the King's room the day before, and he knew I must have taken the piece of paper from the bedside table because it had been there earlier. It was because of the cufflinks. He was checking on them and he saw the paper had gone, and had seen me leaving.'

'What did you say?'

She hung her head. 'I lied. I said it wasn't me. Then he said he didn't want to get me in trouble, but if I didn't tell him what I'd done with it he'd have to report it. He said he was giving me a chance. Tell him what I'd done with it and he'd do his best to get it back. If he couldn't, he'd have to report it.'

'Well, I was stuck. I daren't lose the job, I need the money. And Mr Bothwell said I'd most likely go to prison, but he wanted to save me from that.'

'So you told him.'

She nodded. 'He knew where Billy's butcher shop was because he used to live in Whitechapel. I told him I'd given it to Billy's son, Fred.'

'And then?'

'I guess he went off to Whitechapel to get hold of it.'

'Have you spoken to Fred or Billy since?'

'No. I wanted to stay out of it.'

'Even when you heard that Mr Bothwell had been killed and his body found in Shadwell Basin?'

'No, that made me even more not want to get in touch with them.'

'And they haven't contacted you?'

'No.'

'Even though you only live a few streets apart?'

'I suppose they're staying away from me for the same reason I am from them. A bloke's died.'

'Miss Chalk, it is my duty to remand you in custody on a charge of theft of property from Buckingham Palace,' said Coburg in formal tones,

'It was only a bit of paper!' she burst out, agonised.

Edward Crosby sat in the tower room and weighed up his situation. There was no way he could escape from this. Only two people had been recorded as having escaped from being imprisoned in the Tower of London, and both of them had been in the eighteenth century. No one had managed to break out of the tower in modern times.

Crosby had been imprisoned before, both times in Latin America, where a bribe had been sufficient to obtain his freedom. That wouldn't be the case here. No, if he was to get out of here, it meant doing a deal with the MI5 man, Inspector Hibbert. But to do a deal meant Crosby had to have something of value to offer, and right now he couldn't think of anything he could offer MI5 that they didn't already have.

It was time for some serious thinking, and planning. He knew he was good at deal-making. It was how he'd got the job with the *Reporter*. It was a skill he'd developed at Harrow. It depended on two things: finding out what someone else wanted, or what their weak spot was.

What did Hibbert want from him? Or . . . what was the inspector's weak spot?

CHAPTER THIRTY-ONE

With Maud Chalk in the custody section at Scotland Yard, Coburg left Hibbert to wait for him in reception while he went to his office to find Sergeant Lampson.

'Inspector Hibbert and I are going to Whitechapel to make a couple of arrests in the Bernard Bothwell murder,' he told Lampson. 'I'd like you with us in case we need more people.'

'Maud Chalk gave someone up?' asked Lampson, getting to his feet and taking his coat from the hook.

'Her brother and her nephew,' said Coburg.

The three men made for Whitechapel, Lampson driving. They picked up Sergeant Harker at the police station and told him about Maud Chalk being remanded in custody. 'We're now going to arrest Billy and Fred Chalk on suspicion of the murder of Bernard Bothwell. We'd like you to accompany us as you know the two men, and we'd appreciate you bringing some of your own men with us in case they prove difficult.'

'You really think it was them?' asked Harker.

'All the evidence points to it,' said Coburg.

They drove to the butcher's shop in a procession of two cars. The shop was empty of customers, with just a middle-aged man working in the shop, cutting up meat, who looked at them in surprise as Coburg and Hibbert walked in, accompanied by

Sergeant Harker. Lampson had been asked to wait in the car, ready for action if called on.

'William Chalk?' asked Coburg.

Chalk looked at him suspiciously, then at the unhappy Harker. 'What's going on, Joe?'

'I'll let them tell you,' said Harker. 'They're Detective Chief Inspector Coburg from Scotland Yard and Inspector Hibbert from MI5.'

Coburg took his warrant card and showed it to the butcher. Hibbert remained unmoving, watching.

'MI5?' demanded Chalk in astonishment. 'What's this about?'

'William Chalk, I am arresting you on suspicion of being involved in the murder of Bernard Bothwell.'

Chalk stared at him, stunned, then burst out, 'You're mad!'

Coburg produced a pair of handcuffs. 'Regulations say we have to handcuff you for the car journey to Scotland Yard.'

'You're not taking me away in no handcuffs!' said Chalk angrily, and he snatched up a large knife.

'Is that how it happened, Mr Chalk?' asked Coburg calmly. 'You lost your temper and stabbed him?'

Chalk hesitated, then scowled and put the knife down on the counter. He held out his hands towards them. 'Go on, then. Handcuff me. It won't be the first time the fascist police have taken some poor innocent working man away in irons.'

Coburg pulled Chalk's hands behind him, then slid the handcuffs on his wrists and snapped them shut.

'Where's your son, Mr Chalk? Where's Fred?' Coburg asked.

Chalk looked at him defiantly. 'What do you want Fred for? He hasn't done anything.'

256

'I asked you where he was.'

'He's out with the van, doing deliveries.'

'In that case, Sergeant Harker, will you wait here with Inspector Hibbert for him to return? DS Lampson and I will escort Mr Chalk senior to Scotland Yard. Perhaps you'll join us there when you've put Fred Chalk under caution. Sergeant Harker will provide an escort to accompany you on the journey. Will that be alright, Sergeant?'

'I've got a constable outside the shop, sir,' said Harker. 'He'll go with Inspector Hibbert and Fred.'

'You've got no right to bring Fred in,' protested Chalk. 'He hasn't done anything.'

'And you have?' asked Coburg.

Chalk glared at him. 'I'm saying nothing more until I've got a solicitor present. And one of our own. Not one of your corrupt lot.'

'If you give me his name, we'll contact him,' said Coburg.

'No,' said Chalk. 'I'll talk to him. I'm allowed a phone call. I'll call him when we get to Scotland Yard.'

At the forensic laboratory at Curtis Green, Arnold Ridley was making a telephone call to Scotland Yard. After identifying himself to the switchboard operator, he asked to be put through to DCI Saxe-Coburg. There was a pause full of clicks as the operator tried to connect the call, then she reported, 'I'm afraid there's no one in his office at the moment.'

'In that case, could I leave a message for him? It's quite important. Would you tell him we've examined the fountain pen he left with us, and have found an inscription carved on it. The initials W and D, and a date: 21st June 1939. Offer my apologies for the delay in reporting this, but we had to have it thoroughly cleaned first.'

In the Maida Vale studios, a kind of calm prevailed. The anarchy of the Crazy Gang had subsided temporarily, the comedians heading to the canteen to grab a cup of tea and a bun. Now Rosa and Eric were on stage with Vera Lynn as she sang 'We'll Meet Again'.

As she listened to Lynn sing, Rosa was filled with admiration for her. She must have sung 'We'll Meet Again' hundreds, if not thousands of times since it came out as a record in 1939, but even after all that time she sang the song with such care and artistry as if singing it for the first time.

Lynn was only just twenty-four years old but in her relatively short life she'd had an astonishing career. Born in East Ham, the daughter of a plumber and a dressmaker, she'd nearly died from diphtheritic croup when she was just two years old. But just five years later, at the age of seven, she began singing in public, and by the time she was eleven she'd joined a juvenile troupe called Madame Harris's Kracker Kabaret Kids. By 1933 she'd joined Billy Cotton and his band as vocalist, then Joe Loss, and recorded her first record with Howard Baker. She'd then joined Bert Ambrose. Each time she'd been invited to join a really top band as their vocalist, and finally in 1940 she turned solo, and was now, without doubt, the country's most popular singer. And here she was, singing with just Rosa and Eric as her accompaniment.

When she finished, she smiled happily at Rosa and Eric. 'That was wonderful,' she said.

'Not too thin for you?' asked Rosa. 'It must be so different from the backing of a full orchestra.'

'It is,' said Lynn, 'but it allows me to try out new phrasings, holding a note a different way, without worrying that it'll throw the band and their arrangement. I think it's because you, Rosa, and Eric, are both jazz musicians and used to working with people who improvise, so you sometimes have to improvise too. All I know is, it's a real pleasure working with you both.' She smiled. 'I must admit, when I heard about your drummer, I was a bit worried. But now, I think it's worked out even better.'

'I agree,' said John Fawcett, appearing from the back of the theatre and joining them on stage. 'It sounded absolutely perfect. Well done. I also want to thank you, Vera, for coping with the antics of the Crazy Gang. They can be a bit wearing.'

'Not for me.' Lynn chuckled. 'I love them. And they have such good hearts. Honestly, John, this show is a pleasure for me. I'm so glad you asked me to appear.'

So am I, thought Rosa. For a show to become a series it had to have that extra quality that made the audience at home want more, and Vera Lynn and the Crazy Gang certainly gave it that. Which raised the question: if it did become a series, how could they follow this?

Rosa looked at John Fawcett, who was talking to Eric, suggesting a solo bass run in between numbers, to which Eric nodded. *If it happens, we've got the right producer*, she decided. *Fingers crossed the audience like it.*

At Scotland Yard, Coburg and Lampson escorted Billy Chalk up to their office. Once there, Coburg unlocked Chalk's handcuffs, then pointed to the phone.

'If you give me the name and number of your solicitor, I'll get him on the phone for you.'

'Why can't I call him myself?'

'Because all calls go through the police operator,' said Coburg. 'They'll only take instructions from official personnel. What's your solicitor's name?'

'Felix Ford.'

'And his telephone number?'

Chalk opened his wallet and took out a dog-eared sheet of paper, which he unfolded.

'Got a pencil?' he asked.

Lampson pushed a piece of paper and a pencil towards him, and Chalk copied a number down from his sheet of paper before putting it back in his wallet.

'There's the number,' he said. 'It's the office of the Whitechapel Communist Party.' He gave a smirk. 'I'm surprised you haven't got it already. You lot are always following us about!'

'I hate to disappoint you, Mr Chalk, but frankly we're too busy solving crimes to bother about keeping a watch on you and your pals. Like, for example, the murder of Bernard Bothwell. A working man, like yourself. I'm sure you approve of us investigating his death.'

'Working man!' scoffed Chalk. 'Dressing the King? Call that a job?'

Coburg didn't react; instead he picked up the receiver and gave the operator the telephone number Chalk had given him. When the telephone was answered by a woman, he said, 'This is Detective Chief Inspector Coburg at Scotland Yard. Is Mr Felix Ford there? I have a William Chalk who wishes to talk to him.' He listened, then said, 'Yes, it is urgent.' He turned to Chalk and Lampson and told them, 'She's gone to look for him.'

'That won't take her long; it's only a small office with a

handful of people working there. Not like this place, with Lord knows how many hundreds of people you've got here. All at the taxpayer's expense. If he's not there, leave a message. I don't want anyone else except Felix Ford looking after me.'

Coburg listened as a man's voice said, 'Felix Ford here.'

'Mr Ford, my name is Detective Chief Inspector Coburg at Scotland Yard. I have a William Chalk who wishes to talk to you. If you hang on I'll bring him to the phone.'

He handed the receiver to Chalk, who said, 'Felix? Billy Chalk. I've been arrested on a charge of murder. They claim I killed a man. I'm at Scotland Yard. I need you here urgent.' He handed the receiver back to Coburg and told him, 'He's on his way.'

'In that case we'll take you to the detention rooms until he arrives.'

'Lock me in a cell?' said Chalk aggressively.

'Call it what you like. Detention room. Cell. But it's where you'll be when he arrives. After all, we don't want you thinking we're not going to be fair with you and subject you to pressure without your solicitor being present.' He turned to Lampson. 'Will you take Mr Chalk to the detention rooms, Sergeant?'

Inside the cell at Whitechapel police station, Bazzer Jenkinson sat with the three remaining members of his gang, Tommy Duggan, Arnold Kemp and Shug Pirie. The boys had all been in a state of shock when they learnt that Jerry Trump had been murdered. 'Why?' had been the plaintive question repeated by Duggan, Kemp and Pirie, each time directed at Jenkinson. But Jenkinson had remained silent.

The truth was, he was as bewildered as the others, but he

didn't show it. His role as leader of the gang meant he never admitted he didn't know. He was supposed to be the fount of all knowledge.

A uniformed officer appeared bearing a tray with four cups on it, which he passed through the bars of the cell to the boys.

'When are you gonna let us out?' demanded Shug Pirie. 'You can't keep us here.'

'We can,' said the constable. 'You're charged with attempted murder. Anyway, you sure you want to be let out? The last one of you lot we let out got killed. I'm guessing that someone out there is after bumping you all off, for some reason.' He grinned at them. 'If that's the case, you're safer in here.'

The constable left. The boys looked at one another in alarm, then Kemp turned to Jenkinson. 'Did you hear that? They reckon someone's after killing us. First Jerry, then the rest of us. Why, Bazzer? Who'd want to kill us?'

Jenkinson said nothing at first. The fact was, he didn't understand what was going on. Then he said derisively, 'That's rubbish. No one's after killing us.'

'Then why won't they let us go?' asked Pirie nervously.

'It's about those two blokes we done,' said Duggan.

'The Nazi spies?' said Pirie.

Duggan shook his head. 'I don't reckon they was Nazi spies. They were some sort of undercover people. Like Special Branch or MI5. This is the government getting its own back on us for doing them over.'

'Shut up!' snarled Jenkinson suddenly. 'You don't know what you're talking about!'

'Then why was Jerry killed?' asked Duggan.

'Who knows?' retorted Jenkinson defiantly. He glared

forcefully at them. 'Nothing's changed. We still don't say anything. Got that?'

There was silence from the other three, doubts in their faces, and Jenkinson repeated it even harder: 'Got that?'

'Got it, Bazzer,' said Pirie.

And the others nodded in agreement.

Fred Chalk pulled up in the van outside the butcher's shop. As he got out of it, Joe Harker came out of the shop accompanied by a short, stocky, middle-aged man who had officialdom written all over him. Fred looked at the pair suspiciously, and asked, 'What's going on, Joe?'

'This gentleman is Inspector Hibbert from MI5.'

'MI5? What do MI5 want with me? And where's my dad?'

'He's in custody,' said Harker. 'He's been taken to Scotland Yard.'

'Where I'm taking you,' said Hibbert. 'Frederick Chalk, I am arresting you on suspicion of conspiracy to murder Bernard Bothwell.' He produced a pair of handcuffs. 'I need to put these on you. I would advise you not to struggle or it will make things worse for you, with a charge of resisting arrest.'

'How's my dad?' asked Fred urgently.

'You'll see him soon, you can ask him,' said Hibbert. He held out the handcuffs. 'Hands behind your back, please.'

CHAPTER THIRTY-TWO

There was a knock at Coburg's office door, then a uniformed constable appeared with a slip of paper.

'A message for you, Chief Inspector, from Mr Ridley at Curtis Green.'

'Thank you, Constable,' said Coburg.

He read it. So, the fountain pen had been engraved with an inscription. *W. D. 21st June 1939.* W. D.? Wesley Dixon had fallen in the alcove in the tunnels when he interrupted the killer at work. Coburg looked again at the inscription. Often, an inscription was engraved on a present for a special occasion. A twenty-first birthday, for example.

He picked up the telephone and asked to be connected to Whitechapel police station. Sergeant Harker answered it.

'Sergeant Harker, can you do me a favour? Can you look up Wesley Dixon's details and let me know his date of birth?'

'Certainly. If you'll hang on a second.'

Coburg heard the sound of papers being flicked over at the other end, then Harker said '3rd May, 1919.'

Not Wesley Dixon, then. A thought struck him.

'How much older than Wesley was his brother, William?'

'A year,' said Harker.

'So William was born in 1918?'

'That's right.'

'You don't happen to know the date?'

'Actually, I do, only because Agatha was always talking about it. She used to call him her Midsummer's Day baby.'

Midsummer. '21st June?'

'That's it,' said Harker.

'Thank you, Sergeant,' said Coburg.

'Not at all,' said Harker. Then, curious, he asked, 'Anything to concern us here?'

'I don't think so. When I examined the scene after PC Dixon was stabbed, I found a fountain pen. It was covered with blood and muck. I've just got a report back on it from forensics. They found it was engraved "W. D. 21st June 1939". It sounds to me like it might have been a twenty-first birthday present for William.'

'Which he passed on to Wesley,' said Harker. 'Sounds likely. And Wesley dropped it when he was trying to get hold of the killer.'

'That's how I see it,' said Coburg.

After he hung up, he thought *That's one way of looking at it. Or there is another.*

Coburg and Lampson sat looking at Billy Chalk, who sat facing them from the other side of the bare wooden table in one of the interview rooms in the basement of Scotland Yard. Two uniformed officers were standing just behind Chalk's chair in case the butcher tried anything violent, but Chalk just sat and regarded the two detectives placidly. The handcuffs had been taken off him. Lampson had a large notepad open in front of him and held a pencil, taking notes. Chalk's solicitor, Felix

Ford, sat next to the butcher. Ford had already protested about this interview taking place and had told Chalk in front of the detectives not to make any statements or answer any questions, but Chalk had ignored this advice.

'All I want you here for is to see that proper justice is done,' Chalk had told Ford when the solicitor arrived in the room. 'That no one beats a false confession out of me.'

'We don't do that,' said Coburg calmly.

'You may not, but plenty of coppers do,' retorted Chalk.

With that, the questioning had begun.

'Bernard Bothwell,' said Coburg.

'What about him?' asked Chalk.

'He came to your shop to recover a piece of paper that your sister, Maud, had taken from Buckingham Palace. He came looking for your son, Fred.'

'Fred wasn't there,' said Chalk. 'I was.'

'How did Bothwell die?' asked Coburg.

'I killed him,' said Chalk. 'It was an accident. He came in and started to get violent, attacked me. I was holding a knife and I held it out to try and warn him off. He fell on it.'

'Once again, I must caution my client against saying anything else,' said Ford, tight-lipped with anger.

Coburg ignored him and asked Chalk, 'How did you get Bothwell's body to Shadwell Basin?'

'In the van.'

'With your son's help?'

Chalk shook his head. 'No. I did it on my own.'

'Lugging a dead body around is heavy work for one man.'

'Not for me. I can carry pigs, sheep, anything like that.'

'Again, I must protest, Chief Inspector,' interjected Ford. 'You are harassing my client.'

'He is perfectly within his right to refuse to answer questions,' Coburg told the solicitor. 'You've already advised him of that. If he chooses to ignore your advice, that's his prerogative.' He then turned back to Chalk and asked, 'Where does Fred fit in?'

'He doesn't. He wasn't there when it happened. He came back to the shop while I was out dumping Bothwell's body.'

'Did he ask where you'd been?'

'I said I'd been making deliveries.'

'Where had Fred been?'

'I don't know,' said Chalk. 'I didn't ask him.'

There was a knock at the door of the interview room, then it opened and Inspector Hibbert walked in.

'Sorry to interrupt, Chief Inspector,' he apologised, 'but I've got Fred Chalk next door.'

'He had nothing to do with this!' exclaimed Chalk, starting to rise from his chair, before the two uniformed officers hurried to him and pushed him back down.

'The thing is, he says he doesn't have a solicitor,' said Hibbert. 'So I'll need to get one of ours in.'

'No,' said Chalk firmly. He turned to Felix Ford. 'This is your job. Go and take care of Fred.'

'But I'm here defending you,' protested Ford.

'Against what?' asked Chalk. 'I've already told them I did it.' He looked at Coburg. 'If I need a solicitor to make this legal, you get one of your public defenders in for me. Though I can't see the point as I've already said I did it.'

'We need to know why, and lots more,' said Coburg.

'Then ask me and I'll tell you. But Ford here goes to look after Fred.'

Coburg nodded. 'In that case, Mr Chalk, we'll have you taken to a cell while we arrange for a duty solicitor to come in to represent you.' He looked at Hibbert. 'This is Mr Felix Ford, Inspector. He is to be the solicitor for Fred Chalk.' He looked at Ford. 'I assume you agree to represent him?'

Felix Ford stood up and packed his notepad and pen away in his briefcase.

'I do,' he said. To Chalk, he said, 'I'll see you later, Billy. But you're talking yourself into a hangman's noose.'

'I know what I'm doing. Take care of Fred!' Chalk called after the solicitor as he walked towards Hibbert. 'He's innocent! Tell him not to say anything!'

Inspector Hibbert leant on the wooden table and studied Fred Chalk's face. Felix Ford had taken his place beside his client and had issued the same warning to Fred that he'd given Billy: make no statements, and when asked questions, to reply each time, *No comment*. He soon discovered that his exhortations had as little effect on Fred Chalk as they'd had on his father. Even before Hibbert had begun his questions, Fred Chalk said, 'I killed Bernard Bothwell.'

'For God's sake, didn't you hear what I said!' burst out Ford in disgust at his client.

'Why?' asked Hibbert.

'He was threatening me.'

'About what?'

'That's neither here nor there,' said Fred.

'We have reason to believe that Mr Bothwell had gone to

the shop to demand the return of a piece of paper that your aunt, Maud Chalk, had taken from Buckingham Palace.'

'What piece of paper?' demanded Ford.

Chalk ignored Ford and looked firmly at Hibbert. 'If you know that, you know why he was there and threatening me.'

'You admit you had that piece of paper?' asked Hibbert.

'I'm admitting nothing,' said Fred.

'At last!' exclaimed a grateful Ford.

'Except that I killed him. It was an accident, not murder. He attacked me and I held out the knife I was holding to warn him off, and he stumbled and fell on it.'

'Where was your father when this happened?'

'My father? He was out.'

'Where?'

'I suppose he was doing deliveries. You'll have to ask him.'

'How did you get the body to Shadwell Basin?'

'In the van.'

'But if your father had the van for doing deliveries, that must mean he helped you.'

Fred scowled. 'Dad had nothing to do with it. He wasn't there.'

'Where was he?'

'I've no idea. Like I said, you'll have to ask him. Maybe he was with a fancy woman.'

'Has he got a fancy woman?'

Fred scowled again, then said, 'I've told you what happened. I killed Bothwell, but accidentally. That's all I'm going to say.'

Afterwards, Coburg and Hibbert got together.

'So, their stories are the same. Except, according to Billy, he was in the shop on his own when Bothwell arrived and he stabbed him while defending himself. And according to Fred, *he* was the one in the shop when Bothwell arrived. Both of them claim they were on their own when it happened, and each of them claims he was the one who took Bothwell's body to Shadwell Basin in the van and dumped it.'

'So the dad's protecting the son and the son's protecting his father,' groaned Hibbert. 'A clever ploy. My guess is they did it together, but if they both plead it was them on his own and not the other, the prosecution will have a hard time persuading a jury which of them did it.'

'Then it's down to us to find evidence on which of them was actually at the shop on that particular Friday,' said Coburg. 'If it was both of them, then we can prove conspiracy to murder. If it's alright with you, I suggest you leave this to us for the moment. I'll have a word with Inspector Harker and get his men to talk to the people in Whitechapel and find out if any of them went to Chalk's butcher's on that Friday, and if so, who was in the shop: Billy or Fred.'

'So what will we do?'

'We remand them both in custody, but locked in separate cells so they can't confer. We tell their solicitors we're gathering further evidence, and we'll recall them when the time is right for us to resume questioning the suspects. I'll be in touch as soon as we've got more evidence.' He looked at his watch. 'But right now I have to go to Maida Vale.'

'Maida Vale?' said Hibbert. 'What's there?'

'Rosa's doing a live broadcast from the BBC theatre,' said Coburg. 'Along with Vera Lynn. I promised her I'd be there for it.'

CHAPTER THIRTY-THREE

Coburg had given his seat at the Maida Vale theatre to Malcolm and gone to stand at the back, beside the large window looking into the production booth where the producer and engineer and the producer's assistant sat. A uniformed commissionaire had come up to him and told him he wasn't allowed to stand there, at which Coburg had shown his warrant card and told the man that he was there on official business, sent by Scotland Yard to act as security. 'But I'm undercover,' Coburg had added, 'so we don't want to make a big thing about it.'

The audience was full, and Magnus, to his delight, had been provided with a seat in the front row.

The plush red curtains concealing the stage were closed and the short dapper figure of the producer, John Fawcett, stepped through the gap between them onto the apron of the stage to address the audience.

'Good evening, ladies and gentlemen,' he declared. 'My name is John Fawcett and I am the producer of this brand new show for the BBC, *Rosa Weeks Presents*. Each week Rosa Weeks will introduce her special guests, and this evening her guests are very special indeed, and shortly I will be bringing them onto this stage. We will have the first lady of song, the nation's very own favourite, Vera Lynn.'

On cue, the elegant figure of Vera Lynn appeared from behind the curtains and joined John Fawcett, giving a curtsey followed by a graceful bow, at which the audience broke into hugely enthusiastic applause, which Fawcett let run for a few moments, before Vera waved at the audience then disappeared behind the curtains. 'Vera will be joining us later.' Fawcett beamed, and waved his hands gently to calm the continuing applause down. 'We have also advertised our other guests as that immensely popular duo, Bud Flanagan and Chesney Allen.'

At this the spontaneous applause was even louder, with one or two cheers being heard.

'However,' said Fawcett, and at this ominous word that usually prefaced some bad news there were distinct murmurings from the audience. 'However,' the producer repeated, with a bright smile, 'we have one or two extra even more special guests. The reason for this is because, sadly, Bud has been struck down with a serious throat infection, which means he's lost his voice.' At this there was an outcry of disappointment, which the producer moved swiftly to quell. 'But that won't stop him appearing.' This caused a burst of relieved reactions, and a round of applause. 'For your entertainment Bud will be appearing with Chesney, and to add vocals to the performance there will be a few old friends.'

At this the curtains were suddenly drawn, and there on stage were Bud Flanagan and Chesney Allen, along with the rest of the Crazy Gang: Jimmy Nervo, Teddy Knox, Charlie Naughton, Jimmy Gold and 'Monsewer' Eddie Gray. The audience went wild, getting to their feet and clapping madly, as well as whistling and cheering.

'Don't overdo it, moi old cockers!' Gray grinned. 'We might not be that good.'

'Yes you will be!' shouted a man in the audience, and this was greeted with more cheers.

Fawcett gave the line of comedians a thumbs up, and they departed from the stage, waving and blowing kisses at the audience.

'Those are our guests,' said Fawcett. 'Now let me introduce you to your host for the evening . . . ladies and gentlemen: Rosa Weeks!'

To the sound of loud applause, Rosa walked on and went to the microphone at the front of the stage, giving a curtsey and a bow, just as Vera Lynn had done.

'Ladies and gentlemen,' she addressed them, smiling. 'Tonight we will be conducting a little musical experiment. All the guests have agreed for us to present the musical accompaniment as a small jazz club duo, with myself on piano and the brilliant Eric Pickup on bass.' Rosa gestured towards the side of the stage, and Eric walked on, smiled and bowed to the audience, then walked to where his double bass was propped on its stand waiting for him. In her turn Rosa walked to the piano, sat down on the stool and ran her fingers over the keys, while Eric echoed the sound of the piano with a walking bass for a few bars, before bringing it to a smooth finish.

John Fawcett stepped towards the microphone. 'There, ladies and gentlemen, you have our personnel for this evening's show, with the exception of possibly the most important ingredient: you, yourselves. The audience. In a few moments the red light will go on, which signifies that we will be broadcasting live, to the nation. And this is where you are one of the most important aspects of this evening. Your participation, your appreciation of the performers, your applause. Without that, the listeners at home won't feel they are listening to a live show, one in which it is up to you to convey the feeling that you are having *fun*.' He looked expectantly out at the audience. 'Are you? Are you having fun?'

'Yes,' came a few calls. Fawcett shook his head.

'It doesn't sound like it to me,' he sighed. 'The people at home will think there's no one here. I need you to *sound* as if you are having fun. Let's try some applause. That's what the listeners at home want to hear.' And he began to slap his hands together, urging the audience to join in, gradually increasing the rate of slapping his hands together, exhorting the audience to increase their pace as well, until the whole theatre echoed to the sound of clapping and a few whistles and cheers.

'Excellent!' Fawcett beamed, gesturing for the clapping to end. 'That's the sound we want to hear from you. Remember, these are hard times; it's you and our guests tonight who are needed by people to brighten things up. Your country needs you!'

Then he pointed at the side of the stage where a red light bulb on a stand had just come alight. Fawcett then pointed to Rosa at her piano, who leant in to her microphone and said, 'Good evening, listeners. I'm Rosa Weeks and this is *Rosa Weeks Presents*. In tonight's show you'll be hearing from my special guests, Vera Lynn, and Flanagan and Allen, along with some very special surprise guests. I hope you enjoy the show.' With that, Rosa played the opening bars of 'Up A Lazy River' while Eric joined in with his virtuoso bass playing. As they played, John Fawcett mimed clapping his hands, and the audience responded, the sound of applause filling the theatre. As Fawcett gestured for the audience's applause to fade down, Rosa began to sing, and the show was under way.

To say the show had been a success was an understatement; that was the view expressed as Coburg and Rosa drove Magnus and Malcolm back to their flat. Magnus, especially, continued his delighted memories of the evening as they entered the flat for a farewell celebratory drink.

'That was one of the best entertainments I've ever seen,' enthused Magnus. 'You were wonderful, Rosa. And whatever gave you the idea for just you and a bass player playing the music? It was inspired! Brilliant! And to actually see the Crazy Gang up close!' He turned to Malcolm. 'Come on, Malcolm, even you have to agree they were really good.'

'They were better because they were controlled,' said Malcolm. 'They weren't allowed to run riot like they usually do.'

'They ran riot enough for me,' admitted Rosa. 'I wasn't sure what they were going to do next. But luckily, they kept to the songs.'

'I hadn't realised that Bud Flanagan could play the drums,' said Magnus. 'What a pity he only played them on "Underneath the Arches".'

'That was because he knows the number inside out, as he wrote it,' explained Rosa. 'The other numbers he'd have been less familiar with, as far as putting in the drum parts.'

'I liked Eddie Gray.' Coburg chuckled. 'That fake French cockney stuff he does always make me laugh.' And he mimicked the comedian, breaking into '*Je got 'ere un packet de cards, cinquant deux in numero!* And the other three laughed joyfully at the memory Coburg's mimicry invoked.

After they'd dropped Magnus and Malcolm at their flat, as Coburg and Rosa drove home, Coburg commented, 'Echoing what Magnus said, the performances tonight were inspired. Everyone worked so well together. Even Vera Lynn joined in with the Crazy Gang and seemed to enjoy herself.'

'Much of it was down to the producer, John Fawcett. He really is a remarkable professional. He's also a classically trained pianist, so he has a deep understanding of music, as well as appealing to an audience.'

'You didn't tell Magnus and Malcolm the real reason it was just you and a bass player,' said Coburg. 'I'm guessing your drummer fell off the wagon in the end.'

'Sadly, yes,' said Rosa. 'He arrived in the studio absolutely out of it. But that's just between us. I'm not going to tell tales about him. The accepted protocol is, whatever happens backstage stays between the performers. Poor Wally will be in a bad enough state without the story sneaking into the press.'

CHAPTER THIRTY-FOUR

Wednesday 9th April

The following morning, the magic of show business had faded, and once more Rosa was in the ambulance with Doris, heading for an address to pick up someone with a broken leg to take them to Paddington General Hospital.

'I listened to your show yesterday,' said Doris.

'I'm not sure if it can be called my show, with all the guests on it.'

'It's called *Rosa Weeks Presents*, so it must be your show. Anyway, I thought it was brilliant. That business with the Crazy Gang! Wonderful! How did you manage to get them on it?'

'That was down to Bud Flanagan. He'd got laryngitis and couldn't sing, so his friends turned up to help out.'

'Well, it was a smash. And so was Vera Lynn. What's she like? Is she as nice as she sounds?'

'In person, she's even nicer. Not starry at all. It was so lovely working with her; she made it so easy for me.'

'Well, I thought it was fantastic. Who have you got on next?'

'I'm not even sure if there'll be a next one,' said Rosa with a slightly wistful sigh. 'That was what they call a pilot show, to see how it works, before they commit to more.'

'Well, they'll be mad if they just leave it at that,' said Doris. 'Like I say, I thought it was brilliant!'

In the police car on their way to Whitechapel, Coburg was hearing similar sentiments from Lampson as he drove.

'Eve and I listened to Rosa's show last night on the wireless. Absolutely fantastic! And my mum popped round this morning to pass on the same. She and my dad listened to it. We all think Rosa's got a winner there.'

'I think so, too,' agreed Coburg. 'Considering the problems they had on the night, she did a remarkable job.'

'What problems?' asked Lampson, intrigued.

Coburg just stopped himself in time from telling his sergeant about the alcoholic drummer. Instead he said, 'Bud Flanagan caught laryngitis, so he couldn't sing. That's why the Crazy Gang stepped in at the last minute.'

'Which turned out to be even better,' enthused Lampson. 'I love "Monsewer" Eddie Gray. The way he pretends he's speaking French and completely mangles it! Brilliant!'

Coburg got a similarly enthusiastic reaction from Sergeant Harker when they arrived at Whitechapel police station.

'Heard your missus's show last night, Chief Inspector.' He beamed. 'That's what the country needs at this moment to cheer people up. And, I've got to say, she sure can play that piano. Tell her that from me.'

'I will indeed,' said Coburg. 'She'll be most flattered, I know. But right now we have the problems of the Chalks, father and son.'

'Both of them insisting that they alone killed Bernard

Bothwell and the other had nothing to do with it.'

'Exactly,' said Coburg. 'Now, we could just charge them both with murder, because it's possible they both could have been in the shop at the time Bothwell was killed. But it's equally possible that there was just the one of them, and it wouldn't sit easy on my conscience if an innocent man hung for a crime he didn't commit.'

'Even though he wants to?' said Harker.

'If that's the case, one of them is just doing it to save the real culprit,' said Coburg. 'And I'd really like to establish which of them it was.'

'It could have been both of them,' said Harker.

'It could, but I'd like to look into it,' said Coburg. 'Bothwell left home in Pimlico at six o'clock. He'd have got to the palace by seven and sought out Maud Chalk. He'd have then left for Whitechapel, again using buses, arriving at about eight o'clock or thereabouts. So we need to know if both Chalks, father and son, were in the shop at eight in the morning until, say, ten o'clock, or just one of them. If only one, which one?'

Harker nodded. 'I'll have a word with the men who were on patrol in that area that Friday morning and see if any of them know which of the Chalks was in the shop.'

'Thanks,' said Coburg. 'Ted and I are on our way to the power station to have another word with the man who found Bothwell's body.'

'Desmond Downs.'

'That's him. I'm hoping he might have seen something he didn't report before.'

They drove to the power station, where they found Downs lounging around outside with other workers on a cigarette break. Coburg hailed Downs over and the man reluctantly climbed into the rear of the police car, while his work colleagues looked on with unabashed interest.

'I don't like this,' Downs complained. 'They'll think I'm being arrested.'

'You can tell them you're not,' said Coburg. 'And this way it means no one can hear what we say. I'm sure you'd prefer that.'

'It depends on what you're going to say,' said Downs warily.

'Just a few questions,' said Coburg. 'You said you go fishing when it's your day off.'

'Yes,' said Downs.

'You were at Shadwell Basin last Friday, so is Friday usually your day off?'

'Yes,' said Downs.

'So you were there the Friday before?'

'Yes,' said Downs.

God, thought Coburg, *this is like pulling teeth*.

'What time did you get to Shadwell Basin on the Friday before?'

Downs looked thoughtful. 'It must have been about quarter to ten in the morning.'

'Did you notice a van parked near there, near the water?'

Downs thought it over, dredging up his memory, then finally said, 'I did, now you come to mention it.'

'Did it have a name on it? Most shops and firms do.'

'Yes. I can't remember the name, but I do remember it said *Best Butcher in Whitechapel*.'

'Did you see anyone with the van?'

'Yes. Two blokes. One old, one young. When I got there they were just getting into the van and they drove off. I remember that because I was glad to see them go. When you're fishing you don't want people hanging about, starting car engines and things. It disturbs the fish.'

Coburg nodded in appreciation. 'Thank you, Mr Downs. Hopefully we won't need to trouble you again.'

As they headed back to Whitechapel, Coburg said, 'So Billy and Fred dumped the body together.'

'But did they kill him together?' asked Lampson.

'Either that, or one killed him and the other one turned up and realised what had happened.'

'So which one did what?'

'To get the answer to that, it's back to Whitechapel to find out which one made the deliveries on that Friday morning.'

When they got back to Whitechapel, they found that Sergeant Harker had already got some reports from his men about that Friday morning. The trouble was there were conflicting reports: some witnesses saying that Fred was in the shop, others it was Billy. Four people had said that when they went to the shop between nine o'clock and ten, it was closed, with a sign on the door saying *Back shortly*.

'Who usually does the deliveries?' asked Coburg.

'Billy,' said Harker. 'But if something comes up that prevents him, then Fred does.'

'But no one's certain who did the deliveries on that Friday?' asked Coburg.

'No,' replied Harker ruefully.

'Then let's try and bluff it out and see what we get,' said Coburg.

CHAPTER THIRTY- FIVE

Having delivered their patient to the hospital, Rosa and Doris arrived back at Paddington ambulance station and found Chesney Warren waiting for them.

'Rosa, there was a telephone call for you,' said Warren.

'Oh?'

'Yes. A John Fawcett from the BBC. He was the producer of your show last night, wasn't he?'

'He was.'

'My wife and I listened to it. It was wonderful! I felt so proud, knowing I worked with you! I was thinking of contacting head office and getting them to put a piece about it in the *St John Ambulance Newsletter*, about the fact that you are a radio star, and you drive an ambulance for us. Would you mind?'

'Not at all,' said Rosa. 'Did Mr Fawcett say what he was calling about?'

'He asked if you'd call him.' Warren handed her a piece of paper. 'He left his phone number. You can use the phone in the office.'

Rosa went into the office, picked up the phone and asked the operator for the number. It was answered by the elegant clipped tones of John Fawcett himself.

'Rosa!' he said in obvious delight. 'How are you this morning?'

'Very well,' she said.

'I have some good news,' said Fawcett. 'The Powers That Be at the BBC are delighted about last night's show. They tell me it had one of the best audience reactions in that particular time slot and they are keen to turn it into a series. They'd like another five shows, to start as soon as possible. I've checked and the theatre at Maida Vale is available from two weeks' time for a run of five weeks on Tuesdays, for a live broadcast at seven thirty, the same as last night's. Is that alright for you, with your other commitments?'

'I'm sure it will be,' said Rosa. 'I'll confirm it with my manager, Mr Warren, and get back to you in a moment or two. So, they liked it?'

'Better than that! And not just the BBC, I've already had phone calls from some top agents asking if their clients can appear on it. Billy Cotton, Anne Shelton, Arthur Askey, even Noël Coward. I think we have the making of a top-class series.'

'It won't be easy equalling what we did yesterday,' said Rosa cautiously. 'In a way, we were lucky that Bud got laryngitis.'

'True, but now everyone knows what the tone of the show is, anyone who comes in as a guest knows they can enjoy themselves. Well done, Rosa. It's well-deserved.'

'Thank you, Mr Fawcett,' said Rosa.

'John, please,' said Fawcett. 'With this show, the time for formality has gone.'

Coburg and Lampson returned to Scotland Yard, where they had Billy Chalk brought from the detention cell to the interview room. When he entered the room he walked to the table where the two detectives waited and sat himself down on the chair

283

opposite them, looking arrogantly at them, challenging them to disprove the statement he'd given them the previous day.

'We've established a timetable for what happened on the Friday when Bothwell was killed,' Coburg told him. 'You were out making deliveries when Bothwell arrived at your shop. Fred was in the shop. Bothwell demanded he hand over the piece of paper your sister, Maud, had stolen from the palace and given to Fred. We know she gave it to Fred because she admitted it.'

'Fred told me about it, so I knew about it.'

Coburg ignored this interjection and continued. 'Fred and Bothwell had a row. Fred killed Bothwell. It may well have been an accident, but Fred killed him.'

Billy shook his head. 'I killed him. I came back from making my deliveries and found them arguing. It was me and Bothwell got into a scrap. Bothwell was threatening Fred. I stepped in, picked up a knife and stabbed him. And you can't prove it wasn't me, no matter how many witnesses you've got.'

True, thought Coburg ruefully. A good barrister could play with the timeframe, especially about the time the van would have arrived at the shop after Billy had finished his deliveries.

'We have an eyewitness who saw you and Fred at Shadwell Basin with your van, after you'd dumped Bothwell's body.'

'So what?' asked Billy. 'Yes, Fred helped me because I told him I needed help to move the body, but that don't change the fact that I killed him. Fred was just an accessory after the fact. And he did it under duress, because I ordered him to. He didn't want to do it.' He looked at Coburg defiantly. 'Anyway, Bothwell deserved it. He was a traitor.'

'A traitor?' said Coburg. 'He died defending the King.'

'A traitor to his class,' said Chalk. 'The working class have

284

been the victims in this war, a war that was started by the ruling class.'

'Buckingham Palace has been bombed,' pointed out Coburg. 'Last September five bombs were dropped on it, causing major destruction. Five people were injured, including one who died.'

'Yes, servants,' snorted Chalk. 'Were the royal family injured?'

'They were there,' said Coburg. 'Afterwards, they went out to the East End to see the damage there.'

'And utter platitudes,' sneered Chalk. 'Meanwhile they had the safest possible air raid shelters. What did we have in the East End? Bugger all! Eighty thousand people dead here. Two million homes destroyed. We weren't even allowed in the Underground stations at first, not until my crowd invaded the Savoy and forced the government to allow us to use them.'

My crowd, thought Coburg. *The communists.*

'You've got air raid shelters now,' he said.

'Not enough. That's why I put that petition up in my shop.'

'But you didn't send it to the Prime Minister; you sent it to the Home Secretary.'

'It would have been a waste of time sending it to Churchill; he'd just have thrown it in the bin. He hates working people. Remember Tonypandy?' Then he gave a sneer as he added, 'Though I doubt if you even know about it, being part of the ruling class yourself, with your posh public-school accent.'

Yes, thought Coburg, *I know about Tonypandy, and not just the biased one-sided propaganda the communist and trade unionists put out.*

In 1910, when Churchill had been Home Secretary, the

coal miners of South Wales had gone on strike. The protests by the miners had led to violent confrontations between the miners and the local police. After some buildings had been badly damaged and many injured on both sides, the mine owners had appealed to the government to send in troops to deal with the disorder. Initially, Churchill ignored the request and instead ordered more police from outside the area to attend, including some from London's Metropolitan Police. The confrontations between miners and police became more violent. At Tonypandy, police defences had been thrown around the houses of the mine-owners to protect them. As the confrontations became more violent, Churchill acquiesced to a telegram from a local magistrate pleading for troops to be sent, and ordered a company of Lancashire Fusiliers and a squadron from the 18th Hussars to go to Tonypandy to quell the disorder. During the riots one miner had died after being struck on the head, possibly by a police truncheon, although it could well have been an accidental blow from a weapon by one of the rioters. With the arrival of the troops the riot was brought under control, and many of the miners were arrested and charged. Although there were no reports of the troops having injured anyone, the rumour spread that some of the miners had been killed by soldiers. Ever since that day, Churchill had been labelled 'the man who sent the troops in to kill the miners of Tonypandy', a falsehood that had dogged Churchill's political career and had become part of anti-Conservative folklore. Coburg knew it wasn't worth trying to argue this with Chalk, but he did say, 'Your petition was passed to Churchill by Herbert Morrison, and as a result Churchill authorised my elder brother, the Earl of Dawlish, to find places for more air raid shelters in the East End, starting with Whitechapel.'

'Rubbish!' snorted Chalk derisively. 'That's just lies and propaganda put out to appease public feelings in the East End.'

'Sergeant Joe Harker will confirm it,' said Coburg. 'He gave my brother and his companion a local copper to go round with them and inspect the area for the most likely places to turn into air raid shelters. Unfortunately, when they were going around, they were attacked by a gang of locals, and my brother's companion ended up unconscious in the London Hospital. If you don't believe Joe Harker, you can always send someone to check at the London Hospital. The man who was attacked is called Malcolm Grant.'

Chalk sat and studied Coburg, a surly look on his face. Finally, he said, 'Window-dressing. If they meant it, there'd have been air raid shelters in this area already when the war started. Everyone knew that the docks was going to be the main target for the Germans.'

'How do you feel about Soviet Russia being in partnership with Hitler's Germany?' asked Coburg. 'Stalin's good friend and comrade bombing the East End?'

Chalk shook his head. 'I'm not playing stupid word games with you,' he said. 'You've got no idea what life is like in the East End.'

Coburg was tempted to tell Chalk that he'd been at the Savoy during the famous invasion by East Enders the previous September, investigating a murder, and he'd been sympathetic to, and helped, the invaders. But then he realised it would be a waste of breath. As far as Chalk was concerned, Coburg represented the enemy. And they weren't here to discuss differing political and philosophical opinions; they were here to talk about a murder.

Coburg had Chalk returned to his cell.

'Our problem's the same: both of them confessing to the actual murder,' sighed Coburg.

'We might have to put them both in the dock for conspiracy to commit murder,' suggested Lampson.

Suddenly Coburg smiled. 'No! I've been missing a trick,' he said brightly.

'Oh?' asked Lampson.

Coburg rose to his feet and made for the door. 'I need to talk to Inspector Hibbert and bring him in on this.'

Coburg's phone call to Inspector Hibbert had the desired effect.

'I think I know how to find out which one actually did the killing,' he said. 'The key is the scrap of paper we found on Bothwell.'

He outlined his thinking to Hibbert, and within half an hour the MI5 inspector had joined them at the Yard. At Coburg's suggestion, they'd switched investigators: Coburg would now question Fred Chalk, while Hibbert talked to his father, Billy.

'What happened to the piece of paper?' was Coburg's opening question when he was faced with Fred. Once again, the solicitor, Felix Ford, accompanied Fred in the interview room.

'I told you I killed Bothwell; I'm not saying anything else,' said Fred.

'That's the problem,' said Coburg calmly. 'Your father says he killed Bothwell, and, as he's the older and counted as more responsible, it's highly likely he'll hang.'

'He didn't do it,' said Fred stubbornly.

'Then prove it to me,' said Coburg.

'How? I've told you I did it.'

'Then answer the question: what happened to the piece of paper?'

Fred looked at Coburg warily. 'What do you mean?'

'It's a simple question. Bothwell came into the shop. You were there, your dad was out, according to you. Bothwell demanded you give him the piece of paper that your aunt Maud had given you. What happened to it?'

Fred looked at Felix Ford and asked, 'Do I have to answer that?'

'You do if you want to save your dad from hanging,' said Coburg, before the solicitor could reply. 'Only the person who killed Bothwell knows what happened to it. We're asking your father the same question. If he killed him, he'll be able to tell us. If he didn't, he won't get it right. And the thing is, Fred, I know where that piece of paper ended up, but I'm guessing only one of you knows how it got there. Unless you were both in the shop when it happened, in which case your dad will hang for murder.'

Ford looked at Coburg, puzzled. 'I don't understand your line of questioning, Chief Inspector.'

'No,' said Coburg, but keeping his eyes on Fred Chalk. 'But your client does. Prove to me it was you who killed Bernard Bothwell.'

'Fred, I strongly advise—' began Ford, but Fred cut him off.

'Like you say, Bothwell turned up and said he wanted back the piece of paper my aunt Maud had given me. At first I denied I had it, or that she'd given it to me, but then he said she'd confessed to him that she'd taken it and given it to me.

He said if I didn't he'd bring the police in and have me arrested for treason, which is a hanging offence. He said both me and my dad would hang, as would Aunt Maud.

'I told him he was mad. Then he picked up one of my knives from the counter and pointed it at me. He said if I didn't give it to him, he'd kill me and take it back. I could tell by his face he meant it. But I wasn't going to give him the piece of paper back. It meant a lot to my dad. So I tried to reason with him. I told him the piece of paper was just that, a scrap of paper; the words on it didn't mean or say anything important. To show him what I meant, I took the piece of paper out of the drawer under the counter where I'd put it and showed it to him. "It's just scribble," I said. "It doesn't mean anything." I did that because I didn't want him going to the police about it. If he told them Aunt Maud had taken it from the palace it was likely they'd charge the three of us with treason. But then, the lunatic snatched the scrap of paper from my hand and put it in his mouth and started chewing it! Then he took it out and stuffed it in his trouser pocket!'

'And then you stabbed him?'

'I had to get it back. It was the evidence that could have hung us! The trouble was, when I realised he was dead, I panicked, so I didn't take the ball of wet paper out of his trouser pocket. To be honest, I didn't think it mattered any more. The last thing I wanted was it found. I knew we'd have to dump the body, so the ball of paper would be gone with it.'

In the other interview room, Hibbert was asking Billy Chalk the same questions.

'What happened to the piece of paper?'

'What piece of paper?'

'The one your sister, Maud, took from the palace and brought to your shop and gave to your son, Fred.'

'She didn't give it to Fred. She gave it to me. Fred wasn't even in the shop.'

Hibbert nodded. 'Alright, she gave it to you. And Bothwell turned up to try and get it back. What happened?'

'I've already told you, I killed him.'

'And what happened to the piece of paper?'

Bily Chalk hesitated, weighing up his answer, then he said, 'I threw it away. I didn't want it in the shop. It was evidence that could have been used against us.'

'Where did you throw it?'

'I can't remember! In the bin.'

'So where is it now?'

Chalk hesitated, then said, 'I burnt it. I put it on the fire.'

'Would it surprise you to learn that we've got it?' said Hibbert. 'It was in Bothwell's pocket.'

Chalk shook his head. 'No it wasn't,' he said. 'I took everything out of his pockets before I dumped it in Shadwell Basin, so if the body was found no one would be able to identify him. You can't fool me like that.'

'You took everything out of his jacket pockets. This was in his trouser pocket.'

'There was nothing in his trouser pockets! I patted them and they were empty.'

'They may have felt empty, but they weren't.'

'You're lying. You're trying to trick me but it won't work. I killed Bothwell and that's all there is to it. Yes, Fred helped me get rid of his body but only because I made him.'

CHAPTER THIRTY-SIX

With both father and son returned to their cells, Hibbert, Coburg and Lampson went to Coburg's office to discuss what their latest round of questioning had revealed.

'So, it was Fred who did the actual killing,' said Coburg. 'Billy comes back and finds the dead body, and takes charge. He empties Bothwell's pockets, but misses the wet screwed-up paper in the trouser pocket. Fred's in too much of a panic to tell him about Bothwell chewing it and putting it in his trouser pocket. Anyway, the main thing is we've got something to tell Churchill he can pass on to the King. The good news is that the valet was loyal to the King and honest, and died trying to get the paper back. Do you want to pass on the news to Churchill?'

Hibbert shook his head. 'I'd rather you do it. These political types make me uneasy.'

'Even the Prime Minister?'

'Especially the Prime Minister. There's still going to be awkward questions to answer. Like, do we put Billy Chalk's sister on trial for theft and treason?'

'I'd prefer it if there was a way round that.'

'So would I, but Churchill is bound to bring it up. You're better at handling these people than I am.'

'I don't agree,' said Coburg.

'That's because you come from the same class as them, so you don't see it,' said Hibbert.

'You sound like Billy Chalk in one of his communist rants.' Coburg smiled.

This time, Coburg's visit to Down Street led to his being admitted immediately into Churchill's presence.

'You can reassure His Majesty that his valet was innocent of stealing the note,' Coburg told him. 'In fact, his attempt to recover it led to his death. He discovered that someone among the palace staff had taken the note and passed it on to a butcher in Whitechapel.'

'To what end?'

'The butcher is an ardent communist and he was looking for anything he could use to discredit the royal family.'

'Do you have this butcher in custody?'

'We do. A father and son who were involved in this together. The son did the actual killing, and his father helped him dispose of the body.'

'And the person who stole the note from the King and gave it to them?'

'We're still investigating that,' said Coburg carefully. 'Both men refuse to disclose their identity, and unfortunately Bothwell is dead, so he can't tell us.'

'This person needs to be apprehended,' said Churchill. 'We can't have someone like that running free inside the palace.'

'Absolutely, sir,' said Coburg. 'But for the moment I thought you'd like to reassure His Majesty that his valet was completely loyal to him, and that loyalty cost him his life. I believe his widow could be deserving of some sort of pension, or at least compensation. Bothwell left two young children.'

Churchill nodded. 'I'll see what can be done.'

When Coburg got back to Scotland Yard, he found Lampson studying the reports from Drs McKay and Webb on the victims: Bothwell, the three women, Trump and Brown.

'So the Chalks killed Bothwell, while someone else killed the three women, and Jerry Trump and Brown,' said Lampson.

'Someone using a bayonet, if the doctors are right,' said Coburg thoughtfully.

I've seen a bayonet recently, he thought. *In a photograph.*

Then he remembered the photographs on the sideboard in the Dixons' house. One showing the family standing together as a group, another with Mr Dixon in uniform from the First War, posing with a bayonet. Sometimes soldiers kept mementoes of their time in the forces, usually pistols. No one he'd ever known had actually brought a rifle back. But what about a bayonet?

He stood up and made for the door.

'Come on, Sergeant,' he said. 'I think we may be able to put the New Ripper to rest.'

'Where are we going?' asked Lampson, picking up his coat.

'Whitechapel,' said Coburg. 'That's at the heart of everything.'

Their first call when they got to Whitechapel was to Maud Chalk.

'It was your nephew, Fred, who killed Bernard Bothwell, when Bothwell went to the butcher shop and demanded Fred give him back the note you'd given to Fred,' Coburg told her. 'Your brother, Billy, helped Fred dispose of Bothwell's body.'

She looked at them, her face haggard. 'What will happen to them?'

'That depends on the court. Fred will plead guilty but claim self-defence.'

'Will he hang?'

'That depends on the court,' repeated Coburg.

'And Billy?'

'The same, I'm afraid. He may not have done the actual killing, but he's involved in a conspiracy to murder.'

'And me?' she asked tremulously. 'Will they hang me? Taking that note from the King's room was treason, wasn't it?'

'It could be interpreted as such. The problem is, when it comes to court, the prosecution barrister may well ask Fred and Billy where they got the letter from. They might refuse to answer, but it will make the case against Billy worse. To be honest, Miss Chalk, I'd like to protect you, but if I'm called to the witness stand I'd have to tell about your part in it. As will Inspector Hibbert.'

'What should I do?' she asked, desperate.

'Officially, I have to advise you to give yourself up.'

'But they'll hang me! This is treason!'

'Maybe, maybe not.' He hesitated, then said, 'Unofficially, and I'll deny saying this if I'm asked, the other option is for you to disappear.'

'Disappear?'

'Leave the area. Go somewhere far away where no one knows you. Change your name. Say you lost your identity cards and everything in a bombing raid. Get a job far away under a different name.'

'Away from my family and my friends?' she said, horrified.

'It's up to you. Fred and Billy will be in prison, if they're lucky. You're not married, so you've got no family to consider. And maybe, in a few years when this is all over, you can come back to London. But that's only my personal opinion. Or you can stay and face whatever is thrown at you. It's up to you.'

Coburg and Lampson left the small terraced house and got into their car, Lampson driving.

'What d'you reckon she'll do, guv?' asked Lampson.

'I don't know,' admitted Coburg. 'If she's got any sense, she'll take my advice and do a runner. But somehow I doubt if she'll do that. I suggest we let things run their course, see what happens. The main thing is, the murder of Bernard Bothwell is wrapped up. Now, let's do the same for this so-called New Ripper.'

'You know who it is?' asked Lampson.

'I think I do,' said Coburg. 'Wesley Dixon.'

'The copper who got stabbed?'

Coburg nodded.

'Are you sure?' asked Lampson.

'I will be after I've spoken to Sergeant Harker, if he gives me the answers I'm expecting,' said Coburg.

As they drove to the police station, Coburg told his sergeant what had led him to think the killer was the young police officer. 'I'm telling you all this now because I'd like you to stay with the car while I go and see Joe Harker. I'm still not convinced this is a safe place to leave a police car unattended.'

When they got to the police station, Coburg got out. 'I hope I won't be long,' he said, 'but if I am, don't get alarmed. If I'm right, I'll need to tell Sergeant Harker everything, because we'll need him on our side when we make the arrest.'

Sergeant Harker was at the reception desk when Coburg walked in.

'Any news on the Chalks, Chief Inspector?' he asked.

'Fred killed Bothwell; Billy helped him dispose of the body,' Coburg told him.

'So it was nothing to do with the women being killed,' said Harker.

'No,' said Coburg. 'But that's why we're here. Ted Lampson's outside, making sure no one does anything to our car.'

'Still worried after what happened to your brother and his pal?'

'Let's just say I'd rather be safe than sorry,' said Coburg. 'I'm here to learn about the Dixon family.'

'What about them? You've met Wesley and his mother.'

'What about his father? Was he in the First War?'

'He was. He was wounded in the trenches in Flanders. I believe the same happened to you?'

'It did,' said Coburg. 'What sort of man was he?'

'A wonderful man. Devoted to his missus, and his two sons. Agatha was heartbroken when he was killed. Fire-watching. He was a hero to the end.'

'Was Wesley's brother, William, killed in the same incident?'

Harker hesitated, then asked, 'Is that what Wesley told you?'

'That's the impression he gave me.'

Harker nodded thoughtfully.

'I'm guessing there's more to it than that,' prompted Coburg.

'Yes,' said Harker. 'William didn't actually die fire-watching. He caught a disease that killed him.'

'What disease?'

'Syphilis. It developed into GPI. General paralysis of the insane. He was in Bethlem mental hospital in Beckenham. That's where he died. No one talked about it. Everyone was happy to go along with the story the family put out that he'd died fire-watching. The family is well-liked and respected around here.'

'When did he die?'

'A year ago, not long after the war started. He'd been in Bethlem for a year before that.'

'How did his brother, Wesley, take his death?'

'He was devastated. Him and his mum kept hoping he'd recover.'

'Did they visit him in Bethlem?'

'Wesley didn't go much; it was too hard for him. Same for his dad, Walter. Agatha went, when she could.'

Coburg nodded thoughtfully, then said, 'How's this for a theory? Wesley's brother, William, dies as a result of getting syphilis from a prostitute. Wesley is devastated; he loved his brother. Night after night, when he's on duty at the air raid shelter, he sees the prostitutes at work, picking up men in the tunnels. It all brings back memories of his brother. He wants revenge, and he also wants prostitution in this area to stop. He decides to use scare tactics. He kills and butchers one, hoping the word will spread and put the prostitutes off, and the men who use them. He copies what he knows about the original Jack the Ripper, hoping it will get the publicity. And everyone will hear about it. But these are different times. There's a war on and people are more worried about the bombing raids. So he kills again, in the same way. He deliberately leaves clues pointing back to the original Ripper, the old surgeon's case, the leather apron. Both doctors, McKay and Webb, say they think a bayonet was used to strike the first blow in the heart. On the sideboard in the Dixon house was a photograph of Mr Dixon in uniform, holding a bayonet. I think Wesley found it and kept it and used it.'

'What about when he was stabbed?'

'He did it to himself to put us off the scent. He was ideally placed to hunt down his victims, on night patrol at the shelter.'

'But McKay and Webb think the same person who killed and butchered the women also killed Charlie Brown and Jerry Trump,' said Harker. 'Why kill them?'

'I'm hoping Wesley will tell us,' said Coburg. 'My own thought is Charlie Brown was asking difficult questions and might have been getting close to the truth, so he had to be silenced.'

'And Jerry Trump?'

'Someone told the gang that my brother and Malcolm were Nazi spies. Why? Because they thought that Magnus and Malcolm were here to investigate the murders on behalf of a government office, say the Home Office. Magnus and Malcolm didn't tell anyone what they were really doing here.'

'Nor did I,' said Harker, 'The only one I told was Bert Watts, and I swore him to secrecy.'

'So Wesley sees these two guys walking around with Bert Watts, asking questions, and decides they need to be put out of action. So he tells Jenkinson and his gang this lie about them being Nazi spies, and suggesting they ought to do something about it. The boys believe him because he's a copper, he knows about this sort of thing.'

Harker nodded unhappily. 'When you look at it like that, it all adds up. I should have seen it.'

'You were too close to him. He's one of your officers, and a good one. You trust him. You've known the family for years.' Coburg stopped and added, 'Of course, I could be wrong.'

Harker shook his head. 'I don't think you are. So, do we bring him in?'

'We do, but we'll take him to Scotland Yard for custody. This is Dixon's local nick. People could try to spring him, or kill him.'

CHAPTER THIRTY-SEVEN

It was a small convoy of two police cars that pulled up outside the Dixons' house, Coburg and Lampson in one, Sergeant Harker and two police constables in the other. When Mrs Dixon opened the door to them and saw the two Scotland Yard detectives, accompanied by a team of uniformed officers, she frowned, obviously concerned.

'What's going on?' she demanded.

'We need to talk to your son, Mrs Dixon,' said Coburg.

'You can't,' she said. 'He's resting.'

'I'm afraid we must insist,' said Coburg.

Mrs Dixon tried to stand in front of them to prevent them from going into the house, but Coburg nodded to Lampson, who moved her gently to one side.

Wesley Dixon was sitting in the living room reading a newspaper.

'What's up?' he asked in surprise as the policemen entered the small room.

'Wesley Dixon, I am arresting you on suspicion of the murder of Marjorie Wethers, Georgia Brand and Sarah Mars,' said Coburg.

'No!' shouted Mrs Dixon. 'You can't!'

'It's alright, Mum,' said Dixon calmly. 'Let them do what they have to do.'

'No!' she shouted again, and rushed to her son and wrapped her arms around him. 'You're not taking him.'

Coburg turned to the uniformed officers and told them, 'Remove Mrs Dixon's arms from around her son and take her into another room.'

'I won't go!' she shouted.

'In that case, take Mrs Dixon to the car. I'll deal with her after I've dealt with Wesley.'

The two policemen took hold of Mrs Dixon and managed to prise her arms from her son, then hauled her out of the room and out of the house. All the while she shouted abuse at them, and called plaintively to her son. 'I'll get you out, Wesley!' she yelled. 'This is wrong!'

Coburg waited until she'd been taken out of the house before continuing with his formal caution over the arrest.

'You don't have to say anything, but anything you do say may be taken down and may be used against you in a court of law.'

'I understand,' said Wesley calmly.

'You'll also understand that we need to handcuff you for the journey to Scotland Yard,' said Coburg.

'I do,' said Wesley, still calm. He held out his hands and Lampson put a pair of handcuffs on his wrists.

'We'll take Wesley to Scotland Yard now,' Coburg told Sergeant Harker. 'You can let Mrs Dixon go once we've departed.'

Harker nodded. Coburg and Lampson escorted Wesley Dixon to their car. Coburg got into the rear seats with the handcuffed Dixon, while Lampson slid behind the steering wheel. As they drove past the other police car, Mrs Dixon glared venomously at them and shouted angrily, but they couldn't her what she was saying, and Wesley Dixon remained unmoved.

At Scotland Yard, Coburg and Lampson faced Wesley Dixon across the bare table in the interview room.

'Your brother Willliam didn't die fire-watching, did he?' said Coburg. 'He caught syphilis from a prostitute and died in Bethlem Hospital as a result of it developing into GPI, general paralysis of the insane.'

Dixon didn't respond, just looked back unflinchingly at Coburg.

'You were very close to your brother. Following his death you felt an overwhelming sense of anger and rage against the women who'd caused his death. Prostitutes.'

'They were scum,' Wesley said.

'So you took your revenge.'

'It wasn't just revenge; it was stopping them spreading that disease to other people.'

'By ripping them apart and removing their internal organs.'

'It was the only way to try and stop these women from doing what they were doing. If they thought they were going to be butchered in that way, the chances were they'd stop plying their filthy trade.'

'So you confess to killing those women?'

'Yes,' said Dixon.

'And after the last one, Marjorie Wethers, you made up that stuff about catching the killer. You stabbed yourself in the arm, and then rolled about in the blood and muck.'

Dixon shrugged. 'It seemed like a good idea.'

'Do you admit to also killing Georgia Brand and Sarah Mars?'

'Yes,' said Dixon. 'They were prostitutes. The sort who killed my brother.'

'Marjorie Wethers wasn't a prostitute,' said Coburg.

'How do you know?' demanded Dixon.

'We've been told so by her sister.'

Dixon gave a scornful laugh. 'And you believe her?'

'There's no record of Mrs Wethers being arrested or prosecuted for soliciting.'

'But she was with a man,' said Dixon. 'I saw her.'

'Who was the man?'

Dixon shrugged. 'I don't know. I'd never seen him before.'

'And what did you do?'

'I waited till he'd left her.'

'And then you attacked her.'

Again, Dixon shrugged. 'Attacked her. Took retribution for the men she'd infected. You call it one thing; I call it another.'

'Where's the knife you used?'

'I threw it away.'

'Where?'

Again, the shrug. 'What does it matter? I've said I did it.'

'What sort of knife was it? Describe it.'

Dixon hesitated, then he shook his head. 'I'm saying nothing more until I've got a solicitor with me.'

'Do you have a solicitor?'

'No, but I can get one. There's a few in Whitechapel. They look after the local villains.' He thought about it for a minute, then said, 'Peter Musgrave. Contact Sergeant Harker. He knows Musgrave. Tell the sergeant I've confessed to the killings, but I need a solicitor and I want Musgrave.'

'What about Charlie Brown and Jerry Trump?'

'What about them?'

'Did you kill them as well?'

Dixon didn't reply, and Coburg could see a dilemma in the young man's face.

'Did you kill Charlie Brown and Jerry Trump?' he asked again.

'I've already confessed to killing those three women at the air raid shelter,' said Dixon. 'I'm saying nothing more until I've got a solicitor with me.'

Sergeant Harker's conversation with DCI Coburg was brief and to the point. At the end he hung up the telephone and gestured for a constable to take over from him at the desk.

'I've got to go and see Agatha Dixon,' he said. 'Wesley's mother. If anyone wants me, I'll be back soon.'

He walked through Whitechapel to the Dixons' house, mulling over what Coburg had told him, and wondering how Mrs Dixon would take it.

'Where's Wesley?' Mrs Dixon demanded angrily when she answered the door to his knock.

'At Scotland Yard,' Harker told her. 'He's confessed.'

'Confessed to what?'

'To killing the women in the air raid shelter.'

She shook her head. 'He didn't do it,' she stated firmly.

'He said he did,' Harker told her.

'He didn't do it,' she said doggedly. 'He's not guilty.'

'That's going to be for a jury to decide,' said Harker. He looked at her sympathetically.

'I'm sorry, Agatha,' he said. 'There's not much more we can say, except sorry, now Wesley's confessed.'

'Your lot beat it out of him,' she said accusingly.

'Oh come on,' protested Harker. 'You know me better than that.'

She glared at him, malevolence written all over her face. 'I'll hire the best solicitor there is,' she said. 'I don't care how much it costs. Wesley's innocent, and I'm going to prove it.'

'You've got every right to try that,' said Harker. 'But I think you'd be foolish to waste good money on it.'

'Wouldn't you do it if it was your son, Joe Harker?' she demanded.

'According to DCI Coburg, Wesley's asked us to get him Peter Musgrave to act for him,' said Harker.

Mrs Dixon shook her head.

'Musgrave's no good,' she said. 'Wesley deserves better than Musgrave.'

'He's the one that Wesley asked for,' said Harker.

'I don't care,' said Mrs Dixon. 'I'll find one.'

With that, she shut the door.

CHAPTER THIRTY-EIGHT

Thursday 10th April

The next morning, almost immediately when they arrived at Scotland Yard, Coburg had a phone call from Sergeant Harker.

'There's been another one,' said Harker. 'Another woman killed during the night.'

'Where?'

'Whitechapel Road station again. Same injuries. Internal organs carved out. Womb, bladder, intestines.'

'Where's the body?' asked Coburg.

'At the London Hospital.'

'Who's the medical examiner? McKay or Webb?'

'Neither was available when I rang, so I had the body sent there to be looked at.'

'In that case, I'll head there now. I'll be in touch after I've seen whichever doctor is handling the case.' He hung up and looked at Lampson.

'Joe Harker at Whitechapel,' he told him. 'There's been another woman killed there during the night. Same sort of injuries as the others.'

Lampson looked at him, bewildered. 'But Dixon's been under lock and key here.'

'I know,' said Coburg, getting up. 'So we're off to the London

Hospital to see what the doctors say about the injuries.'

When they got to the London Hospital, they were told that the doctor who'd taken charge of the latest victim was Dr McKay.

'What can you tell us about the injuries the victim suffered?' asked Coburg.

'Would you like to see her?' asked McKay.

'To be honest, I'd prefer to hear your professional opinion,' said Coburg. 'How similar are her injuries to the other killings?'

'Identical.'

'You're sure?'

'I am. From the bayonet in the heart to the way the excisions were carried out. I've discussed them with Dr Webb and he agrees that the lacerations are identical. In the same way that a surgeon can tell another surgeon's work by the incisions they make and the stitches and suturing, the cuts and incisions made to this woman and to all the victims have the same signature.'

'So the same person killed all the four women in the air raid shelter?'

'That is what I am saying, yes,' Dr McKay told him. 'The same person killed all of them.'

Coburg and Lampson's next call was to Whitechapel police station. When they told him what Dr McKay had told them, Harker stared at them in disbelief.

'But how can that be?' asked Harker. 'Dixon was securely locked up at Scotland Yard last night.'

'Because he didn't kill any of them,' said Coburg.

'What do you mean?' asked Harker, uncomprehending. 'Why did he confess?'

'It's similar to the business over who killed Bernard Bothwell,' said Coburg. 'He's protecting the person who did it because it's someone he's close to.'

'Who?'

'His mother.'

'Agatha?' said Harker, stunned. 'I don't believe it!'

'Look at the evidence. William Dixon died from syphilis he caught from a prostitute. When Wesley Dixon told us he saw the person who did it and struggled with them, and was stabbed, I thought he was doing it to cover up for the fact that *he* was the one who did the killings. He was ideally placed to do it; he was on duty at the air raid shelter when the first victim was killed, and Mrs Wethers. I made the wrong assumption that Wesley wanted revenge on these women because he was close to his brother and he blamed prostitutes for William's death. But this latest killing done while Wesley was in custody means it can't have been him. So it's someone else who has the same feelings of revenge because of what happened to William. The clincher here is the mess Wesley got into when he said he tried to catch the person he caught doing the butchering. Covered in muck and blood. He did that to himself, because the person he found doing the butchering was his mother, so he told her to scram and then made up the story about the killer. It was the business of the bayonet that made me suspect Wesley, after seeing it in the photograph of his father, but it would have applied equally to Agatha.'

'So Agatha carried out this latest murder knowing that it couldn't be laid at Wesley's door because he was in custody,' said Harker.

'And she thought it would also convince everyone he wasn't guilty of the other murders either.' Coburg nodded.

'I can see her motive for killing the prostitutes, revenge for

308

William getting infected, but what I don't understand is why she killed Charlie Brown and Jerry Trump,' said Harker.

'The same reason I thought it was Wesley: to silence them. Brown was nosy; he knew something. As for Jerry, we were hoping he'd tell you who told him and his pals that Magnus and Malcolm were Nazi spies.'

'Agatha Dixon? But why?'

'My guess is she noticed these two men going around Whitechapel asking questions, and because they'd been told not to say what they were really up to – looking for suitable buildings for air raid shelters – she assumed they were government types come to investigate the killings. Magnus and Malcolm have that official-looking air about them.' He thought it over, then asked, 'After Jerry Trump, which one of the gang is most likely to talk?'

Harker thought about it, then said, 'Tommy Duggan. He's the quietest, but deep down I've always thought he'd be alright, if he could be got away from Jenkinson.'

'Is he still here?'

'All of them are. We were hanging on to them until we knew what you wanted done with them. For one thing, another night in the cells might make them think twice before they do anything like this again.'

Coburg nodded.

'Can you bring Tommy Duggan to the interview room?' he asked.

'You think he'll talk?'

'I hope so.'

Tommy Duggan looked apprehensive when he was escorted into the interview room. Coburg gestured for him to sit in the chair opposite him and Lampson.

'The person who told you that the two men you attacked were Nazi spies was Mrs Dixon, wasn't it? PC Dixon's mother.'

Duggan looked at him, obviously surprised, but also wary.

'Who told you that?' he asked. 'Jerry?'

'Jerry was killed to stop him telling us who told you about the Nazi spies business, because the person who told you that was the same person who killed all those women at the air raid shelter. She needs to be locked up, otherwise she'll kill you and the rest of the gang to ensure your silence. If it was her who told you, of course. Or was it someone else?'

Duggan shook his head. 'It was her,' he said. 'We thought we was being patriots.'

Coburg looked at the attending constable. 'That's all we need. Take him back to his cell, Constable.'

A short while later, Coburg and Lampson, along with Sergeant Harker and a team of constables, arrived at Agatha Dixon's house, where Coburg had her formally arrested. Sergeant Harker and two constables took her to the police station, while Coburg and Lampson gave instructions to the team of officers 'Search the house and all the outbuildings. Especially the outbuildings. We're looking for a bayonet.'

The bayonet was discovered in the coal shed, partly hidden beneath a pile of coal.

The detectives took the bayonet to Whitechapel police station and Coburg laid it on the table so that Mrs Dixon would see it when she was brought in to be questioned.

A local solicitor was organised to represent Agatha Dixon.

'You were at the shelter last night,' said Coburg.

'Of course I was,' said Dixon. 'So was half of Whitechapel. Where else would I be when there's an air raid?'

Coburg pointed at the bayonet lying on the table. 'Your fingerprints are on this.'

'Of course they are. It's my late husband's. He kept it as a memento of the war and now I keep it as a memento of him.'

'Willliam didn't die fire-watching, did he? He died in Bethlem Hospital of general paralysis of the insane, as a result of catching syphilis from having sex with prostitutes.'

'Lies,' she said. 'You've been listening to lies.'

'I've checked the medical records,' said Coburg. 'He died insane from syphilis and that reporter, Charlie Brown, knew about it. That's why you killed him, to stop him writing about it in the paper. And you killed that woman last night to protect Wesley. You'd been told he'd confessed, so you killed her to show it couldn't have been him because he was in custody. That's why you did it quickly. In case Wesley was released on bail.'

She looked at him defiantly. 'I would never have let him be charged. As for the women, I have no remorse. They were scum. It was their sort that killed my son William. I wanted to make sure they didn't kill other men, infecting them with filth the same way.'

'Wesley caught you doing it, didn't he?' said Coburg. 'He told you to leave and he'd take care of it. He stabbed himself in the arm, then came up with that false description of a tall man.'

She said nothing, just glowered at him.

'How do you know so much about anatomy?' asked Coburg.

'I was a nurse during the last war. That's where I met Walter when he was wounded. I helped at operations, including some on women.'

* * *

After Agatha Dixon had been formally remanded into custody, Lampson was detailed to take her to Holloway prison.

'I'll see you back at the Yard,' Coburg told him. 'I just have to wrap up something here.'

Lampson was allocated two WPCs to act as escorts to help him take Agatha Dixon to Holloway. After they'd gone, Coburg asked Sergeant Harker to bring Barry Jenkinson to the interview room.

'Mrs Dixon played you for a fool,' he told the young thug when he'd been placed in the chair opposite him.

Jenkinson looked at him, puzzled. 'What do you mean?' he demanded.

'She told you that the two men you attacked were Nazi spies.'

Jenkinson scowled. 'I'm saying nothing.'

'You don't need to. But it was a lie so you'd attack them and you fell for it. The truth is, the reason they were here in Whitechapel was on the orders of the government to find more places to serve as suitable air raid shelters. Orders from Churchill, no less. But they'd been told not to let anyone know what they were doing in case some dodgy property owners put the price of their buildings up.'

'Rubbish!' snorted Jenkinson.

'If you don't believe me, ask Sergeant Harker. He knew the truth and he supplied them with a constable to walk around Whitechapel with them looking at possible sites.'

'The chief inspector's right,' said Harker.

'But Mrs Dixon didn't know this; she thought they were looking into the murders, and she didn't want that happening,' continued Coburg.

'Why not?' asked Jenkinson, curious in spite of his attitude of defiance.

Coburg shook his head. 'You and your pals will find out why

in due course. But right now, you're in serious trouble. Your act in attacking those two men will very likely put a stop to any more air raid shelters here in Whitechapel. You'll be responsible for the deaths of hundreds, if not thousands, here in this area from the air raids. That's treason, that is. Helping the enemy. Killing your own people.'

'No!' burst out Jenkinson, agitated. 'It can't be true! She's just an old woman! Why would she do that?'

'Like I said, you'll find out in due course. And once word gets out about what you and your pals did, and the outcome of the lack of air raid shelters, you are going to be deeply unpopular. You might even be safer in prison, because people here in Whitechapel are going to hate you. Everyone with a loved one who's died in the bombing will come looking for you.'

'No!' said Jenkinson, even more agitated. 'It's not my fault.'

'Being stupid is not an excuse,' said Coburg. 'But once word gets out, I don't think your gang will be following you and your orders any more,' He turned to Sergeant Harker. 'You do the business, please, Sergeant. Charge him. Then, afterwards, charge the rest of them. Assault and battery. Grievous bodily harm.'

'My pleasure,' said Harker. 'Whitechapel will be a better place with you off the streets, Jenkinson.' He fixed the distraught teenage gang leader with a steely gaze, then said, 'Barry Jenkinson, I am arresting you on charges of assault and battery and grievous bodily harm.'

'No! I was being a patriot!' protested Jenkinson.

'You don't have to say anything, but anything you do say will be taken down and may be used in evidence against you,' continued Harker, unmoved.

CHAPTER THIRTY-NINE

Inspector Hibbert walked into the room that housed Edward Crosby at the Tower of London.

'I got your message that you wanted to see me,' he said.

'Indeed. Thank you for coming, Inspector. The fact is, I've been considering my position.'

'In what way?'

'I'm incarcerated in the Tower of London. I'm not allowed legal representation. My guess is you haven't informed anyone that I'm here for reasons of what you'd call "national security", and that includes my employer and close friends and family.'

Hibbert didn't respond, just sat watching Crosby, waiting for him to continue.

'The fact that you don't deny it suggests to me I shall be here for the duration of the war. Not because I've done anything wrong, I know I haven't, but because you are concerned as to what I might do, or write.'

Still, Hibbert didn't respond.

'The danger for you is, surely, that when I am finally released I will then write about the injustice and unfair imprisonment I suffered for however many months or years I am here. As I see it the only way to stop me doing that is to kill me. Which is something I really don't wish to happen. So, I have a proposal that I feel could be to both our advantages.'

'Go on,' said Hibbert.

'First, I will sign a legal undertaking that I will not write anything derogatory about any member of the royal family, nor their staff, with the proviso that if I break it I understand I can, and likely will, be imprisoned for an indefinite period of time.' Hibbert opened his mouth to say something, but Crosby held up his hand to stop him and added, 'However, I don't believe you will trust me to keep to it. You possibly think that at the first opportunity I will decamp to somewhere like, say, America, and then write about it there. So, my additional proposal is this: that I work for you. Either in an official or unofficial capacity.'

'What as?' asked Hibbert.

'A spy. You are MI5 after all. You already know who I am and my background. I move in many circles with people that might interest you: politicians of all sorts, royalty, the aristocracy, the media, show business. I know many secrets. Who is having an affair with who. Who is secretly supportive of the enemy. Which MPs and peers are the most corrupt and will sell their soul to the highest bidder. Which members of the church engage in suspect moralities. Which high-up members of the police force and military are tainted. Some of them you will know about, but I am an insider and have the inside track. The information I already have about these people will fill many desk drawers at MI5. But put me back among them, and there will be a harvest of such information you will not believe.'

'You'd sell out your so-called friends?' asked Hibbert.

'I have no friends,' said Crosby. 'And those I have, I would sell out in a heartbeat if it meant my freedom.' He gave Hibbert a benign smile. 'Well, Inspector? What do you say?'

Hibbert frowned. 'Promises are easy to make, but for how long?'

'As long as you like,' said Crosby. 'The proof of the pudding is in the eating. I will provide you with inside information. You check on it and confirm its veracity. And, as long as you're happy, so will I be. I will also brief you on any gossip I intend to write about, so you can approve it, or ask for it to be kept under wraps.'

'What about your editor?' asked Hibbert.

Crosby laughed. 'Sandy McCaig? He's as corrupt as anyone. I think we could let him know what our agreement is and he'd be amused and very supportive.'

Hibbert fell into a thoughtful silence, then said, 'I need to think about this. Run it by a few people.'

'Understood.' Crosby nodded. 'But I'd be careful about who you run it by. The Under-Secretary of State for Home Security, for example. I'd avoid discussing it with him, especially in view of his unusual and definitely illegal sexual preferences.' He smiled. 'I throw that in as an example of what I can supply.'

Hibbert got to his feet and nodded. 'Very well. I'll be in touch shortly.'

Crosby watched the inspector as he left the room and shut and relocked the door.

'So far, so good,' he murmured to himself.

ACKNOWLEDGEMENTS

Writing this book gave me an opportunity to pay homage to BBC Radio light entertainment. All television broadcasts were suspended for the duration of the war and did not resume until 1947, so the only broadcast communications were on BBC Radio.

I was born in 1944, six months before the end of the Second World War, and for quite a few years after it the primary form of entertainment for the British public was still radio. Very, very few houses had a television set (my family did not, and nor did our neighbours), and those that had one could only watch the one channel, BBC. Consequently I grew up listening to comedy and drama on the radio on the Home Service and Light Programme. In fact, I didn't live in a house with a TV set until I was in my thirties. As a result, when I began my writing career in 1971, it was writing for radio comedy (a situation comedy called *Parsley Sidings* with Arthur Lowe, Kenneth Connor, Ian Lavender and Liz Fraser). I went on to have two hundred and fifty radio scripts broadcast, including winning my first award writing for a Ronnie Barker radio comedy series, before turning to television scripts, and then writing novels. The great pleasure for me was writing for people I had grown up listening to on the radio (e.g. Deryck Guyler) and, during breaks in rehearsals, listening to their memories of those golden days of radio.

In the character of Rosa's radio producer, John Fawcett, I also pay homage to my own radio producer from 1971 to 2008, the late John Fawcett Wilson, a true genius of radio.

Alas, I never worked with or met Flanagan and Allen, or the other members of the Crazy Gang (although I did co-write with Vera Lynn about a book on the final days of World War Two), but I heard them on the radio, and worked with producers and studio engineers who'd worked with them. By the late sixties, radio production hadn't changed much since the war years; it was the digital audio technology in the eighties that changed some studio practices. So the sub-plot with Rosa and her radio show is my faithful depiction of what radio used to be like backstage, having experienced the tail end of the process.

As an afterthought to this story: the old Whitechapel Road Tube station (also known as St Mary's), which had been heavily bombed during the Blitz, was finally destroyed by a German bomb that blew up just outside on 19th April 1941. Eight people died in the blast, and as a postscript, I decided that one of those who died would be Maud Chalk. She did not flee but stayed at Whitechapel, and sought refuge at the air raid shelter on the night of 19th April.

Subsequent to the destruction of the former Whitechapel Road Tube station, a tunnel was dug from the remains of the stairwell of the old station through to the sub-basement of the building next door, creating a new entrance to the shelter. After the war, the site became a wasteland. However, there is, at the time of writing, still stairway access to the former platforms, with the brick screens at the edges to show their conversion to air raid shelters.

JIM ELDRIDGE was born in central London towards the end of World War II, and survived attacks by V2 rockets on the Kings Cross area where he lived. In 1971 he sold his first sitcom to the BBC and had his first book commissioned. Since then he has had more than one hundred books published, with sales of over three million copies. He lives in Kent with his wife.

jimeldridge.com